Praise for
New York Times and *USA Today*
Bestselling Author

Diane Capri

"Full of thrills and tension, but smart and human, too. Kim Otto
is a great, great character. I love her."
Lee Child

"[A] welcome surprise… [W]orks from the first page to 'The
End'."
Larry King

"Swift pacing and ongoing suspense are always present… [L]
ikable protagonist who uses her political connections for a good
cause… Readers should eagerly anticipate the next [book]."
Top Pick, *Romantic Times*

"…offers tense legal drama with courtroom overtones, twisty
plot, and loads of Florida atmosphere. Recommended."
Library Journal

"[A] fast-paced legal thriller…energetic prose…an appealing
heroine…clever and capable supporting cast…[that will] keep
readers waiting for the next [book]."
Publishers Weekly

"Expertise shines on every page."
**Margaret Maron, Edgar, Anthony, Agatha, and Macavity
Award-Winning author and MWA Grand Master and Past
President**

FATAL SHOT

by DIANE CAPRI
with
NIGEL BLACKWELL

Published by: AugustBooks
http://www.AugustBooks.com

Print ISBN: 978-1-942633-97-6
eBook ISBN: 978-1-942633-96-9

Original cover design by: Cory Clubb

Published in the United States of America.

Visit the author website:
http://www.DianeCapri.com

ALSO BY DIANE CAPRI

The Hunt for Jack Reacher Series

(in publication order with Lee Child source books in parentheses)

Don't Know Jack (The Killing Floor)

Jack in a Box (*novella*)

Jack and Kill (*novella*)

Get Back Jack (Bad Luck & Trouble)

Jack in the Green (*novella*)

Jack and Joe (The Enemy)

Deep Cover Jack (Persuader)

Jack the Reaper (The Hard Way)

Black Jack (Running Blind/The Visitor)

Ten Two Jack (The Midnight Line)

Jack of Spades (Past Tense)

Prepper Jack (Die Trying)

Full Metal Jack (The Affair)

Jack Frost (61 Hours)

Jack of Hearts • (Worth Dying For)

Straight Jack • (A Wanted Man)

Jack Knife • (Never Go Back)

Lone Star Jack • (Echo Burning)

Bulletproof Jack • (Make Me)

Bet on Jack • (Nothing to Lose)

The Jess Kimball Thrillers Series

Fatal Distraction

Fatal Demand

Fatal Error

Fatal Fall

Fatal Game

Fatal Bond

Fatal Enemy (*novella*)

Fatal Edge (*novella*)

Fatal Past (*novella*)

Fatal Dawn

Fatal Shot

The Hunt for Justice Series Due Justice

Twisted Justice

Secret Justice

Wasted Justice

Raw Justice

Mistaken Justice (*novella*)

Cold Justice (*novella*)

False Justice (*novella*)

Fair Justice (*novella*)

True Justice (*novella*)

Night Justice

The Park Hotel Mysteries Series

Reservation with Death

Early Check Out

Room with a Clue

Late Arrival

The Michael Flint Series:

Blood Trails

Trace Evidence

Ground Truth

Hard Money

Short Reads Collections

Hit the Road Jack

Justice Is Served

Fatal Action

FATAL SHOT

CAST OF CHARACTERS

Jessica Kimball
Henry Morris
Carter Pierce
Mandy Donovan
Alphonse Norton
Theo Kahler
Lynette Tierney
Ross Tierney
and
Peter Kimball

Even the simple is never easy.

CHAPTER 1

Saturday
Big Peak, Colorado

THEO KAHLER HATED WORKING backup. It was insulting. He was the gang's only sniper and ranked among the top half dozen snipers in the country. Army trained. Eight years in those places they talk about on TV doing things they don't mention on TV.

Pay was better now, of course. Much better. Which was why he put up with whatever job the boss gave him to do.

It still rankled. He could shoot the wings off a fly. He deserved to be the go-to guy, not the cleanup guy.

Yet here he was, lying in the Colorado snow, perched on the side of a mountain, waiting for one of the gang's goons who claimed to be an expert driver to screw up.

Still, he'd put everything the army taught him to good use.

The day before, he'd scoped out the area to choose the best setup position. He'd measured the six-hundred-yard distance to the target with a laser range finder. He'd cleaned and loaded his gun and wrapped it in white fabric to blend its dark silhouette into the surrounding snow.

Wildlife was sparse, so nothing would draw undue attention.

Dressed in white snow gear and white gloves, Kahler had settled into a white sleeping bag an hour before. At regular intervals, he shifted his weight, rolled his shoulders, and flexed his fingers to keep limber in the January cold.

His phone dinged. A single code word text.

"Hello."

Which meant the target was minutes away.

He slipped off his gloves. Two small heating pads fell out. The sort that activated in air. He tucked them in his coat so as not to waste the warmth.

Kahler's gun was ready.

A Kalabar K10 Precision Rifle. Over four feet long, it promised accuracy and a scary destructive force. Properly adjusted, the skeleton stock was more comfortable than it looked. His Leupold sight was equally well adjusted.

"Backup my ass," he muttered under his breath. "No way the target gets away on my watch."

The target would exit a short tunnel in a restored '60s Plymouth muscle car, probably at high speed because an aggressively driven Chevy Camaro would be pressuring the hell out of him.

From there, the Camaro would push the target's vehicle to the side of the road at a sharp bend.

The guardrail would crumple at the first touch. Kahler had weakened the once strong structure by removing its bolts.

The target vehicle would drop and roll a hundred feet before coming to rest, hopefully in a flaming mass.

Kahler shuffled, settling his legs and resting his chest on the snowbank he'd built to steady his weight. He leaned forward, wrapping his arm around the stock and resting his finger on the trigger guard.

If the Camaro failed its mission, Kahler was ready with the Kalabar.

He sighted the tunnel with the scope. An SUV exited the tunnel and took the curve with ease. Another car followed without mishap.

And then he heard the roar of big engines being pushed hard reverberating through the air.

Kahler paced his breathing and curled his finger against the trigger.

He felt the pressure of the mechanism. The delicate balance of light touch and instant response thrilled him.

The engine noise grew in a rush. A yellow and black Plymouth burst from the tunnel, a red Camaro beside it. At eighty plus, the cars crossed the small distance to the corner in a flash.

Kahler didn't blink. Breathing slowly, he tracked the vehicles.

The Plymouth turned. The Camaro didn't.

The Camaro speared into the Plymouth's front wheel, jolting both cars.

The Plymouth's brakes squealed, but the car didn't slow.

Instead, it slammed through the barrier, flying for the first fifty feet before landing nose first on the steep slope.

The hood crumpled and the whole car folded around the passenger compartment.

Not because of crumple zones and careful engineering designed to absorb the forces. But because in the sixties, no one cared about the dangers of a big block engine hurtling backward through the passenger compartment.

Glass flew in all directions. The doors burst open, torn off as the car rolled.

The gas tank exploded as the car cartwheeled down the rocky face.

A final impact brought the vehicle to a stop, sending a jet of flame across the snow.

The Camaro screeched to a halt and reversed fast to the point of impact.

The driver leapt out, grabbed a section of the Camaro's bumper that had broken off, stashed it inside the car, and raced off.

The Camaro's big engine wailed as it disappeared into the distance. The driver would dump the car on a deserted back road in Utah and burn it to an unrecognizable black shell.

Kahler kept his attention on the burning wreckage below. The high-powered scope provided a ringside seat to the slaughter as he waited to be sure the flame-engulfed target did not survive.

Over several minutes, oncoming cars drew to a halt on the road. A few curious drivers gingerly looked over the edge at the damage and turned away in horror.

Kahler rolled his shoulders. The cold was getting to him. The target hadn't survived, for sure. He moved his weight, shifting his elbows, ready to bring himself to a kneeling position.

He knew his mistake as it happened and when it happened.

Knowing didn't stop the consequences.

Kahler still had his finger on the trigger.

He hadn't moved it to the guard as he'd been trained. The simple safety protocol ingrained in every soldier, especially snipers.

A small force was all it took. Three pounds for the briefest instant.

Unintentionally, he pulled the trigger.

The gun bucked, the stock thumping against his shoulder. The exhaust blast threw a plume of snow upward and a sharp crack cut the crisp air.

He shifted his gaze down the barrel, desperately searching the area around the burning car for his round.

Nothing moved, no cloud of snow, no rocks shifted from the bullet's impact on the target.

He checked through the scope. Flames still engulfed the car, and glass and metal surrounded it. The flames reached a tree, adding to the destruction.

Kahler blew out a long breath. Destruction of the target and surrounding area. He had to hope it would be enough.

Emergency vehicle sirens sounded in the distance. Time to go.

He wrapped his gun in the bag and slung the weight over his shoulder. He had a mile-long hike to get to his SUV, parked far enough away to avoid connection with the crash.

With just one small exception, the boss had received exactly what he wanted. There'd be an investigation, of course. But no one would use the word "assassination."

The target's death would be classified and forgotten. A simple fact of modern life.

Road rage.

CHAPTER 2

Tuesday
Colorado Springs

JESSICA KIMBALL WALKED INTO Bergmann-Ross High School. The familiar scent of school meals and disinfectant met her nose. Rows of lockers lined the corridors, just as they had done in her day. A hand-painted sign welcomed visitors to Science Night. She followed directions and found the exhibits in the cafeteria.

Throngs of parents wandered past exhibits that spanned three walls. It took less than a moment to spot the one that most interested her.

She'd finally found her son after years of searching and she'd tried to do everything possible to make up for the missing time. It was a balancing act.

At fifteen, Peter was used to both his adoptive parents and his own freedoms. Another adult interested in his life was good, as long as she didn't cut too much into those freedoms.

This wasn't one of those nights when he wanted to be independent from his biological mother.

Tonight Peter would be pleased for the extra attention, Jess knew. She just had to remember to use the name his adoptive parents had given him. Steven.

"Mom said I had to come," said a voice. Jess turned to see Michelle, Steven's adoptive sister.

Jess smiled. Sibling rivalry was nothing new. Michelle and Steven's was definitely the healthy kind. "I thought you were off at college?"

"Family vacation. Dad's paying and I'm a poor student. Besides, my tutor agreed the trip can be incorporated into my classes."

"Want to see what he's done?" Jess asked, smiling.

"Steven? I've seen it. He always has some sort of project going for this event. Every year he monopolizes the garage for a couple of weeks to make it. Which means Mom has to park in the driveway every night. Which means I'd be freezing going to school every morning when I lived at home."

"Your mom mentioned that."

"Did she also mention that she had to walk to school every day, uphill both ways?"

Jess laughed. "She didn't, but I'm guessing she told you it builds character."

Michelle rolled her eyes. "There must be some special school adults go to learn all these lectures."

"It's called life."

"There you go with another one."

Jess gave Michelle a friendly nudge. "Let's go talk to Steven before we get any older."

"And yet another. How do you do it?" Michelle teased with a grin.

Jess led the way through the crowd to her son's exhibit, smiling all the way.

Two girls stood in front of Steven's table, watching as he turned over a small contraption in his hands and pointed out things that obviously interested him more than they interested the girls.

"Mom tells me they're the Oslo twins," Michelle whispered.

One girl had straight blond hair that reached her back, and the other had red curls.

"Twins?" Jess asked.

Michelle shook her head. "Exchange students from Finland. Apparently, the nickname just stuck."

"But Oslo is in Norway."

"Yeah, but you name somewhere in Finland."

"Helsinki."

Michelle stared and frowned. "How do you know…? Isn't that a syndrome?"

"That's Stockholm. In Sweden."

Michelle exhaled. "I'm so glad I'm doing art."

The Oslo twins left, giggling as they went.

"Oh, to be fifteen," Michelle said.

"You're nineteen," Steven deadpanned. "Barely."

"And don't you forget it."

"So what have you got?" Jess said, feeling the need to interrupt the rivalry.

Steven held up what appeared to be a circuit card covered with wires and helicopter-like propellers. "A drone."

"Are we talking about your conversation style or that bunch of wires?" Michelle said with a look of mock seriousness.

Steven scowled.

"So you've built a drone," Jess said, hoping to get the discussion back on track.

"Hasn't that been done?" Michelle teased.

"With four blades," Steven said. "But mine has three. Makes it lighter. And I did the software to make it stable in flight."

He tossed the device into the air, where it flipped the right way up and hovered at head height.

"Cool," Jess said, rightfully impressed.

"That's it?" Michelle asked.

"Nope." Steven held his phone out to Jess. A box appeared on the display, outlined in red. "Draw a route."

"To where?"

"Just do a loop of the room."

Jess looked at the crowd. "You can't fly it around here."

"Trust me."

She stared a moment. He seemed confident, so she drew a path around the box. Go appeared on the display.

"Press it," he said.

Jess tapped the button, hoping she wasn't about to cause an accident.

The drone bleeped and set off around the room. People stared.

It tilted left and right, weaving around obstacles. It stopped and backed up to go around a group of boys who tried to form a wall to block its progress.

One of the boys reached for it and the drone shot upward, clearing the group before descending and continuing the journey.

"Ultrasonic sensors and a bit of programming," Steven explained when he saw Jess's astonishment. "Actually, quite a lot of programming."

"Amazing," Jess said as the drone returned to settle on the table. "It's just a circuit card."

"Adding a shell would make it too heavy."

"You built all this?"

He nodded.

Jess leaned closer to examine the aircraft. The parts were tiny.

"Multicore ARM processor," Steven said, a note of pride in his voice. "A gig of flash, six sensors, and three servo motors."

"Arm?" said Jess.

"ARM. Same sort of processor you have in your phone."

"Right," Jess said with confidence as if she had any clue what he was talking about.

"I usually just nod at this point," Michelle whispered.

"She wanted to paint it," he said.

Michelle picked up the drone. "I thought red with a white racing stripe."

Steven took back the drone. "I'll keep it as is, thanks."

"Your mom tells me you're going skiing in Utah," Jess said.

Steven nodded. "Snow all around us and yet we're going to Utah."

"It's Sundance," Michelle said. "It has some of the—"

"Best art in the West. Or something. Yeah, yeah," he said.

"It's part of my art course," Michelle said. She leaned close to Jess. "He's just disappointed he won't be able to see the twins while we're gone."

"No. No. It's not—" Steven's face reddened with embarrassment.

Jess held her hands up. "Okay, okay. It should be great. The art, the skiing, everything."

One of Steven's teachers arrived and engaged Jess in conversation. Michelle drifted away to see old friends visiting their one-time high school. The Oslo twins paid a second visit to Steven.

Too soon, Science Night was over.

Jess left Bergmann-Ross High bursting with emotions.

After years of worry, her search had found her son in a loving family, well adjusted and safe. She had an amicable agreement with his adoptive parents for visitation.

The dark dread that had for so long inhabited the corners of her mind had been replaced with unrestrained joy about her son.

CHAPTER 3

6 days later
Denver

JESS PULLED TO A stop in her parking spot at the *Taboo Magazine* offices, glad the building had underground parking. She'd traded her Charger for a white Jeep. It was a little older than the one she'd used to rescue her son, but it was roomier and still had the big V-8 engine and manual transmission. All of that had proven useful on the weekends she'd gone skiing with Peter and Michelle.

She grabbed her bag and hustled inside, taking the stairs up two floors to the ground level and the main elevators.

The doors opened when the elevator reached the tenth floor. Occasional pools of light spilled from offices and cubes into the dim hallway. Early birds getting a head start on the day.

Her assistant, Mandy Donovan, smiled and waved from across the room, holding up a mug with steam wafting from the surface.

Jess hurried over, took the mug, and smelled the aroma of fresh coffee. "You're a treasure."

"And you're earlier than ever."

Jess checked her watch. "Six forty-five and the coffee's ready. You're not exactly slacking."

"I live two blocks away. Besides, we're doing podcasts now."

Jess frowned. "Podcasts?"

"Like recorded radio shows."

"I know what podcasts are. I—"

Mandy leaned close. "Have you seen the audio engineer?"

Jess shook her head.

"Well." Mandy shrugged. "He doesn't usually get here till nine thirty, but it's worth the wait."

"O-kay."

"What about you and Henry?"

Jess stiffened at the mention of Henry Morris. She didn't discuss her personal life at work. "Henry likes coffee, too."

Henry was a rising star in the FBI. They'd clicked when Jess was researching an article in Dallas. She had never decided whether his move to the FBI's Denver Field Office had been fate, or he'd requested the transfer.

Either way, his move had given their relationship time to evolve, professionally and personally. There were decisions to be made and she just didn't want to talk about it here.

Mandy shrugged. "Just wondering."

When Jess didn't reply Mandy took a deep breath, looked at her monitor, and got back to business. "You have a seven thirty with Carter."

"He wants to talk about my new assignment."

"Right." Mandy broke eye contact and hummed.

"What?"

"You're not going to like it."

"Why?"

"You know what the Rockies play?"

Jess frowned. "Baseball."

"It's not that." Mandy raised an eyebrow.

"It's not what? Oh no. He's got some softball—"

"What?" said Carter Pierce, the magazine's owner and editor. Wealthy, he didn't need to work, but he wasn't one to sit idle. The magazine wasn't a plaything for him. He took responsibility for the livelihoods of the entire staff. He'd steered the ship through rocky times and made it all work with both his business and integrity intact. Jess admired and appreciated him. Truth be told, they all did.

Mandy turned back to her computer, busying herself with typing as he walked over.

"Can't a man keep anything secret around here?" Carter said.

Jess gripped her coffee mug harder. "You've got some softball assignment for me?"

Carter ignored the question and stared at Mandy, who shrugged without looking up.

"Open floorplan offices," she said. "You can't not hear things."

Carter looked at the coffeepot on the corner of her desk. "That fresh?"

Mandy grabbed a mug, filled it, and held it out. He took a sip. "Not bad. Bit like the audio engineer." He winked. "At least, so I hear."

Mandy mumbled something while staring at her keyboard.

Carter turned to Jess. "Let's talk in my office."

Jess followed and took a chair while he sat behind his desk. In the corner, a new grandfather clock ticked. A soft, dignified click, entirely appropriate for Carter's personality.

"Softball doesn't sell magazines, Jess," he said. "You know that, and I know that. Let's get that idea out of the way at the start."

"So what is it?" Jess and Carter had long ago passed the point where she took on any assignment he offered. She chose her work carefully, and he knew that.

"Road rage."

Jess stared. "You're kidding."

"Do I choose topics for giggles?"

"No."

"So why don't you want to do it?"

"Look, Carter, nobody likes road rage. It's wrong and some incidents end in tragedy, but what can I do to stop it with an article on the subject? Everybody already knows the facts. You want me to document known facts?"

Carter scowled. "For what I pay you, I sincerely hope not."

"But there's no story. Road rage events are one-offs. Some driver gets ticked and slams into another driver and speeds away. A brief police investigation followed by—sometimes, eventually, hopefully—some sort of prosecution that brings a measure of justice."

Carter nodded reasonably, "And you don't want to try to make a difference?"

"I...*Taboo* should be more than the local newspaper. The legal system might be flawed, but it metes out justice. Eventually. We need to—"

"Raise public awareness? Highlight the very real human costs of a driver's momentary lapse of reason? Plead with the public to be more considerate of other drivers? More careful?" Carter said. "You can write that better than anyone."

"Hard to find more than a lot of boring statistics and scolding drivers who won't read *Taboo* anyway for their abominable behavior."

"So find the humanity, Jess. The real stories behind these incidents. You know there's more to the story. *Try* to make the world a better place."

Jess said nothing.

Carter arched his eyebrows as he sipped the coffee. "Those were your goals, once. No more?"

"Hoisted by my own petard, eh?" The grandfather clock ticked. Jess pressed her lips together. "You think we're playing chess and your move is check, don't you?"

He slid a thick folder across his desk. "Fifty-seven cases reported in the last month. And one death."

"In the United States?"

"In Denver."

"That's a lot," Jess said, genuinely surprised. She picked up the folder, hesitating before she opened it. "Oh, right. In Denver. I get it. You're worried about separating me from Peter. Well, he's skiing this week. In Utah."

Carter shrugged. "Even so, it's not been very long since you found him. Only a couple of months. You need some time to get used to the changes."

"And they've been the best times I can remember. But we've talked. Me, Peter, the Tierneys. They understand what I do. Peter's almost fully grown. He'll be out in the world on his own soon, anyway. I'm not looking to relive all the years I've missed. That's not even possible. Even if that were my preference. Which it's not."

Carter inched the folder closer to Jess. "Then I'm sure Peter will appreciate you helping to make his world a better place."

Jess exhaled. Carter knew her almost as well as she knew herself. Only one sign that he was both a good editor and a good friend.

He'd maneuvered her into a corner with her own words.

And he was right.

Or maybe she was right. People didn't read her articles in *Taboo Magazine* for sorrow and statistics. They read Jessica Kimball's byline because they wanted to believe in and help to create a better world. For themselves, for their children.

That was the force that had driven her for over a decade as she searched for Peter. Having found Peter, that force hadn't disappeared.

"Checkmate, I believe." She picked up the folder and stood.

Carter laughed as he watched her leave his office.

CHAPTER 4

JESS MOVED TO HER desk and started to work. Carter's folder contained names, addresses, summary reports, and in some cases links to videos of road rage incidents. Jess extracted the one incident that had resulted in death and buzzed Mandy to collect the rest.

"Can you organize the addresses in the most efficient route for interviews?" she asked, head down, already engrossed in the Rooney case.

A picture of the deceased from social media showed a clean-shaven man in his mid to late twenties with brown hair and green eyes.

Justin Rooney's biography included a degree in computer science and IT work at a couple of obscure internet services companies before he ended up at a local bank.

Unmarried, he lived in a condo in Broomfield, on the north side of the city.

Looking him up online, Jess found pictures of a young man interested in old cars more than his friends. A couple of sites posted photos of Rooney smiling as he turned rust buckets into competition vehicles. Probably not a cheap hobby, but it didn't look like he'd spent his money on much else.

Mandy returned with a map and pointed out several routes. "Red line for cases where there was some sort of injury and video. Blue for injuries and no video. Green for just a report of aggressive driving with no injuries."

Jess ran her finger over the lines. "North, south, east, and west. Freeways and surface roads. Downtown and suburbs. No distinct pattern."

"But…" Mandy placed another page on the desk, a spreadsheet with graphs. "Peak in cases around rush hour. Morning and evening. There's a dip on the weekends, obviously."

"You got this from the documents in Carter's folder?"

Mandy nodded. "But no surprises, right?"

"That's my problem. We know all this. How do I make anything more out of these events than spreadsheets and graphs?"

"Well…" Mandy shrugged on her way out the door. "You're the ace reporter. I'm going to have to leave that to you."

Jess pushed the spreadsheets aside and picked up the Justin Rooney report. It was the obvious case to investigate, the one most likely to have issues that might resonate with the magazine's readers. Focusing on avoiding tragedy might save lives.

But Jess was no ambulance chaser. Never had been, never would be. A young man's life had been cut short. Parents and siblings and friends would be struggling with loss. They'd be planning a funeral, tidying up finances, closing down credit cards, the million and one things left to do after a bereavement.

There'd likely be anger, too. A desire for justice, at least. Nothing would bring Rooney back, but whoever killed him shouldn't get away with it.

Jess shuffled the papers into a neat stack. Justice. Where she always started. Why should this assignment be any different?

CHAPTER 5

THE JUSTIN ROONEY FILE listed the accident location between mile markers 36 and 37 on Highway 44W. Jess knew the route to the Big Peak ski resort, an ironic name given its limited number of ski runs.

Highway 44W curved through the mountains and a couple of small tunnels along the way. Steep sections of the roadway along that route displayed great views, but the road was frequently closed during snowstorms, much to the chagrin of the Big Peak Ski Company since their business was literally built on the availability of snow.

Jess called a contact at Denver PD. The Rooney case was being handled by Detective Alphonse Norton. "Goes by Al," he said.

Norton worked in the newly formed Denver Coordination Unit, a group designed to liaise and support some of the smaller police departments surrounding Denver.

She dialed Norton's number. "Detective Norton, this is Jess Kimball. I'm a reporter with *Taboo Magazine*." She mentioned her contact's name for good measure.

"I doubt this is a social call. What's up?" Norton said in a no-nonsense way.

Jess preferred the get-to-the-point style, too. "Justin Rooney."

"Killed out on 44W a week ago, but you probably know that."

"I do."

"Went over the edge. Big drop. Didn't stand a chance."

"A second party involved?" Jess asked.

"Possibly. An unknown party," Norton replied. "And to what extent they were involved, we don't know."

"Witnesses?"

"That bend in the road is a long way from civilization. A minivan driver called in the accident, but the driver didn't see it happen."

"If it was an accident."

He paused a moment and then said, "I have an open mind."

"Did forensics tell you anything useful?"

"Some initial things." His rapid-fire style slowed. "Gonna take time for a more in-depth report."

Jess waited until it became apparent that he wouldn't volunteer more. "I'm looking for a way to make Rooney's death a cautionary tale about road rage, Detective. Help me out here."

"Look," he replied, "It's an ongoing investigation and I don't really have a need to involve the press at this point. No offense, but once we've got things tied up, or when we need information from the public, I'd be glad to talk. Before then…"

"You realize I'm going to look into this myself."

"Glad to hear it." Norton's grin came through the phone. "We need all the help we can get."

"And if I find something?"

"Then I hope you'll do the law-abiding thing and let me know."

Jess didn't want to push him too far too fast, so she thanked him and hung up with a promise to keep him informed.

She needed to get out to see the accident site. She stopped at her apartment to change into heavy boots and add a couple of extra layers to her outfit. It was winter in the Rockies and still damned cold outside. Ten minutes later, she was on the road.

Monday-morning traffic was light. The Jeep's winter tires had no problem climbing the slope to Big Peak. The brawny V-8 barely rose above a steady rumble.

She watched the mile markers and found the spot where Rooney's car went over the guardrail after exiting a short tunnel.

Tire tracks raked across the pavement. Fresh unpainted guardrail had been installed to cover the gap where Rooney's car flew over the edge.

Jess slowed until she found a place to pull in and park about a hundred yards farther on.

The outdoor air temperature gauge on her Jeep said ten degrees below freezing. She donned a fleece hat and thermal gloves before stepping out.

Norton was correct. The crash site was a long way from civilization with no possibility of CCTV out here.

Jess walked back to the crash site, keeping close to the outside of the gravel shoulder near the guardrail. The metal guardrail was the only barrier to a steep drop.

As she rounded the bend she could see down to where Rooney's car finally stopped falling. A near sheer face of rock on a craggy plateau.

The destroyed vehicle had been removed. But burned tree branches and mud-churned snow marked the spot unmistakably.

She waited for an SUV to pass before walking to the middle of the road to photograph the guardrail and tire marks. Tires left black lines of rubber angled into the barrier. Rooney's car, presumably. More tire marks had been laid down beside them.

She walked back and forth, examining the road, shooting photos. As a van approached, she moved out of the way onto the shoulder.

The second set of tire tracks was wider than Rooney's. They weren't easy to read. The tracks also suggested a car traveling in the opposite direction might have come to an emergency stop. Why?

Was Rooney trying to avoid oncoming traffic? If so, the other driver had been on the wrong side of the road.

She stood at the point where Rooney's car must have gone over the edge.

If Rooney had been trying to avoid another vehicle, why didn't he just stop? The two vehicles might have impacted, but maybe the crash would have only damaged the corners of the two cars. Instead, a man was dead, and the other driver would live with that forever.

An SUV passed Jess's position. The driver accelerated as he rounded the corner.

She knelt to stare across the tarmac.

The tire tracks pattern from Rooney's accident wasn't as she'd first thought. The second car hadn't braked to a stop. The second car was already stopped. And then raced away, wheels spinning, laying rubber on the road.

So was the second car involved, or was the second set of tracks left by a driver who'd stopped momentarily and then left? Was that why Norton had been cagey about saying a second party was involved?

She aimed her camera over the mountain's edge, all the way down to where the car had come to rest. Rooney's last moments would have been terrifying.

The fire had followed the impact. On the rocky slope, there were few trees, which prevented the fire from spreading. She hoped Rooney had passed long before the fire began.

Jess walked back to her Jeep, stopping along the way to take pictures of more tire tracks. This group seemed the mirror image of the previous set. As if the car had braked hard and then reversed fast.

"They match," a male voice called out.

Jess looked up. A short, square-shouldered man in a weatherproof blue police jacket approached. "Detective Norton. You're Jess Kimball, right?"

"Yes." She shook the hand he offered.

"Recognized you from the TV," he said. "You were on the morning show a while ago."

Jess considered sharing how her son's appearance was so like her own, but Norton's demeanor suggested he wanted to talk about other things.

"Rooney went over right there." She pointed to the tire tracks and the new guardrail. "A second car braked to a halt here, raced back to where Rooney left the road, and then tore away in a cloud of smoke."

"Seems so."

"Then there was a third vehicle?"

Norton pressed his lips together and stared for a moment, deciding what to say. "Lady in a minivan was passed by Rooney and a Camaro, speeding fast. They raced out of sight."

"Okay," Jess said, visualizing the incident.

He pointed to the tire tracks. "That rubber compound matches the tires used on a Camaro, which is what the minivan driver said the second car was."

"Let me guess. The same tires are also used on other cars."

"Twenty-seven different models. And still doesn't mean any of those tires were involved in what happened to Rooney."

"Which is why you're noncommittal on the Camaro."

"Minivan driver thinks there was something going on between Rooney and this Camaro. That's all we've got."

"Going on?"

"Racing each other, specifically."

"Why did Rooney's car go through the barrier?"

"Good question." Norton's chin jutted toward the guardrail. "Seems the barrier had somehow lost a lot of bolts."

"How do you lose a bolt?"

"Another good question," Norton said. "Temperature extremes can make it happen. So they tell me."

"But there must have been plenty of bolts missing to make the guardrail fail like that."

He nodded.

Jess took a breath. "You think someone removed them?"

He grunted. "That would make this incident premeditated murder."

She shrugged.

"No, I'm not saying that," Norton replied.

"Because?"

"Because you're a reporter." He turned away. "Want to look at the impact site?"

"Sure." Jess had no real desire to examine where Rooney had met his end, but Norton's vague answers to her questions set off all her internal alarms.

There was more to this story. Norton undoubtedly knew things she needed to know, too.

CHAPTER 6

JESS WATCHED NORTON GRASPING for handholds as he slipped and slid along the rocky slope downward to the impact site. She was glad her boots provided a better grip on the steep and muddy path.

Rooney's car had come to rest on a plateau perhaps fifty feet wide. Beyond the plateau the mountain continued down for another hundred feet before forming into a gently sloping valley.

Rocks of various sizes littered the plateau floor, proving random rock falls were a threat here. The ground was scorched where the car had landed in the center of the plateau.

She walked the perimeter, occasionally glancing up at the guardrail far above. "He fell straight down."

"CSI reckons he was only doing twenty-five when he launched over the road's edge."

Jess understood. "So he was braking."

"Another few feet and he'd probably still be alive." Norton nodded like she was a particularly apt pupil.

"Twenty-five miles an hour isn't fast. Why couldn't he steer away from the danger?"

"You really are full of good questions," Norton replied without snark.

She stared at him in return, eyebrows raised.

"Why did he go through the guardrail rather than turn the wheel?" Norton asked, as if she already knew.

Jess looked up again, this time seeking the answer. "He knew what was happening. He was braking and trying to avoid going over the crest. Which means he tried, but he couldn't turn away."

It was Norton's turn to raise his eyebrows, encouraging her on.

"Something blocked him from stopping."

"Exactly." Norton hummed. "We found a lot of debris. Plastic, paint, metal. The usual bits and pieces that come from a crash."

Jess said, "He was forced over the edge."

"That would make it murder."

"Is that how you're treating it?"

Norton sighed. "The evidence is still circumstantial."

"But?"

"There's something you should know before you go running off to print any kind of story based on what you hear from me."

Jess frowned and cocked her head.

"Four years ago, my wife died when a guy in a pickup rammed her car. He had those big bull bars on the front. Solid rods of steel. Went straight through the driver's side door. Went straight through…" He turned away, squeezing his lips together.

His wife. He didn't need to finish the sentence.

Norton clenched his fists. His breath hissed through his nose.

Jess stood still, patient, waiting for him to compose himself.

He took a deep breath and turned back. "Driver got off. His lawyer threw out all sorts of bullshit. Left the court smiling. Waving to the cameras."

"I'm sorry."

"I still go to Santiago's."

"The boxing place?" Jess asked to be sure she understood the non sequitur.

"Work off steam. Started the day after the judgment," Norton said. "Put a picture of the guy's face on the heavy bag."

"I can understand."

"Still do. Sometimes."

Jess nodded.

"Word gets around, you know?" Norton took a pause for a bit and then grunted. "People think I'm fixated. Biased. Hell, they might be right. So save us both some grief. You don't want to go around quoting me."

"Thanks for the heads-up," Jess replied. "Why did you get this case, if your department is worried about your objectivity?"

"I never want another family to go through what happened with my wife's death. I took this case on willingly. I take as many serious traffic cases as I can." He nodded. "I work the cases hard. Collect the evidence, tie it with a bow, and hand it over. That's all I can do."

Jess knew what it meant to detectives to close a case, to offer the victims justice. She felt that need herself and always had, even though she wasn't a cop.

When he couldn't close a case, it had to hurt. Perhaps he spent a little longer hitting the heavy bag on those days.

"Four convictions from six fatal traffic crash cases," he said. "So far."

"Two-thirds. That's a good average for cases that were undoubtedly difficult," Jess replied. "Why are you telling me this?"

"I know your magazine. Read some of your stuff." He gestured to the impact point, where, they both believed now, Rooney was pushed off the road to his death. "The motor vehicle fatality issue needs a spotlight."

There was no arguing with the logic, but she couldn't give him false assurances. "I've only just started. Don't know where this story is going. Might not lead to a publication or conviction."

"This one has a different feel," he said.

"How?"

He gestured up to the road. "The tire marks."

"Almost looks like the driver passed, reversed, came back to see what happened."

"Or to make sure it had happened," he said quietly.

Jess whistled. "Barbarous."

"That's a fancy reporter word for it."

"Any video? From sky cams over the freeway, maybe?"

He shook his head. "Nothing."

She circled the impact site. Tree-lined valley walls extended a good mile, and the floor of the valley was hidden by the plateau.

"Forensics turn up anything worth pursuing?"

"Still waiting."

Jess stopped at a small tree. Thirty feet from the fire, several of the branches had been singed and the six-inch trunk had split.

She ran her fingers over the freshly exposed wood. A straight line seemed to cut through the jagged break. She stretched up to peer into the gap. The sharply cut line stopped at a dark lump.

Jess looped her arm around the tree and used a bulge on the lower part of the trunk to lift herself up for a better look.

"What?" said Norton.

"It's…" She peered closer. Dark metal glinted. "A bullet."

Norton grunted. "Hunters. Gun people. There's nothing out here that hasn't been shot at."

Jess slid back onto the ground. The straight line in the tree pointed upward. She followed the imaginary line over the edge of the plateau to a group of trees on the far valley wall. "Why would anybody shoot a tree?"

"They'll shoot at anything."

"The shooter was somewhere over there." She pointed to a group of three trees on the valley wall.

"Impressive." Norton nodded. "Long shot."

"And the impact is high up in the tree. Crazy aim. Couldn't have been shooting at wildlife."

"Unless the animal was in the tree. Or the target was way out of the shooter's skill range."

Jess dusted the grime from her gloves. "Maybe."

Norton's phone rang. He walked off to answer the call.

It hadn't snowed in a week, and Jess could see the faint shadow of a trail toward the group of trees where the shooter must have stood. Someone had trod a path there. She looked for more tracks in the snow in the area. The guy must have left by walking along the same trail.

Norton finished his call. "I've got to go. They need me back at the station. Keep in touch, okay?"

"Yeah. You, too," Jess replied, watching him jog up the slope toward the road.

It was cold out there and she needed to move. She headed back, too, turning at regular intervals to check the view from the group of trees where the shooter might have stood.

By the time she reached the road, she felt confident she could walk up there.

She waited for a silver Nissan Pathfinder to drive by. It slowed. A nice gesture, given the spray it churned up from the sloppy pavement.

Jess returned to her Jeep, donned snow pants and boots, and set off in search of the shooter's nest.

The valley had accumulated a couple of feet of snow. Time had hardened the surface. The walk was a slow slog.

Her boots broke through the crust and compressed the softer snow beneath as she trudged through. The effort increased her body temperature and strained the muscles in her legs. At this point, the cold air felt good on her face.

She kept going.

After a few minutes the burning feeling in her muscles diminished as her body warmed to the effort.

The smooth white snow on the surface hid dips and climbs beneath. She had to detour a couple of times around trees and brush. But she finally made it. She checked her watch and was surprised to see she'd made the walk in just over ten minutes.

The person had definitely used the same path in and out. Between the trees, the snow was well trodden. She saw no trash.

The snow was packed into a smooth slope, like someone had camped there. She knelt to inspect it closer. The smooth section sloped upward at one end.

She lay down on her belly on the smoothed area. The raised end supported her chest.

Jess wriggled forward. At her right shoulder, the slope dipped. She raised her arms as if cradling a rifle.

A perfect spot.

Jess felt comfortable and her arms were free to operate the imaginary weapon. When she leaned her head to one side, the aim of her nonexistent weapon lined up perfectly with the split tree on the plateau.

Hunters, Norton said.

Why would a hunter aim toward a bare plateau beneath the road?

Traffic noise would likely keep wildlife away, wouldn't it?

She looked down the valley. Portions of the area were forested. A happy hunting ground compared to the plateau.

Norton had dismissed the bullet, but the hunter hypothesis made no sense.

Jess shuffled to her knees. Light glinted from a small hole in the snow down the slope to her right.

She climbed between the trees and retrieved a spent cartridge. The heat from firing the bullet must have caused the metal casing to melt the snow when it landed. Jess wasn't a hunter, but it was two inches long, so probably a rifle cartridge. She zipped it into an empty pocket in her jacket.

Jess followed the footsteps through the snow. Twenty minutes later, the track ended at a parking spot on the side of a road. She looked around. No businesses or homes or much of anything that might have had CCTV.

"Nothing else to do right here," she said into the quiet. "But let's get that bullet."

She returned to her Jeep and found a screwdriver in the Jeep's tool kit. She hiked back to the tree, dug the bullet from the trunk, and zipped it into another jacket pocket.

CHAPTER 7

THEO KAHLER DROVE HIS silver Nissan Pathfinder into the tunnel on the route down from Big Peak. Half a mile later, he emerged on the long run back into Denver.

He punched the first speed-dial button on his burner phone and put the call on the phone's tinny speaker. If he'd connected it to his SUV's Bluetooth system, it would leave digital tracks. Not happening.

The call clicked and buzzed and rang. Erich Miller picked up in his usual no-nonsense way.

"What?"

"Kahler. I just rolled down 44W. People getting interested in the view."

"What people?"

"Cop and some woman."

"Names?"

"Damn. I should have stopped to ask."

"You watch your mouth," Miller growled.

Kahler waited. Sometimes he couldn't decide if Miller was just stupid or if he enjoyed arguing. Miller was dangerous either way.

"Watch the woman," Miller said. "I have a man who can give us a name on the cop."

"Want me to do anything else?"

"Yeah. Watch."

"I mean if she becomes a risk."

"And why's she going to become a risk?"

"Who knows?"

"We do. Snout handled the schmuck. All accident, no evidence."

"Right."

"Something different you want to tell me?"

"Nothing," Kahler said, twisting his tone to emphasize his sincerity.

"Exactly. Anybody worried, send them to me. Got it?"

Kahler swiped a palm over his face. "Clear as a bell. I'm in. Hundred percent."

"Peachy," Miller said sarcastically. "First shipment's almost here. You better be at the top of your game. After tonight we're in the big leagues."

"I'll be there."

"Good. And no mistakes. Got it?"

"Got it," Kahler replied, but Miller had already disconnected.

CHAPTER 8

JESS USED THE DRIVE time returning to Denver to call Henry. Their relationship had cooled after she found her son. Henry joked about two men competing for her attention, but he was right. She didn't have much free time and now most of it went to Peter.

Henry had adapted to the changes in her life. They still talked regularly. But she hadn't seen him in a while. Too long, probably.

She waited as his office phone clicked, routing the call through to his cell. He answered on the second ring. After a moment's catching up, she ran through what she'd seen on the mountain.

"A lawyer's going to make that sound like a lot of guesswork," Henry said.

"I found the casing. That's solid evidence."

"Evidence of what? It's a casing. For a bullet that might have ended up stuck in a tree. In the vicinity of an accident," he replied reasonably.

"But—"

"I'm not being negative, Jess. Norton doesn't have a suspect, even. No one connected to the crash. You know what we'd be up against if we tried to make an arrest with nothing more than that bullet. Even your magazine wouldn't publish such speculation."

"Justin Rooney died," Jess said flatly.

"You know I care about lost lives, Jess." Henry's weary tone reminded her just how hard he worked. "Someone died in every case on my desk. Sometimes you just run out of steam."

Jess exhaled slowly. She did know how much he cared. She couldn't fathom how he handled the pressure and grief and stayed sane. But he did. And she felt safer because of Henry and others like him.

"Look," Henry said, his tone conciliatory. "Take the casing to Detective Norton. See what he makes of it."

"I'm not sure he's going to do anything with it."

"Why so?"

"He was pretty dismissive of the idea when we were out there on the mountain. Thought the bullet came from hunters."

"Not exactly prime hunting ground out on those steep slopes."

"My point exactly."

"But he needs the bullet either way. The casing, too. Chain of custody and all that."

"Of course. I just don't want him to toss it in a drawer to gather dust."

"All right." Henry sighed. "There's an expert we use. Here in Denver. Keshawn Goodwin. Might give you a quick analysis before you hand everything over to Norton. You can tell him I sent you."

Jess thanked him and they hung up. A moment later Goodwin's address pinged onto her phone. She punched it and GPS indicated a thirty-minute drive.

Following the navigation route, she arrived at a short block of single-story industrial units exactly on time.

Each unit had a single entrance door beside a roll-up door. One or two displayed fancy signs. Goodwin's unit was identified as KG INDUSTRIES.

Jess parked her Jeep and walked to the entrance. The door was locked. She pressed an intercom buzzer beside it. A moment later a metallic voice came from the speaker.

"Yo?"

"Jessica Kimball, *Taboo Magazine*. Looking for Keshawn Goodwin."

"A reporter?"

Fearing the way the conversation might head, she played the best card she could. "Henry Morris said Mr. Goodwin might be able to help with an investigation."

"Wait a minute."

The speaker clicked dead. After a minute she pressed the buzzer again.

"Wait," said the metallic voice, so she waited.

A van passed. The roll-up door a few units to her right opened, and the van drove straight inside. The door descended, rattling and clanking.

"You coming in?" said the metallic voice followed by an unmistakable buzzing sound.

Jess pushed the door open and stepped inside. The door closed behind her to the sound of electronic bolts locking in place, which made her a little nervous.

The floor had been coated with a smooth and spotless gray epoxy paint. Giant lights hung from the ceiling, making the room brighter than outside. Lab benches stretched three rows in front of her. Machines and equipment filled each bench. A long vat of water was placed on the last bench at the end.

A tall man in jeans and an orange polo sweater descended metal steps from a second-floor office at the back of the unit. The bright lights gave his skin a bluish-black appearance. His close-cropped gray hair had geometric patterns shaved into it.

"Sorry 'bout that," he said as he approached, waving at the door. "My business attracts a lot of…let's say different people. Had to check with Morris."

Jess shook Goodwin's extended hand. "I understand, but I'm not working for the FBI."

"Pity. Coulda charged their account." He grinned. "Anyway, welcome to the BRL."

"BRL?"

"Ballistics Research Laboratory."

"You do research here?"

"Some." He looked across the arrayed equipment, smiling. "Henry said you have a cartridge?"

Jess nodded and unzipped her jacket pocket.

"Wait," Goodwin said, snapping on a pair of nitrile gloves. "You touched it?"

"Sorry to say."

"Not a problem for me. We'll leave someone else to look for fingerprints."

He grabbed a thin rod that looked like a short knitting needle. "Do you mind?" he said, gesturing to Jess's pocket.

She held the pocket open, and he hooked the bullet by inserting the rod into the open end of the cartridge and then lifted it out.

Goodwin inspected the metal and sniffed. "It's a .338 Lupua Magnum. Two to three hundred grains. Fired recently, but not today. New when fired, not a reload. Good for a couple of thousand yards in the right hands. Marks on it are good enough. Might be able to identify the make of gun."

"I have the bullet," Jess said, unzipping another pocket.

He placed the casing in a pillbox. With a pair of tweezers, he picked the bullet from Jess's pocket and peered at it for a while.

"Hollow point. Some scrapes." He looked at Jess. "How did you get this?"

"Dug it out of a tree."

Goodwin grimaced. "That explains the shiny marks."

"I didn't have much choice. It was well above my head in a tree trunk on one of the rocky slopes out toward Big Peak."

"That's what CSIs are for." He gave her a dubious look. "Well. The bullet could be a match for the casing. Give me a bit and I should be able to say."

Goodwin dropped the bullet into another pillbox. "You know what this bullet is?"

Jess shook her head. "That's why I'm here."

"Sniper bullet. Designed for the military to take targets at one to two thousand yards. Sold commercially now. No shortage of guns take this round. Some hunters use them. Hollow points reduce the chance of collateral damage because it stops the bullet inside the target. Where did you get it?"

"From an accident on the road to Big Peak. Car went over the edge. A big drop."

"Ow. Did the gun go off in the crash?"

She shook her head.

Goodwin frowned. "So not connected with the crash?"

"Don't know. Like I said, the bullet was in a tree beside the impact site. The cartridge is from a hideout on the other side of the valley."

"So we don't know if the bullet and casing are connected."

"True."

"And a hideout?" he said.

"In the trees. Snow had been smoothed to make a stable platform pointing directly to where I found the bullet."

"Sounds professional. But there's plenty of how-tos on the internet these days. An amateur could have done it. Any sign of shots to the car?"

"Hard to say. The car burned. We're waiting for Denver PD forensics," she said, making a note to prompt Norton.

"It'll be a long wait. They must be stacked. Been sending me twice the normal number of cases lately."

He picked up the two pillboxes. "So you got nothing to connect the crash and this bullet?"

"Just weird coincidence."

He cocked his head. "You find a bullet and you think it might be related to a car crash. Kind of a big jump, don't you think?"

"The crash might not have been an accident."

"Ah."

"Can you link the bullet and casing?"

"Possibly." He nodded. "If you think the car crash wasn't an accident, you're thinking what? Maybe someone wanted to make sure the driver didn't walk away?"

Jess shrugged. "The car dropped more than a hundred feet. Rolled on the way to the bottom. The driver died on impact."

"And if none of that had happened?"

"You mean the sniper would have shot him? As some sort of backup?"

Goodwin shrugged. "Best I can offer."

She nodded. It was a solid answer. "But why did the bullet end up in the tree?"

"Sighting shot? Boredom? Who knows?"

"If you can match the bullet and casing, we'll know something more than we know now," Jess said slowly. "But a sniper in position, just in case the driver survives after a crash like that? Takes serious planning."

"Yeah," Goodwin said. "And there was me thinking only the military took the five Ps to heart."

"The five Ps? You mean like marketing? Product, price, place, promotion, packaging?"

Goodwin chuckled. "You can boil it down to proper planning prevents poor performance."

Jess shrugged. "Yeah, well, this time proper planning didn't do the job, did it?"

CHAPTER 9

AFTER LEAVING HER PHONE number, Jess left Goodwin inside the BRL, sat in her car, and called Detective Norton.

"What's up?" he said.

"You had a witness in a minivan. Can you give me the name?"

"Naya Bozeck. She didn't witness the accident. Just that Rooney and the Camaro were racing when they passed her."

"Still worth a shot," she said, regretting her choice of words the moment she uttered them. It didn't seem to faze Norton.

"We already have her statement. I can send you the address if you tell me what you get."

"Fair enough."

"And keep my name out of it."

"I got the message. Anything from forensics?"

Norton sucked in air, the sound loud over the phone. "First-look report tomorrow. But don't get excited. I'll have to assess it first. See what, if anything, I can release. I'm all for the help, but don't go thinking we're partners."

"Roger that. You should know I'm not one to give up easily."

"So it seems. I looked you up," Norton replied flatly.

"Don't believe everything you read on the internet."

"Just remember you're a public citizen in a city with a fully functioning police department," he warned.

"No matter what you've read, just know I'm a reporter looking for justice for victims who don't often get any," Jess replied. "I don't go after the cops. Not my style."

"Then we should get along just fine."

With their uneasy truce restored for the moment, Jess decided not to rock the boat again. She decided not to mention the bullet at the BRL until she had some more information from Goodwin.

Next she dialed Mandy, who answered with her usual crisp enthusiasm.

"Rooney's crash might not be an accident," Jess said.

"Definition of road rage, isn't it? Intentional damage done by a ticked-off hothead, right?"

"Might be more than that in this case. If I'm right, someone wanted Rooney dead."

"Really? Who? Why?"

"All good questions. Which is where you come in."

Mandy paused. "You want to meet the family?"

"No. They just lost a son—"

"Actually, his father passed away a few years ago."

"Very sad," Jess said quietly and paused. Then she took a breath. "Let's not talk to his mother just yet. I might be wrong about the whole thing. First let's see what you can dig up online, public records, every database we've got. Find friends and contacts in the area and make me a list. Include bars he frequented, too. Anywhere people would have known him. And, if you can, set me up to talk to his employer."

Mandy's voice became serious. "Okay, so you want me to get road rage statistics going back the past few years."

"No, his friends and employer," Jess corrected.

"Five years. Check."

Jess rolled her eyes. "Is my softball guardian standing by your shoulder?"

"Yeah…No problem. I'll email it ASAP."

Mandy hung up.

CHAPTER 10

KAHLER WATCHED HER JEEP pull away from the industrial unit. He waited for a couple of cars to pass before following.

She'd spent fifteen minutes in a place called KG Industries. The name belied the fact that the owner, Keshawn Goodwin, was interested in only one industry. Guns.

According to Kahler's quick scan on the internet, Goodwin called the place the Ballistic Research Laboratory and modeled it after the original army lab in Maryland. Goodwin was the very definition of a wannabe in Kahler's opinion, but that didn't matter now.

The woman didn't look like a cop, but she had gone straight from the crash site to Goodwin's. Could be a whole slew of reasons for that, but one possibility needled Kahler's conscience. Evidence. Could she have found his stray bullet?

He cussed silently. He should have gone back to the site. Searched it himself. If some random woman could find it, he'd have located the damned thing in a quick snap.

Kahler's burner phone rattled in the cupholder as he went

over a pothole. He gritted his teeth against the bounce.

Tonight was the night. Miller's plan to get into the big leagues as he called it. The man was an idiot, no question. But if the plan came off, they'd all be rich damned quick. And rich was the goal, with or without Miller and his half-assed bunch of goons.

Which meant Kahler had to deal with the woman. Clean up the situation and eliminate any evidence she might have acquired. He only knew one way to do it.

And he was more than fine with that.

CHAPTER 11

TRUE TO HIS WORD, Norton sent Naya Bozeck's address via text. Twenty minutes later Jess arrived at a smart-looking seventies-era split-level home. Brick cladding covered the lower half of the building, and freshly painted white siding covered the walls above the brick.

A young boy stared out from a picture window as Jess walked the winding brick path from the curb to the house. She rang the bell. A round-faced woman with dark blond hair opened the door.

"Naya Bozeck?"

The woman held the boy back behind her as he pushed forward to see the visitor. "Who are you?"

Jess held up her press card and explained she was investigating the Rooney accident.

Ms. Bozeck sent the boy to the kitchen. "Sorry about that. He's got another year before school, but he's dying to go. Very social boy. Never met a stranger and all that." She held out her hand. "I'm Naya."

They shook hands. Naya led the way into the family room and gestured to a large sofa. "Please."

Jess sat on the edge of the cushion to avoid falling deeper into the seat and having to climb out again.

Naya took the armchair opposite. "I told the police everything I know. Which isn't much. We were heading to my mother-in-law's home. In the van. Me and the kids. A beautiful yellow classic car passed me before we reached the tunnel—"

"The tunnel immediately before the crash?"

"Right. It passed me maybe a minute before I got to the crash site. The car looked pristine. You know how hard it is to keep a car clean this time of year. The guy must have spent every weekend detailing it."

"Going fast?"

Naya shook her head. "Sixty, maybe? But the next car—"

"The Camaro?"

"Yeah. Red. I recognized it. Neighbor has one. Except this one was all sported up."

"Sported how?"

"Big wheels. A spoiler on the back. Probably other stuff." Naya shrugged. "Sorry. I'm no expert."

"Anything unique about the Camaro? Identifiable?"

Naya shook her head. "No, but he was flying. The draft when he passed was strong enough to shake my van. He went straight down the middle of the road. Right up to the back of the previous guy. I mean really close. Flashing his lights and weaving all over the road."

Jess made a mental note of the pronoun. "How long before the crash?"

"They disappeared into the next tunnel. And that one bends, you know. By the time I was in there, they'd gone. I could still hear their engines making a lot of noise."

"Did you see them again?"

"I didn't." Naya shrugged. "Maybe half a minute later I saw the barrier and stopped."

"The Camaro had gone?"

"Yeah. When I got out of the tunnel, I heard an engine roar in the distance. Probably him but could have been anything. And when I saw over the edge...the yellow car...I had to back away and see to my kids."

"I understand."

"It was a shock. I didn't want them exposed to it."

"Definitely."

"One of the only times I've been glad they both have phones to watch cartoons."

"Right."

Naya shook her head slowly. "I knew that boy couldn't have survived."

"Boy?"

"Yeah. In the classic car. The yellow one. Real young looking."

"Did you see the driver of the Camaro?"

Naya shook her head. "Just a glimpse. That car had kind of small windows. Hard to see into."

"But you did see something."

Naya frowned.

"Was it a woman?" said Jess, trying not to suggest.

"No. A man. For sure. He had a beard." She put her hand to her mouth. "Oh right, I didn't even realize."

"I don't suppose you have a camera in your van?"

"You mean the sort people use if they get in a wreck? No. But I took some photos. Sent them to the police."

Naya pulled out her phone, found the pictures, and handed it to Jess.

Jess flipped through two dozen pictures of the gaping barrier and the burning wreckage below. Several pictures showed the road and debris spread over it. The black tire tracks were there. Jess zoomed in.

"Those," said Naya, nodding and pointing. "I'm pretty sure I wasn't imagining it."

"Imagining what?"

"I could smell burning rubber."

"The classic car was on fire as well," Jess reminded her.

"Yeah, but that smelled different. When I was at the edge by the barrier. It was gas and—" She shivered. "Horrible. But in the middle of the road, by those tire marks was different."

"Do you think the Camaro made these marks?"

"Probably, because no one else passed me. But I didn't see it happen."

"May I?" Jess asked. When Naya nodded, she sent the photos to her email and then handed the phone back. "Did you notice anything else?"

Naya pressed her lips together for a moment, apparently thinking back to the event. She shook her head. "There was noise, but that was from the car on fire. Banging and popping. One time it was real loud, though. Like a gun went off."

"Did you tell the police about it?"

"Yes. Of course."

"When did the gun go off?"

Naya shrugged, speaking slowly as if she were trying to recall. "Don't know. I'd been there a while. I phoned the police and waited for them to arrive. Maybe five minutes later."

"Do you know where the louder sound came from?"

"Out in the mountains?" Naya shook her head. "Everything echoes."

"Distant?"

"At the time, I thought maybe the guy in the car had a gun and the ammunition had exploded. But thinking back now, yeah, it was probably farther away." Naya stopped to think. "And only once. So not like a handgun popping off in the fire. If that's what a handgun does."

Jess waited patiently for a few moments.

Naya pressed her lips together again. Her eyebrows inched down, and lines formed on her forehead. "You know, there was something. Not really strange, but a guy walking. In the far distance. A little later after the crash. Walking away. Which seemed odd because he was not helping, you know?"

"Where did you see him?"

"To the right." Naya waved her hand as if the valley lay in front of her on the carpet. "And you know the really weird thing? Most walkers wear bright colors, stuff to be seen on the snow."

"Yeah?"

Naya nodded firmly. "This man was dressed in white."

CHAPTER 12

MANDY MAILED A SHORT list of Justin Rooney's contacts. From what she'd found, Rooney seemed like a two-dimensional guy.

On social media, most of his friends were either working in IT or heavily involved in various car clubs. His name also appeared several times in computer journals, mainly on topics of encryption and web security.

As requested, Mandy had also arranged a meeting with his employer, First Aurora Bank. Jess hustled to make the appointment.

First Aurora Bank's head office was housed in a stylish two-story building at the entrance to an upscale shopping area. Jess parked in the middle of a sparsely filled parking lot and walked inside.

The two-story lobby soared, and a grand staircase ran along one wall. Glass-walled offices on the second floor overlooked the lobby and soft music filled the area.

Three bored-looking tellers stared at her hopefully. She picked the one closest to the door and walked up to introduce herself.

"I'm Jess Kimball. I have an appointment with Margo Alvarado," she said.

"Sure. Let me call her for you." The teller picked up a handset, pushed a button, and spoke quietly. "She'll be right down."

"Thanks," Jess said, stepping back to wait.

A minute later a woman swept down the stairs and approached. Forty-something with long brown hair and a smooth radio announcer voice. "Ms. Kimball? I'm Margo Alvarado. You're here about Justin Rooney?"

She led Jess up the stairs to a small square office at the back of the building. No glass-walled office for the personnel department.

"Such a shock," Margo said. "Justin was a valued member of the First Aurora family. And such a nice young man. We're all heartbroken."

"How long had he been with the bank?"

She glanced at his personnel file on the computer screen and scrolled through a couple of pages. "Six years, eight months."

"What kind of work did he do here?"

"IT. Back-office stuff, but it's all beyond me." Margo smiled. "I know how to use our computer systems, but I have no clue about the code behind everything."

"Did Justin ever have any personnel problems here?" Jess asked.

Margo scowled. "Heavens no. Everyone liked him. Quiet, kept to himself. Such a nice young man. Sorry, I already said that, didn't I?"

Jess smiled. "And good at his job?"

"Oh yes. A positive star. He developed all sorts of things. Apple of Jerry's eye."

"Jerry?"

"Larson. CEO. Started the bank. He and Justin are responsible for several patents. Though I couldn't tell you anything about them," Margo explained.

"Is that normal? A bank getting patents?"

Margo waved the question away. "We try to be different. And Jerry has a strong background in software."

"Really?"

"Be right back." Margo bustled out to intercept a man in a tailored suit with salt-and-pepper hair, speaking to him quietly.

He glanced into the office as Margo talked. He was about fifty-five. Evenly tanned, suggesting a local tanning salon or a vacation in a warmer climate. Coloradans with a winter tan were regular skiers. They sported untanned hands and a white mask across their faces where ski goggles normally sat.

After a moment's discussion, the man strode into Margo's office with a wad of papers under his arm. "Miss Kimball. Jerry Larson. Pleasure to meet you."

They shook hands.

"I'm familiar with your work, of course," Larson said. "And I'd love to talk, but at the moment there's a lot going on."

"The Justin Rooney incident," Jess said.

Larson's eyes widened. "Don't you mean accident?"

"I believe the police are still holding an open mind on the issue."

Larson's eyebrows rose a fraction as if he held further response in check. "First I've heard of anything like that. Protocol, I suppose. Very sad, either way. Not that I really knew him well. Anyway"—he looked at his watch—"I really have to go. But we should meet again sometime."

For the second time in twenty seconds, Jess shook the man's hand. He rushed out of the office and around the corner out of view.

CHAPTER 13

JERRY LARSON LAID HIS papers down and plopped heavily into the chair behind his desk. The reporter had referred to Rooney's death as an *incident*. She said the police were *holding an open mind*. What the hell?

Surely Justin's driving off the road in the mountains was an unfortunate accident. What else could it have been? A crime? What kind of crime?

Larson briefly considered returning to talk to Kimball but decided against it. Better to keep out of it.

The big problem was Rooney. He'd been a rising computer security star when First Aurora hired him. The business got up and running fast because of Rooney's skills and work ethic. Simply put, Rooney was the essential cog in what Larson considered the mind-numbing job of cybersecurity.

That had been the problem. Starting a bank, installing the equipment, setting up the protocols—all that had gripped Larson's imagination, kept him focused, hard at work.

Then his interest waned. He'd looked for other opportunities. It turned out that Larson chose the worst possible time to expand the business.

First Aurora's business doubled in a year. The finances looked good. Expansion in the US was an obvious move. But Larson wasn't interested in the obvious.

For Jerry Larson, diversification was the name of the game.

So when the opportunity to buy a bank in Colombia came up, he grabbed it. It had been a financial stretch, of course.

"No risk, no reward," Larson had said before he put everything he had into the new venture.

Rooney's skills were an essential piece of the Colombia acquisition.

Integrating different systems was a complex job, the kind of thing Rooney relished and at which he excelled.

Rooney stayed on the payroll and worked hard. He came up with ideas that could be patented.

Since Rooney worked for the bank, the patents were the bank's property.

Larson owned the majority stake in the bank, so of course his name went on the patents.

In hindsight, that had been another mistake. He should have kept Rooney off the paperwork.

Sure, Rooney had profited from the patents. A one-off payment for each one. But Rooney considered himself unique. Above everyone else. He wanted stupid stuff, like a no-interest loan to buy some heap-of-junk car. And working from home.

Larson had acquiesced. It seemed harmless. And the patents kept coming. Two in the past year alone.

But Rooney hardly ever came into the office anymore. Signed out all sorts of IT equipment and Larson didn't object.

But now?

Banks survived on their reputation. On the surface, First Aurora's reputation looked good. New accounts and investments had slowed, but the long-term position was fine.

It was the coming year that worried Larson. He'd taken on short-term loans to purchase the bank in Colombia. Personal loans. Loans that would be coming due soon.

The loans had allowed him to protect his majority position in the bank, but they were high risk. And the international acquisition would mean more oversight by banking regulators.

One slip, one failed payment, one bad piece of press, and the whole thing would collapse faster than Larson could tweet goodbye.

Six months earlier, the looming threat had led him to discreetly move his assets offshore.

A small bank on a little-known island in the Indian Ocean that had no extradition treaty with the United States. When the time was right, a business jet and a boat ride and he would be free.

Free. And very, very rich.

The broker who was shuffling his money out of the country was the woman he'd take with him. The woman he should have married. The flirty, happy-go-lucky one. Not the PTA meetings and soccer mom he'd somehow ended up with.

Larson's mind drifted a moment before he came back to earth. None of that could happen right now.

He wanted more time to consolidate his wealth and move it offshore.

He still had assets to cash in, including the sale of his controlling stake in First Aurora Bank once the loans were paid off.

Rooney's death could generate bad press, but Larson wasn't ready to give in. Damage control was his specialty.

That reporter in Margo's office, Jess Kimball, worked for *Taboo*. Larson had met the magazine's owner at a charity event a couple of years earlier. It wasn't a strong enough connection. Larson couldn't apply appropriate pressure to get the reporter to back off.

But the man who'd introduced them was Senator MacKrell. He could do the job.

Larson called MacKrell. After a few moments of reminiscing over MacKrell's all-expenses-paid fishing trip off the Florida Keys, Larson's mere suggestion was enough.

He grinned. The senator would make a friendly call and Jess Kimball would be assigned a new project.

Larson leaned back in his chair. The reporter had been easy to deflect.

More difficult would be to clean up whatever Rooney had been doing at his apartment.

Banking regulators took a dim view of mavericks like Rooney.

And the people who funded them.

CHAPTER 14

LARSON WALKED INTO A costume shop on the edge of town.
He browsed various theater costumes and eventually chose a jet-
black wig and a walrus mustache.

He tried on the wig and mustache in his car and inspected his
appearance in the rearview mirror. The cheap disguise wouldn't
fool anyone up close. But it only needed to work from a distance
and only for a few moments. He hoped.

Rooney's apartment complex had the usual part rental office,
part clubhouse setup at the entrance. Larson ignored the visitor
lot out front and parked among the residents with his rear license
plate obscured. He walked toward the clubhouse.

Larson's heart raced, and he shoved his hands in his pockets
to conceal their nervous shaking. He found lying easy, but he'd
never tried to deceive with his appearance.

A tall young woman greeted him as he entered the building.
She had a singsong voice and introduced herself as Kelly.

He kept his distance and hung his head down. "I'm…" His
voice trembled with his racing heart. Really it was his nerves,

but the effect was exactly what he wanted. He took a deep breath. "I'm Justin Rooney's father."

The girl's smile evaporated. "Oh, I'm…we were all very sorry to hear…you know…what happened."

"Thank you," he said. "My wife and I are still trying…to come to terms with it."

"Of course. If there's anything we can do…"

He nodded. "Thank you. I just wanted to see his apartment. We're arranging to collect his things. Need to know how much he has to move."

The girl bit her lip. "Well…I'm not sure I can let you in."

He glanced up. "I know. You must have procedures and such. But my wife couldn't cope with the idea of coming here. She… well, and I really don't want to have to do this twice."

"Right." The girl nodded. "I understand." She disappeared into her office and returned with the key. "I'll show you the way."

Larson held out his hand. "It's okay. It's at the rear of the complex. He told us."

"I…Well, all right." She handed the key into his shaky grasp.

"I won't be long. I'll bring the key straight back."

He turned and left.

CHAPTER 15

JESS'S PHONE RANG BEFORE she reached her Jeep. Mandy's name appeared on the display.

"What's up?" Jess said as she picked up the call.

"I confessed."

Jess frowned. "About what?"

"He was trying to be nice, but I had to tell him."

"Carter?"

"Of course."

"And you told him…?"

"That you don't think the Rooney crash was entirely accidental."

"And what did he say?"

"That I need to stop covering, and you need to get a story together. Oh, and he muttered something about being the boss."

"He knows I'm not wasting my time."

"He said something similar. Just thought you ought to know. Anyway, do you know the Mellon Tree?"

"The, er, what?"

"The bar. On Broadway?"

"No."

"Rooney's friends are having a get-together. Seven p.m. It's on social media."

"You want me to crash a wake?"

"It's not a wake. It's a get-together. And the invite says anyone welcome."

It would be a quick way to meet a group of Rooney's friends, and if there was anything suspicious about his death, the quicker she knew everything about him the better. "Okay. I'll see who's there, at least. And I could learn something useful."

Jess finished the call. She ate at a retro-style diner and drank coffee until it was time to join the others. She walked two blocks to the Mellon Tree, which was already loud and busy.

Jess had been to the Mellon Tree before. The setup was three-sided rooms encircling a dance floor that was a step lower than the rest of the room. Which meant she had to step down onto the dance floor to cross the place.

The DJ stand was unoccupied. Background music played through the speakers. Jess crossed the sunken dance floor to the bar on the other side, where she ordered a Perrier and orange juice.

While she waited for her drink, two young men approached the bar. She caught the word "Aurora" in their conversation.

"Are you here for Justin Rooney?" she asked.

They frowned at her.

"You with the bank?" the taller one asked.

She shook her head. "Jessica Kimball, *Taboo Magazine*."

They introduced themselves as Armando and Darrin. They ordered a couple of beers.

"Did you know Justin, or…?" Darrin, the shorter one, let his question hang in the air.

"I didn't know him. Are you with First Aurora?"

"Yeah. So you doin' an article or something?"

"There's been a few cases of road rage lately, and I came across his."

Armando scoffed. "Is that what they're calling it? Road rage?"

"They're still investigating."

"They said he went over the edge. I mean, like a big drop."

"It was a big drop."

"You been out there?"

She nodded.

"Don't they have cameras or anything?" said Darrin.

"No. At least not where the incident happened."

"That's crap." Darrin shook his head. "He was a great guy, you know. Help anyone. Hard to believe."

"Did you notice anything different about him recently?"

Darrin stared. "Why?"

"I'm just trying to understand him."

Darrin gave her a steady glare.

"Journalism one oh one. Build a profile of the victim to highlight the human cost." Jess shrugged. It wasn't a lie, and she didn't want to raise her suspicions with these two.

Darrin nodded. "We go out on Thursdays. Bunch of us. He used to come along. Hasn't shown up for the last few months. But that could be anything. He worked a lot."

"Old Larson called him into the office a couple of times last week. That'd be enough to get anyone down," Armando said.

Jess and Darrin shared a knowing smile.

"I heard Larson liked him. I mean, they shared the patents," Jess said.

"Yeah, right," Darrin replied with a sneer. "Larson liked getting his name on Rooney's patents. Larson gloms onto everything if he thinks there's money in it. He didn't understand anything about what those patents were. Just wanted the glory and the cash."

"Used to tick Justin off," Armando said.

"You sound like you don't like the place? Why work at First Aurora if it's that bad?"

Darrin shrugged. "It's going downhill, that's all."

"So why do you stay?"

"One word, stock options."

"That's two words, idiot," Armando said with a grin, punching Darrin on the shoulder.

"Yeah, yeah," Darrin admitted, hoisting his glass and draining the last of the beer. "A few more months and my options are vested. Assuming they're still worth something by then."

"Why do you say that?" Jess asked.

"Been in one of our branches lately? They're not exactly packed with depositors."

"That's not surprising. Don't people mostly bank online now?" Jess said. "What did Rooney do at First Aurora, anyway?"

"Security and infrastructure," Armando said as he gave the bartender a nod to request another round.

"Which is?"

"Keeper of the keys," Darrin said with a grin.

"Idiot." Armando nudged Darrin in the ribs. "What he means is that Justin looked after the security of our systems. Meaning boxing out a million and one brute-force hackers. But that's the easy part. The keys part is harder. That's how we exchange data with other banks. Encryption. It's what keeps everything secure. Hence, we called him keeper of the keys."

"Like Hagrid," Darrin said. "You know? From *Harry Potter*?"

"Got it," Jess said, forcing a smile, although she only had a vague idea who Harry Potter was, let alone Hagrid. "When you say the banks exchange data, what does that mean?"

"Money," Darrin replied.

"Well, money and other financial information," Armando said. "It all gets encrypted."

"Sounds important."

"Domestic banks are pretty routine. Not a lot of challenge, really. Justin used to say any average IT dude could handle it. But international banks come with another whole set of problems."

"Can First Aurora manage without Rooney?" Jess asked.

"Sure. Lucy Cranfield took over. Hot as hell, that one. In every conceivable way. Master's in enterprise security," Armando said. "So we'll manage, yes. Until something happens that needs international experience. Justin kind of kept that to himself."

"Security." Darrin shrugged. "Comes with the job."

Jess cocked her head. "Does a local bank like First Aurora do much international business?"

"People send money all over the place. Mainly Canada and South America. Most of ours goes to Colombia. First Aurora has a small bank in Cali. Larson bought it."

"One of his great ideas." Darrin's voice dripped with sarcasm.

"It's a nice city. Larson bought a dozen branches," Armando said.

"Closed five in the first year, though," Darrin said.

"Safe to say the bank isn't doing as well as the brochure claims." Armando grinned.

"Brochure?" Jess asked.

Armando explained. "As things were advertised."

"Yeah," Darrin snarked. "Larson sure has the golden touch."

CHAPTER 16

LARSON SAT IN HIS office. His head still itched from the ridiculous wig. His heartbeat had returned to normal after an hour of rapid pounding as if his heart wanted to burst from his chest. The stress of duping his way into Rooney's apartment had been terrifying and the situation devolved from there. Erasing the computers had taken far longer than he'd expected on six company machines.

Rooney's personal computer had lots of LED lights that pulsated when the machine was switched on. It was a gaming laptop with lots of fancy graphics. Not the sort of thing someone would use for work.

Which was just as well since Larson didn't know the password. He left it alone.

As CEO, Larson had an administrator password for the company machines, which allowed him to log on to each of the laptops. His only real difficulty was typing with gloves on.

First, he backed up all contents to his secure private servers.

Then he erased the contents from each of the six company machines.

A simple delete command was all it took to start the deletion process.

Waiting for the laptops to complete the tasks was nerve-racking. They worked fast, but the process seemed to drag on forever.

Larson had sweated every second of the full hour he spent in the apartment as he watched the laptops delete thousands of files. All the while, he worried that the girl from the front desk might come to check up on him.

He practiced holding a picture of Rooney and his pals from the mantelpiece and forcing tears to his eyes. An emotional defense was his best ploy to anyone objecting to his behavior. He hoped.

Larson had wandered the apartment while he waited. Wires, modems, and old computer parts lay everywhere.

A bookshelf held notebooks with handwritten records reflecting Rooney's car restorations, but nothing that appeared to describe the bank's systems.

Rooney had been a geek, all right. His tables were stacked with old modems and network equipment. A couple of pieces looked new. Larson recognized some stuff that must have come from the bank. He wanted to take the equipment, but the stuff wasn't small, and he didn't want to be seen removing Rooney's belongings.

When everything was finally erased from the computers, Larson had meant to return the key. But standing in front of Kelly again seemed too stressful to contemplate. So he slipped the key into his pocket.

Eventually someone would wonder why Rooney's stuff hadn't been collected. Kelly might call the office. He'd come back after the police investigation wound down. Kelly would have lost interest in Rooney by then, surely.

CHAPTER 17

JESS ARRIVED AT HER apartment after nine. Darrin and Armando had been unstoppably talkative after a few drinks. A regular comedy duo. But Jess took it as a sign that they were telling the truth. Making up lies on the fly for a couple of hours was beyond Darrin and Armando. They just weren't that clever.

The pair had dragged Jess to meet their friends. The group had relayed Justin Rooney stories nonstop. Some of the tales were punctuated with pictures held out on phones.

Rooney's small circle of friends shared a social media account that Jess hadn't seen before. Scrolling through the account's entries supported the stories his friends told.

Jess found no indication that Rooney had possessed a secret dark side. He seemed like an ordinary young guy enjoying the fruits of his hard work along with the rest of his life.

Rooney's friends asked her not to use their names in her article, should she publish one. She couldn't promise, but she said she'd try.

After leaving Rooney's friends, Jess felt an overwhelming urge to call her son. He always answered her calls, but she tried not to be clingy. Peter was growing up. Like any teenager, he craved independence. She'd promised herself that she wouldn't check on him every night while he skied in Sundance.

She texted "good night" and got a smiling emoji in return, which was enough to calm her nerves.

As Jess prepared the coffee machine for tomorrow, her entrance buzzer sounded. Her apartment building had a secure entrance on the ground floor and inside the small foyer, a video intercom for visitors to request entry.

She wasn't expecting company, but maybe Henry had decided to stop by.

Jess went to inspect the visitor in the tiny monitor mounted on the wall by the front door.

A disheveled man leered into the camera. His eyes didn't seem focused. "I's suppose-ta say hello," he said drunkenly.

Jess didn't bother responding to the intrusion. Denver's homeless population was getting bolder. Maybe he'd go away if she didn't engage.

She clicked the video off button and the intercom buzzed again.

As she reached to cut off the buzzing noise, an explosion blasted within the wall.

Reflexively, Jess leapt backward.

A cloud of plaster burst into the room from beneath the intercom.

Splinters ejected from the front door flew through the air.

Gunfire came next.

Shots peppered the wall where she'd stood moments before.

"What the hell?" she blurted when she realized the homeless man's call had set her up.

She ran to the kitchen and grabbed her lockbox from a cabinet.

A hard boot hammered against the front door. The damaged wood creaked with each impact.

She dialed the lockbox's four-digit PIN and ripped it open. Her weapon was already loaded.

Two more shots sounded in the hallway.

The front door swung open, slamming back against the wall.

Jess dived for the kitchen range to put the largest piece of metal she could find between her and her attackers.

Firing a high-powered weapon in a populated space like her apartment building was never a good idea.

She scanned the area frantically. What were her options?

Her bathroom was on the opposite side of the hallway.

If she set up to fire toward the bathroom, there was a good chance her bullets wouldn't travel through the bulk and mass into a neighboring apartment.

Heavy boots crunched on debris in the hallway. Quick steps. No caution.

He was planning to overwhelm her resistance.

Out of time, she pushed the muzzle of the Glock close to the wall. She aimed low. Knee height.

Jess counted, mentally visualizing the steps coming closer in the hallway.

When he was five steps away, she fired.

Twice.

Adjusted her angle.

Fired twice more.

The first blast from the intercom followed by gunshots had overwhelmed her hearing.

Even so, Jess heard a single shout ring out when she returned fire.

Followed by an unnaturally quiet moment.

Maybe there was only one intruder. Maybe she hit the guy.

Could this nightmare be over?

She'd begun to breathe a little easier when, without warning, automatic fire tore through the wall above her head.

Drywall tumbled into the kitchen in chunks. Clouds of dust and powder flew like a snowstorm in Aspen.

Jess steadied her breath and her hands. Raising her aim, she fired again, spreading her blind shots to cover a greater area.

More bullets raked the kitchen counter. Appliances and food flew from the surfaces.

The noise overwhelmed all hearing in the small space.

She rolled into the gap and then into the hallway, leading with the Glock as she slid deeper, ready to fire again.

Dust and debris lingered in the air, but the gunman wasn't there.

Jess leapt to her feet, ran to the doorway, and searched for movement.

A heavy door closed nearby. Had to be the fire escape.

The attackers were well prepared. They'd have backup. Chasing them down the fire escape during a gunfight within the confines of the stairwell was way beyond her skill set.

Jess grabbed her cell phone and ran for the elevators. She messaged apartment security on her phone. She hoped other residents had already raised the alarm.

Jess pulled up the building's security cameras on her phone. She switched between the street-level camera views surrounding her building.

As the elevator car finally settled at her floor, one of the rear cameras showed a man in a ski mask exiting in a hurry.

Jess stepped into the elevator car and immediately lost the video signal. She hammered the button for the lobby and stepped out as soon as the doors slid open.

Sirens wailed outside the front doors. Imran, the night shift security guard, had his gun in his hand. He shouted for her to take shelter.

Jess told him the gunman had taken a rear exit.

"Saw that on CCTV," Imran said. "Called it in already. But he's long gone now."

Two patrol cars emptied out and four officers ran up the steps to the building's glass doors.

Jess pulled the magazine from her Glock and handed both weapon and ammo to Imran. Unarmed, she wouldn't be mistaken for the aggressor. Not all the local cops knew her.

CHAPTER 18

JESS POURED A GLASS of tepid orange juice from her bullet-riddled fridge. A couple of blue-gloved crime scene guys were working their way through her apartment, bagging, tagging, and numbering evidence.

Downstairs, officers took statements and reviewed security footage with Imran.

Adrenaline faded from Jess's system, leaving her shaky and depleted as she scanned the damage to her home.

It would take a good long while to restore her apartment. Drywall between the kitchen and hallway was pulverized. Kitchen cabinets sported lines of bullet holes. The room was spray coated with a mixture of flour, jelly, and breakfast cereal.

The attacker's bullets had traveled through the far wall but were stopped inside her neighbor's closet on the other side. The elderly lady who lived there was still terrified. A female officer was with her.

Jess's return fire had destroyed her bathroom. The sink and tub were cracked in several places. One shot had ricocheted upward and embedded itself in the concrete that separated her apartment from the one above.

A small blood splatter on the hallway floor suggested she'd hit her attacker at least once.

"Lucky," Detective Norton said, looking at a bullet hole in her stove.

"Not the word I'd use," said Jess.

He tapped the appliance right next to the hole. "You were crouched here, right?"

Jess nodded.

"Then I'll stick with lucky. Maybe I'd add amazingly to it." He stood. "So, you've told us what happened. Now the question is who did this and why were they after you? Any ideas?"

She shook her head. "I've been racking my brain."

"I reviewed your reporting for *Taboo Magazine*. You've definitely annoyed more than a few people during your career."

"Over the years. Maybe." Jess shrugged. "And nobody lately. Why would any of those people pick *tonight* to blast up my apartment?"

"Opportunity, probably. Most things like this boil down to timing conflicts, in my experience," Norton suggested with a shrug. "If it's payback, why not shoot you down in the street? Much easier that way. Probably would have finished the job."

"You're a bundle of laughs. But I've been wondering about that, too. This guy broke into the building and tried to shoot me through my own front door on the eighth floor."

"Gutsy."

"Stupid, I'd say." Jess nodded. "And desperate."

Norton raised his eyebrows, encouraging her to expand.

"It is a stupid place to attack me, we agree," Jess said. "So whoever did it was desperate. Like they were short on time. Had to do it as soon as possible. But why?"

"Our best line of inquiry is some link to your work," Norton said. "I know about the Rooney case. What else are you working on?"

Jess shook her head. "I haven't published anything lately. I had a couple of months off. Nothing I'm working on now except Rooney."

"You met Naya Bozeck," Norton suggested.

"No chance. She's as far from a gun-toting hoodlum as you can get."

Norton shook his head as he pointed to the destroyed intercom. "You were lured to a predictable spot. The guy was a hitman, not a hoodlum."

"Yeah." Jess looked at the tattered remains of her front door through the gaping space where her kitchen wall had been. "Maybe this is about the bullet I found. In the tree at the crash site. I found the cartridge as well."

Norton scowled. "You didn't tell me about the cartridge."

"You didn't seem interested."

He grunted. "Where did you find the cartridge?"

"Several hundred yards down the valley from where I found the bullet. By a small group of trees."

"That's a long distance. Lots of hunters and gun enthusiasts could have been shooting out there. How do you know the casing you found is actually connected with the bullet you pulled out of the tree at the crash site?"

"It looked like the shooter had prepared an area to lie in wait. Pointed directly at the spot where Rooney's car crashed."

"Still speculative." Norton exhaled and cupped his hand around his neck. "But you should have told me before."

"That's exactly why I didn't tell you. Your skepticism is legendary."

A quick knock on what was left of the door and Henry stepped into the apartment. A crime scene tech gave him directions around the evidence and into the kitchen.

"You okay?" he asked as he approached.

"I will be. Just coming down off a heavy adrenaline spike and"—she gestured to the room—"I'll have some redecorating to do."

"No kidding," he said with a grimace while looking through the gap at the damage. "Amen to that."

Jess stepped out of the protective circle of his arms. "Who told you about all this?"

"I was on the way over anyway." He held out a bottle of Cabernet. "I was thinking we'd have a quiet evening. Obviously, some jerk had other ideas."

She found three unbroken glasses and poured them all a drink.

After his first sip, Henry said, "You were lucky."

She grunted and Norton grinned. "We just had that discussion."

"Right. Sorry."

"The bullet and shell you found out there at the crash site," Norton said, coming back to the point they were discussing before Henry arrived. "Where are they now?"

"Keshawn Goodwin."

"You know Goodwin?" Norton said, surprised. "At the BRL?"

Jess nodded.

"I have some bad news on that front," Henry said. "The BRL had a break-in. Earlier this evening."

Norton cursed. "At the laboratory?"

Henry nodded.

"Goodwin okay?" Jess asked.

"He doesn't live at the lab, and by comparison to Jess's apartment, the BRL break-in was a pretty clean job." Henry nodded. "Goodwin has alarms, but the thief was in and out before one of your cruisers had a chance to get there."

"Video?" Jess asked.

Henry shook his head. "They cut the power and the video system wasn't backed up with a battery."

"You're saying they broke in and stole the bullet and shell Ms. Kimball found out in the woods by the crash site. And nothing else," Norton said.

"Yep."

"You're kidding, right?" Jess said.

"Nope."

Norton looked around the wrecked kitchen.

Jess said, "Still think all this isn't linked to Rooney?"

"Unlikely," Norton replied.

CHAPTER 13

THEO KAHLER CIRCLED AROUND to be sure he wasn't being followed before returning to his apartment. His leg burned. The woman's lucky shot had barely torn his jeans and scraped his thigh. Not even close to lethal.

But she'd hit him, and he'd left blood at the scene.

Which meant they'd have his DNA.

Not good.

Nothing he could do about it at the moment. But a thick layer of ointment and a bandage on the wound and he was good to go.

Thirty minutes later, Kahler pulled into the parking lot at an abandoned burger joint. Following Miller's required routine, Kahler stepped out of the SUV, hands by his sides, while Miller's guys frisked him. Dayton, a classic leg breaker, sat in a rusting pickup truck across the street, head bowed, sending a text message to Miller.

A moment later, Dayton lifted his gaze to Kahler and flashed a thumbs-up. Kahler was cleared for entry.

Meaning Miller's men wouldn't shoot Kahler the moment he walked inside.

Kahler forced himself not to limp. He gritted his teeth against the fire in his thigh, which was burning his pride more than his leg.

Kahler moved through the side door, gagging on the overwhelming stench of congealed fat and age-old fried food. He stood for a moment to let his eyes adjust to the dark interior.

He spied a line of red light filtering beneath a door at the back. Kahler strode toward the red beam. He tapped the door and entered without specific permission.

Eleven men stood in a ragged arc around Miller. Even in the dim light, Miller's half-closed left eye and the malevolent images of serpents and crows tattooed on his neck projected menace and darkness.

Kahler joined the others without comment.

"What the hell's wrong with you?" said Miller.

Kahler shrugged. "Traffic."

"The limp," Miller said with a sneer.

Kahler shrugged. "Walked into a table."

"Really," Miller deadpanned.

Kahler said nothing.

Miller's lips pressed together, and he breathed loudly through his damaged nose. "I *know* you're not moonlighting—"

"Come on, man." Kahler shook his head, as if the suggestion were ridiculous.

Miller was unmoved. "I hear otherwise and you're toast."

"Nothing coming between me and a good payday. And this is gonna be a good payday."

"Yeah. And don't you forget it." Miller surveyed the group. "None of you. Until we wrap up this operation, *no one* does *anything* without my orders. We can't afford any trouble. None at all. Understand?"

Murmurs of agreement rippled from one side of the group to the other.

"Not so much as a parking ticket. Clear?"

Murmurs were joined by nodding for emphasis this time.

"Good. 'Cause we're taking over a business. Clean and efficient," Miller said. "These guys are speculators. They don't like the kind of change we've got in mind. So we got to make it all happen nice and smooth. Don't want nobody scared off. Right?"

The group replied with a series of affirmative grunts. Miller gave them each a long stare and paused an extra moment on Kahler.

"Charlie Finnegan muscled out the competition 'cause nobody stood up to him." Miller took a breath. "Well, we're taking him out. Tonight. Him and his top men."

They responded with muted cheers.

Miller said, "We tipped Finny's guys that we'd diverted his shipment. He's pissed. He'll show up to shut us down."

Snout, the tall skinny guy who had driven the Camaro for the Rooney job, laughed and shook his head with appreciation. "Man, that's brilliant."

Miller smiled. "But the crew bringing in Finny's product is the same crew we use. So he won't lift a finger till they've cleared out and neither will we. Can't afford to hurt our suppliers."

"Moment the suppliers move off"—Miller nodded and jerked his thumb to point to Kahler—"Slick here's gonna take Finny out. Permanently."

"Check," Kahler replied with finality. "He'll be down and dead before he can wiggle his eyebrows."

"How do we know you're going to be able to hit him?" Snout wanted to know.

"Bird's-eye view. Ain't nobody I can't see. Or shoot."

Snout scowled. "Yeah, while the rest of us are standing around like bait."

Kahler held back a grin. Snout was right. They were the bait in Miller's plan. But this wasn't the time to admit it.

"We're all gonna be happy tomorrow, Snout," Kahler said.

Miller held up his hand to stop the bickering. "Once Finny's down, his crew's gonna be outta there fast and we get the product. Ain't no point to fighting when they ain't gonna get paid."

Snout grunted.

"With Finny out of the picture, we own Denver." Miller laughed broadly and then checked his phone. "Five hours to showtime. Don't forget. We *dominate*. Absolutely no hesitation. Blow 'em away. Them suckers ain't family. No blowback for nailing them good."

CHAPTER 20

KAHLER WOUND HIS WAY through the Denver streets driving a stolen Nissan Leaf more silent than a grave. Electric. Couldn't beat it for stealth.

He turned onto J Street. A sign warned No Way Out. That would change when the tower construction was completed. But not today.

He cruised silently up to the construction site blocking the road.

The only tower for a mile in every direction, the building was a monster in the dark. The lower half was bathed in the glow from temporary streetlights. The upper floors were hidden by the darkness. Small red flashing lights on the roof warned low-flying air traffic.

Kahler could see straight through the lower floors' bare concrete and pillars. A fancy facade would eventually adorn the towering edifice. But not tonight.

Despite the building's size, at this stage of the project a single night watchman was on duty. He wore a big black coat with the company name emblazoned on the front and back.

He swung the main gate open and Kahler drove in.

Navigating around construction debris, Kahler reached the rear of the building. He drove the SUV through one of the large open spaces designed to accept heavy equipment.

Massive crates filled half the space. From a previous recon mission, Kahler knew the crates contained motors, gears, and cables, which would become the elevator assemblies.

He pulled on a ski mask and quickly scanned the area. He saw no one and nothing unexpected. The watchman had gone back to his cabin and the rest of the site was deserted. Amazing what a few hundred dollars would buy.

Reassured, Kahler stepped out of his vehicle.

From the cargo section of his SUV, Kahler lifted a pack and settled it onto his back. Fifty pounds. His muscles tensed with the weight. He could handle the load. He'd carried more. Far more.

But this would be a straight-up climb. He wanted his heart rate low and his body calm when he reached the top.

Kahler picked up a four-foot-long plastic case, locked the car, and headed for the stairwell.

Once inside, he slipped on a night vision monocle. Having night vision in one eye and not the other was disorienting and annoying. But he needed to know what the unaided eye could see.

After adjusting to the night vision's green glow, he started up the steps.

Grit crunched under his boots. His leg muscles worked to carry the extra weight.

He stopped every five floors. Resting and breathing. Calming his heart. Avoiding fatigue.

After thirty-three flights he stepped out of the stairwell onto the concrete floor. Absolute darkness filled the empty spaces where windows would one day be installed. A breeze whooshed through and swept welcome coolness across his warm body.

Kahler worked around the stairwell to the elevator shaft. Yellow warning signs and a plastic cord where the windows would eventually be installed marked the dangerous drops.

He retrieved a kernmantle rope and anchors from his backpack. The rope had an inner core for strength and an outer sheath for protection, warranted for a thousand feet. Which meant more than enough for the five hundred feet he needed tonight.

Kahler hammered the anchors into the concrete, attached the rope, and threw the free end into the empty elevator shaft. The rope snaked downward, twisting, turning, and brushing against the sidewalls. Eventually the extra length slapped onto the ground below.

Bitter air chilled his skin, even though the breeze had faded. The city lights spread as far as he could see.

Three- and four-story buildings occupied the area around the new tower. In the first block, family businesses operated in rundown buildings. If the small businesses could hang on a couple of years until the tower was operational, those meager plots would skyrocket in value.

The next street over, an empty warehouse with a parking area consumed the whole block. The parking area was closest to where Kahler was standing in the tower.

From his vantage point on the thirty-third floor, Kahler confirmed only a few lights around the site were burning and they'd been dimmed. "Money well spent," he mumbled.

Kahler laid out a blue canvas tarp and nailed the corners to the concrete floor.

From a pile of wooden crates nearby, he extracted several blocks of polystyrene and stacked them on top of the sheet.

Sitting on the polystyrene, he assembled the Kalabar rifle on its stand and attached a thermal scope.

The scope could be set to offer a massively zoomed view compared to the night vision monocle. With both, he had a reasonably good view of the warehouse and its parking lot hundreds of feet below.

He checked the laser spot and set up the scope as he'd tested days before.

Scanning the warehouse beyond the parking lot, he identified the three heat signatures he'd expected.

Two of Miller's crew, Hassan and Dayton, were doing a good job of blocking their body heat. Kahler only located them occasionally and only with the scope, not the monocle.

Snout was constantly fidgeting, which made him more visible. But at least everyone was in place.

Kahler nodded approval. They had actually listened to his warnings.

"Get in place early. Very early. You can arrive as early as you wish," he'd told them many times. "But if you're even a second late, we fail, and we'll all be dead. Get your affairs in order. We fail, and Finny won't let us survive."

He settled his weight on the polystyrene, tilted his long gun down at an extreme angle, and set his scope.

The plan was going well. Kahler was feeling lucky. Even the wind had died down.

Nothing and no one would get away from him tonight.

An hour later, Finny's men arrived on foot, as expected. Six of them. Kahler scanned the surrounding blocks looking for the vehicle they'd arrived in. He couldn't find one, even though he knew it must be there.

Finny's men split up. Two crouched behind dumpsters on either side of the parking lot.

Two entered the warehouse. A minute later, they appeared on the roof and settled down near the edge overlooking the parking lot.

Everything had unfolded exactly as expected, so far.

The two men on the roof carried assault weapons. The ones behind the dumpsters looked to have machine pistols, not as lethal but easier to operate in close quarters.

Kahler scanned two blocks in every direction. Only an hour to go and there was no sign of Finny.

Kahler kept scanning, alternating between the scope and monocle. At fifteen minutes before the scheduled meet, he texted Miller. "No F."

His phone buzzed in response.

"Go anyway" appeared on the display.

A minute before the scheduled meet, Miller's crew arrived in two large Lincoln sedans. They parked near the warehouse.

Close enough to eliminate angles of enemy approach and provide some protection.

Far enough away to keep Miller's necessary escape routes open.

Three men exited the first vehicle and fanned out calmly. Kahler saw them sweating. One of the men in the back of the second car glowed in the thermal scope, too.

Kahler shook his head. Miller's guys were sitting ducks.

Finny's crew could cut Miller's guys down where they stood, and everybody knew it.

But Finny's men on the roof must have been instructed to hold fire. Question was: Why?

A Tahoe SUV turned into the parking lot. Purposeful, not fast. Drawing to a stop ten feet from Miller's Lincolns.

The delivery vehicle? Probably.

A second Tahoe SUV followed the first, hanging back in a covering position. Four men peeled out of the first Tahoe, two going eye to eye with Miller's men, the other two quickly sweeping for threats.

Miller stepped out of the second Lincoln from the backseat.

The rear door of the first Tahoe opened. A small man got out of the passenger side and beckoned Miller over.

They stood by the rear door as the small man opened a box. Miller took a white brick from the bottom of the box, pricked it with a needle, and dropped the needle into a sample tube.

He shook the sample and shined a small black light at the tube. Kahler could see the glow in his monocle.

There was dubious value in checking a single brick of product because the other bricks could easily be harmless white powder.

But this was a business. Bigger fish needed smaller fish to make sales. Screwing over the small fish would be self-defeating. Finding and training personnel wasn't as easy as it used to be. No small fish, no sales. Simple as that.

Miller and Finny understood the realities.

So testing only one brick would be enough.

Miller nodded. He accepted that the consignment was good.

The small man held out a phone.

Miller stepped to the phone and busied himself typing something. The phone flashed. The small man scowled.

Miller typed on the phone again and a green glow emanated from the screen. The small man checked the display and nodded.

Miller's crew moved the boxes to the Lincoln. Fast. Jogging back and forth.

Movement caught Kahler's eye. An unknown SUV approaching. A block away. Watching, he flicked the scope between the SUV and the parking lot.

The boxes had been transferred. Finny's delivery crew hustled back into their Tahoes. The vehicles headed out of the lot before the doors were closed.

Things were moving fast now.

Kahler could wait no longer.

He settled his scope's red dot on the nearest man on the rooftop and squeezed the trigger. First shot. The force of the bullet's impact threw the man sideways.

The gun pounded Kahler's shoulder, but his hand was already moving, cycling the bolt and reloading.

Second shot. Finny's second roof man was out of the fight as quickly as the first.

The two shots would have been unmistakably loud to both teams on the ground. They scrambled.

The Tahoes sped out of the parking lot. Kahler watched the taillights.

Miller's crew had known the two shots were coming. They dived into the Lincolns, ready to run.

The unknown SUV raced into the lot, headed in Kahler's direction. Kahler's scope lined up on the nearest dumpster. The two men, standing around the corner behind the metalwork, held their guns ready.

Kahler aimed and fired at the front man. The guy's chest exploded, sending the second man staggering back, covered in blood and tissue.

Hassan and Dayton, weapons drawn, sprayed the second man in the back.

Shots blasted from the unknown SUV toward Kahler's location in the tower.

Kahler didn't bother settling his aim. He simply snapped his gun around and fired through the approaching windshield.

FATAL SHOT | 99

The SUV lurched left.

Kahler fired two more shots. The SUV careened farther left, slammed into a lamppost, and crumpled around the concrete.

Two men emerged from behind the far dumpster. Kahler aimed and fired, but missed as they raced toward the wrecked SUV.

Miller's Lincolns rolled closer, too.

Finny's two men slowed as they approached the SUV.

Kahler aimed his red dot squarely on the first man's chest and fired. The bullet's impact pushed the dead man backward before he fell.

Finny's second man dived for the SUV. He must have been unsure about the direction of the fire because he huddled down on the side nearest Kahler.

Taking him out was a single easy shot.

The wrecked SUV's rear doors burst open. Finny and another man leapt out, running in opposite directions.

Hassan and Dayton downed the pair quickly.

Miller exited his Lincoln and stood over Finny's body, firing into him like some Hollywood gangster wannabe posing in slo-mo.

Kahler snorted. Had the dumb schmuck never heard of ricochet?

Snout climbed from his hiding place, crossed behind a dumpster, and fired his first shot into one of the bodies on the ground. Snout annoyed Kahler more than Miller's other sycophants. Snout was a coward and a liability.

Not only that, but Snout expected an outsized share of the profits, which irked Kahler no end.

Right at that moment, he had the chance to eliminate Snout. Permanently.

Kahler turned his gun. Snout had backed himself against the steel of the dumpster. Kahler's red dot glowed nicely on the idiot's forehead as Kahler squeezed the trigger.

Snout went down. Easy as that. Kahler's bullet continued through Snout's thick head, striking the steel dumpster. A bright flash lit up in the thermal scope as the bullet scraped the steel.

Police sirens sounded in the distance.

Miller's team rolled out. The Lincolns left the parking lot at speed, separating at the end of the block.

Kahler surveyed the ground for previously unseen movements. Seeing none, he quickly packed his gun. He threw the polystyrene away and rolled up the canvas tarp, collecting his empty shells.

After he returned everything to his backpack, he scanned one last time. He'd left nothing behind. Confirmed.

He attached the specialized grip to the kernmantle rope secured to the elevator shaft and stepped over the edge.

Squeezing the grip, he could control the speed of descent. But he needed to hurry. The night watchman would be having fits. Kahler needed to get off the premises before the police arrived. He moved faster than he should have.

Kahler landed so hard that the impact jammed his feet onto the unforgiving concrete. He ignored the pain, ripped the grip from the kernmantle rope, and left it in place.

He ran to his SUV, stowed everything in the trunk, and sped away.

The electric SUV moved in silence as Kahler raced toward the exit. The advantages of a silent getaway vehicle were obvious, but the experience itself was uncanny. He wasn't sure whether he liked it or not.

Kahler spied the watchman near the exit, sheltering behind a stack of uninstalled windows. He rose to man the gate as Kahler's SUV approached.

Kahler lifted an MP9 submachine gun from the passenger seat and opened fire toward the watchman.

The windows the watchman hid behind exploded in a storm of glass and packaging.

The watchman dove behind a construction trailer. Kahler released one more burst from the MP9. This time, he hit the target. The watchman's body tumbled forward. He landed facedown in the mud.

Kahler hopped out and used bolt cutters to remove the exit gate lock. He hurried back to his SUV and sped away from the muddy site.

Two blocks later he joined a column of traffic traveling away from the attack. In the opposite direction, a flock of flashing lights raced toward the carnage.

Adrenaline fizzed in Kahler's blood. He counted six definite kills, plus whatever happened to the passengers of that wrecked SUV. At least a couple of them should die, too.

He still had the touch. No one outgunned him. None of Finny's guys had stood a chance. And Snout was a bonus. Kahler's world would be a lot better without that barnacle on Miller's operational belly.

All of which made him feel better. So what about the nosy reporter? She got lucky. The hit didn't go down as planned.

Kahler gripped the steering wheel hard. His anger seethed as he recalled the failure.

Jess Kimball might have squirmed away once.

But he wasn't finished with her yet.

CHAPTER 21

THE HANDS ON THE alarm clock ticked ahead one more minute. The buzzer sounded. Jess rolled over to tap the stop button. She preferred the simple alarm. Nothing digital with multiple buttons to press and a choice of sounds. Just one hand to set the alarm. The same noise every morning. The routine was reassuring, somehow.

Traveling was one of the requirements of her job, and the buzzer reminded her she was home. The cheap plastic device had been with her since Peter was a baby. Back then, she longed for him to sleep through the night until the buzzer sounded in the morning.

And the clock had been with her for the long years after Peter was taken. When she wouldn't let herself sleep through the night in her struggle to find her son.

She rolled out of bed. The apartment looked like a tornado had slammed through during the night.

In the hallway, the Sheetrock and plaster had been brushed to one side. Norton had arranged temporary repairs to the front door, but the effect was all function and no form. The remains of the intercom dangled off the wall. The destruction was a solid reminder of how close the attacker had come to killing her.

The CSI team's plastic bags, tape, and fingerprint dust were everywhere. They had offered to clean up, but she'd insisted they get some rest. Everyone had been exhausted when they'd finally left a few hours ago.

The kitchen was also a mess. The CSI team had probed every cabinet, removing the contents to check for bullet fragments. They had courteously replaced the contents but in different cabinets. Fortunately, the kitchen wasn't huge. She'd find everything soon enough.

The coffee maker had taken a direct hit and was out of commission. But she found a French press in a lower cabinet.

She ground beans on the coarse setting and let the scent wake her senses while she heated the water.

Jess messaged Peter and the Tierneys to explain what had happened. She warned them to be alert to possible dangers until Norton found the man who had tried to kill her.

They messaged back, reporting they were all fine and would take additional care until the situation was resolved.

As Jess poured her coffee, Carter called.

"I just heard," he said. "How are you doing?"

"Might be a while before the neighbors talk to me again."

"But no one was hurt, right?"

"Looks like I might have winged the guy."

"Blood?"

"Not much, but hopefully enough. Denver PD took samples. Should get DNA results in a week," she said, pouring a mug of coffee.

"Why so long?"

"Chain of custody and a full workup. Takes a while."

"Tell me about it," Carter said.

She ran him through events with the bullet and Keshawn Goodwin.

"And I thought I'd be keeping you out of trouble," he said.

She laughed. "Next time I'm picking my own assignment."

"There's one more thing. I got a call. Senator MacKrell. His constituents are complaining. Made it plain that you're harassing people. Not acceptable. His words."

Jess snorted. "Had to be Jerry Larson doing the complaining. He got way too defensive when I asked a few questions."

"Always a good sign you're onto something. Just make sure whatever you get is worth the blowback."

"And what about the senator's complaint?"

"I'll buy him a bottle of whiskey. Keep going," Carter said as he disconnected the call.

Jess tuned to a local radio station and carried her coffee to the shower.

The weather forecast called for a storm coming, heavier over Utah, but Colorado would get plenty of snow. The ski resorts and powder hounds would rejoice. The city dwellers would bundle up and carry on as usual.

The news anchor mentioned a shooting. Several victims. Early in the morning. The police hadn't released details, but the newscaster suggested the FBI would be involved.

After Jess showered and dressed, she texted Henry about the shooting and then flipped on the television. Several minutes later, she received his terse "already there" reply.

Several television stations showed news crews camped out around a warehouse parking lot on the west side of town. Cameras showed a sea of lights and vehicles in the early-morning gloom.

Jess recognized the place. Golden's Shoes, a local chain until the business folded a few years ago. Reporters repeated that the police still had no comment at this time.

She flipped through all the stations, but nothing more was added to the story.

Multiple fatalities in an empty parking lot sounded like a disagreement between gangs. A serious concern, and something Denver PD and the FBI would run to the ground. Not likely to result in the kind of story Carter wanted from her.

Nevertheless, spending an hour at the start of a potential story was better than spending a week trying to track down details at the end. She clicked off the TV and left for the warehouse on the way to the office.

The sun had yet to rise by the time Jess reached the scene. Police vehicles, TV vans, and the inevitable onlookers filled the roads. Two blocks away she found an empty parking place on the street beside a construction site.

Approaching the scene, she recognized a patrolman and joined him. He shook his head when she waved her press badge.

"Too soon and too much going on for press access," he said. "Big scene. Several bodies. Techs've been working all night. Take a couple of days just to finish documenting it all."

Jess thanked him and moved on, walking outside the yellow crime scene tape around the warehouse and parking area.

Two dumpsters sat on either side of the lot. The closest had the outline of a body on the ground nearby. The victim must have been seeking protection behind the dumpster.

She pulled a flashlight from her bag and tried to visualize the man sprawled on the ground. A black-on-yellow logo was painted on the dumpster. She recognized it. Kindermann was a local waste management company.

To the left of the logo, a long scar ran down the dumpster, leading to the outline of the man's body directly in front.

She knelt, playing the flashlight beam over the scar.

The heavy metal was indented, the paint scraped, and freshly exposed silver glinted through. Corrosion was a perennial problem for bare metal in Colorado winters. No corrosion here. This scar was fresh.

Several white disposable circles lay scattered around where the body fell. Markers for bullet fragments most likely. The evidence had already been removed.

Jess checked the dumpster. There were no other bullet holes or obvious indentations where a bullet might have been stopped by thick steel.

Which meant the victim had been felled by a single, fatal shot.

Could have been a lucky round.

Or maybe a well-trained, highly skilled shooter.

Either way, the result was the same. A man had died here.

Skirting around TV crews and bright lights, Jess followed the road. Crime scene tape led her to the middle of the warehouse parking lot.

A Lexus SUV had been impaled on a heavy concrete lamppost. The front of the vehicle stove-in all the way to the steering column. Bullet holes peppered the windshield. Two of the side windows were missing.

Jess spied more outlines on the ground. Two bodies this time, near the vehicle. They managed to get out of the mangled SUV but would have been exposed here in the middle of the lot. Easy shots.

Henry waved from a black Suburban parked on the far side of the street. She walked over as he closed his laptop's lid.

"How you feeling today?" he said.

She put her hands on the open window. "Angry, frustrated, curious, but mostly glad to be alive."

Henry put his hand on hers. "Don't mind telling you I was worried."

"Same."

He gave her hand a long squeeze. "At least Detective Norton is taking your bullet and casing more seriously now. And he's a good guy. If there's something to be found, he'll find it."

"This place is a mess," she said, gesturing to the parking lot. "Looks like a full-scale gun battle happened here."

"Yeah. We're bringing in help." He paused a moment. "We're up to ten now."

"Detectives?"

"Bodies."

Jess whistled.

"Like you said." Henry nodded. "A real mess."

"Messes like this leave a lot of evidence, though. So that's a good thing."

"And we'll find it. Called out all the techs we have. Overtime for the ones that spent the evening at your place."

"Unsung heroes."

He agreed. "This shoot-out has everyone worried."

"Gangs?"

He shrugged. "As good a guess as any. If it's a grudge or turf war, there could be more violence and bodies to come. We've got to dig in and figure this out before it escalates. I'll let you know more when I can."

Jess nodded. His comment was her cue to stop probing. She decided not to be offended because they were both under a lot of pressure. But Henry should know better. She'd never used her relationship with him for unprofessional advantage. She didn't intend to start now, and he couldn't possibly believe otherwise.

They said their goodbyes and she headed toward her Jeep as a sliver of sun lifted over the horizon. Partly to stay out of Henry's way and following a hunch, she moved her Jeep toward the tower. The views of the warehouse scene from the higher floors would give her a better feel for what happened.

The street had filled with an assortment of well-used trucks parked bumper-to-bumper along both sides of the road. Workmen filed through a gate into the tower worksite.

Jess had seen the artist's rendering of the extravagant new tower a few weeks ago. When completed, the tower would be nothing short of stunning.

But now, during the early stages of construction, the building was little more than a stack of concrete floors. It was the tallest structure for some distance in every direction. One day, the people on the top floors would have an impressive view.

Jess found a place to park and stared up at the unfinished structure another moment before following a couple of guys deeper into the site.

She asked, "I'm looking for the foreman."

One guy pointed her to a thin, middle-aged man with a goatee. EMILIANO was embroidered on his yellow jacket.

Jess waved her press card as she approached him to ask if she could climb up a few floors for a better view of the incident.

"No chance," Emiliano said. "Insurance won't allow it."

He shouted instructions to a passing worker.

She pointed to the flashing lights around the Golden's warehouse. "You could be a help to the investigation."

"But you're press, right? Not a cop?"

She shrugged.

"Sorry. Bring a cop and I'll think about it. Right now I've got enough problems cleaning this place up."

She looked at two men wearing heavy gloves clearing away thick shards of glass. "An accident?"

"Break-in."

"Why did they want to break in here?" Jess swiveled her head as if she'd missed the diamonds and gold bullion.

"Broken glass fanatics?" Emiliano hesitated a moment before he continued. "And some joker decided to climb the elevator shaft. So probably kids."

"You think kids did this?" Jess shook her head. "Not likely."

He shrugged. "Not exactly the sort of thing you'd expect to be connected to that shooting down at the old Golden's warehouse, if that's what you're thinking."

"Do you have security cameras?"

He nodded. "And a night watchman, too."

Emiliano's radio buzzed and he hustled off to the rear of the site.

Jess headed back to the gate, detouring around the men cleaning up the destroyed windows. The glass sheets were thick and sturdy. She wondered what kind of impact the killers launched that was powerful enough to cause so much breakage.

Beyond the glass were two portable construction trailers. Cheap, thin-walled steel. The sort of thing that could be thrown together in a few hours.

The foundations were stacked bricks that raised the buildings off the mud. The windows were dark, suggesting the buildings were unoccupied.

Both structures sported an assortment of dents and gashes on their walls.

Two specific marks drew her attention. Were they holes? Made by gunshots?

She stepped around a muddy puddle to get a closer look.

Something dark protruded from between the two buildings. Jess retrieved her flashlight and pointed the beam. A boot. She squatted down to shine the flashlight into the crevasse. A man's body lay facedown under the steel edge. His legs were twisted, and one arm seemed to be reaching for something. Sodden jeans glistened with rain and mud. His black jacket was emblazoned with SECURITY in dirty white letters.

He was dead and probably had been for a good long while.

Jess stood up and backed away, carefully retracing her original steps to avoid more interference with the scene.

The men who had been clearing the glass shards were staring at the body.

"Get Emiliano," Jess said, dialing Henry as they both raced away to find the foreman.

CHAPTER 22

"DAMN," EMILIANO SAID, LOOKING down at the body.

"Your night watchman?" Jess guessed.

Emiliano nodded. "Yeah. Good guy. Totally dependable."

They stood twenty feet from the construction trailer. Denver PD and a couple of crime scene techs were on the way. They'd take charge, secure and process the scene.

Jess looked at the incomplete tower. The night watchman's death had to be related to the warehouse shooting.

Sure, connecting the two was just a guess.

But there was no other reasonable explanation for the dead watchman at the moment. It was a good working theory.

She could stand around and speculate while the police did their jobs. Or she could be proactive.

"I need to get up a few floors," she said to Emiliano.

He replied flatly, still staring at the body. "No."

"If your guy saw something, we need to know what it was."

Emiliano gave her a brief stare. "He only patrolled at ground level. No one's going to break in on the upper floors. What would be the point?"

"Unless he's a joker."

"What?" Emiliano frowned.

"You said some joker climbed the elevator shaft."

"Yeah, but—"

She put her hand on his shoulder and pointed toward the building. "Show me."

Emiliano protested, but he walked with her to the elevator shaft.

Jess looked straight up into a vertical space that soared all the way to the roof. She imagined she might see a bit of sky up there and feel a breeze.

The height of the open space was unnerving, but it was the rope piled on the floor that held Jess's attention.

"Kernmantle rope," she said. "And a lot of it. Used for rescue and climbing. Whoever chose this to use here might have been a joker, but he was no fool."

Emiliano shook his head. "Yeah? Who climbs up a rope when the stairs are right there?"

"Who said he climbed up?"

"You think they hoisted something all the way up there?" Emiliano said, looking up.

"Maybe. Or maybe he came down. In a hurry."

Emiliano shook his head again, still not persuaded. "Why do that?"

"To get out fast. Save energy. Hit the ground running. All reasonable concerns if he'd just shot someone."

"He shot my night watchman? He was at ground level. Why would some joker go up to the roof to shoot a guy who's right here on the ground?"

"I'm talking about the shooting next door. At the warehouse."

He stepped back, still staring upward. "Oh God."

"Let's take the stairs," Jess said, heading up swiftly, with Emiliano following.

She slowed her pace at the tenth floor but refused to rest until they reached twenty.

The kernmantle rope had been placed from a higher point.

Emiliano wiped sweat from his brow and panted. His heavy work gear was made for durability, not aerobic exercise.

At the thirtieth floor they exited the stairwell, checked that the rope was hanging in the elevator shaft at this level, and then climbed the final three floors.

Boxes, wires, and pipes covered the concrete on the thirty-third floor. From the center by the stairs, all Jess could see was a bleak sky faintly illuminated by the rising sun. A stiff breeze hit her back, reminding her of the approaching storm.

A yellow and black cord across a wide opening seemed to be the only visual warning before the building's edge. There was no chance that cord would prevent a fall.

Disoriented by the twists and turns of the stair climb, Jess circled the area to find the entrance to the elevator shaft.

More yellow and black cord lay snapped onto the floor. Three anchors had been hammered into the concrete entranceway and the kernmantle rope was securely attached.

The anchors were high up, which made it easy to grasp the line.

"Definitely made for a quick exit," Jess said, grabbing on to the rope to look down the shaft.

The view was intimidating. Even though she knew the shaft's walls were parallel, from this vantage point, they seemed to converge. Jess shivered as she absorbed the daunting reality.

He had dropped five hundred feet onto the tiny square at the bottom.

This guy was nothing like any thug or gangster Jess had met before. He had skills. Training. Expertise.

A two-way radio on Emiliano's belt buzzed. He walked away while talking into the device.

The sun had risen a few more degrees. In the early-dawn light, the thirty-third floor offered a spectacular view. From one side of the building she could see downtown. On a good day, even the mountains might be visible.

She walked around to the side of the building that looked down on Golden's.

From her vantage point the warehouse parking lot seemed almost straight down. A clear bird's-eye view.

Henry's SUV was still parked on the side where they'd talked. She recognized one of the Denver TV vans and a reporter speaking into a microphone.

Police officers patrolled the crime scene tape, discouraging onlookers as the CSI team, wearing bright blue nitrile gloves, bagged and tagged, and photographed.

Whoever had been on floor thirty-three must have been an essential part of the murders that took place five hundred feet below.

She knelt and scanned the floor with the flashlight on her phone. She found no spent cartridges but did find four more anchors placed in a rough square at the edge of the building. Kneeling, she found blue fibers caught between the anchor and the concrete. She took several pictures with her phone.

Emiliano finished on the radio. "I have to go," he said. "Police are trying to close down our construction site."

Jess pointed to the square arrangement of anchors on the floor. "Is this normal?"

Emiliano frowned. "Nailing things into our concrete?" He shook his head. "That's not part of the planned construction."

"Then we'd better go. Denver PD is going to have to secure this floor, too."

CHAPTER 23

THE AIR IN THE old burger joint reeked. Toppers had gone belly-up five years ago. The owners had simply closed the doors and walked away. The neon signs covering the walls had not been switched on, and a single bulb at the back of the small room was the only source of illumination.

The light, if not the smell, suited Kahler. His jeans and old coat would stink, but he wouldn't be wearing them much longer. He'd soon be rich enough to throw his clothes away every day, Jack Reacher style.

Kahler's leg ached. In fact, it damned well hurt.

Jess Kimball got lucky, for sure. But he had, too. Her bullet tore a quarter-inch chunk from his thigh. An inch or two farther and she'd have hit a vein.

Overnight the injury had become more painful, which he knew was a bad sign. He'd cleaned the wound and applied ointment and a bandage. But the throbbing kept him awake.

The pain in his leg wasn't the only thing that led to Kahler's disturbed night. His mind wouldn't let him forget the potentially disastrous mistakes he'd made.

Kimball had found the bullet from his stupid wild shot out there on the mountain road.

He'd been careless. Sloppy. An unfortunate breach of his expertise, hard-won after years of training.

Even worse, she'd found the damned cartridge he'd left out there as well. Inexcusable.

Other than the huge dent to his pride, her finding the bullet and cartridge wasn't the end of the world. Lots of guns took the same round, and there'd be no way to trace them to his gun.

Well, there might be a way, but no woman would ever figure it out, he'd thought with a sneer when the situation first came to his attention. He'd been wrong.

Turned out Jess Kimball wasn't law enforcement, but she'd acquired some street cred and knowledge of forensics along the way. Plus, she had friends.

All of which meant she'd taken the bullet and cartridge to a ballistics expert.

He'd managed to recover it easily. No harm, no foul.

But if Kimball had known to take the bullet and cartridge to a forensics guy, what else did she know? How much more trouble could she cause?

His leg and Kimball were not the only concerns keeping him awake, either.

Stupidly, he'd shot Snout. Totally on impulse. He wasn't sorry Snout was dead. Not even a little bit.

Snout was a useless piece of trash who would have received a cut of the sizable profit from Miller's crew. Eliminating Snout meant one less piece of the pie and more profit for Kahler.

Not that the rest of the crew would necessarily see Snout's murder in the same way. Snout had his supporters. They would have their suspicions. Which they would have expressed in vengeance. Violently. During the night.

But none of Snout's guys came. Kahler's night had passed quietly. Which meant he'd be okay. Probably.

He opened the door beneath and entered a room full of people. The atmosphere changed as he stepped over the threshold. The stale smell of fried food would remain until the building was demolished, but the pulse of the room shifted.

Eyes swiveled in Kahler's direction. Electricity seemed to crackle in their silence. After a few seconds, chairs and tables creaked as they shifted their weight, probably reaching for guns.

He raised his hands palms out and scanned the room. "Whoa, guys. Easy there."

Return stares were cold and hard.

He knew why. Snout.

Maybe they were waiting for Kahler to confess. Maybe they expected it. Some sort of honor among thieves thing. Except they couldn't do anything much here and now.

Toppers had gone bust, but it was surrounded by other active businesses. There'd be cameras. Police close by. The sound of gunfire inside Toppers right now would bring far too much attention.

Kahler stepped to one side and lowered his hands. "Sorry I'm late."

"This ain't some coffee club," said Miller, poking him in the chest. "You get an order, you follow it. To the letter. Got it?"

Kahler nodded.

"You're sweating," Miller said.

"Hot in here." Kahler pulled at the neck of his polo shirt.

"I don't like people sweating. Means they got something going on."

"What the hell are you talking about?" Kahler replied with what he hoped was precisely the right amount of indignation.

Miller nodded to Hassan. "Frisk him."

"What is this?" Kahler shifted toward the door.

Hassan blocked the exit, lifted Kahler's arms, and patted him down. He double-checked all pockets and pulled Kahler's shirt from his jeans.

Hassan removed Kahler's gun from its holster and placed the pistol behind him on a rickety table. He turned Kahler around.

"Kick off your shoes."

After shaking and poking them, Hassan dropped the shoes on the floor. "Clean."

Miller twisted Kahler around, straightened his shirt collar, and clapped him on the shoulders. "Good. I like clean. Clean is good. Don't you forget it."

"You think I'm some snitch? Wearing a wire after what I did last night?"

"We all know what you did last night," Hassan said in a deep, growling voice.

"Exactly right. I put Finny out of business," Kahler snapped. He kept his face impassive, straining to watch the whole group for the first sign of threatening movement.

"*We* put Finny out of business. But yeah." Miller nodded. "In a game of winner takes all, last night we won."

"Because of me."

"Because of all of us," Miller said.

Someone in the room whooped.

Miller turned. "Hold it down. Ain't all goodness. We lost one of our own."

"Dead wood," Kahler blurted. A knee-jerk reaction he regretted at once.

Miller scowled.

Kahler shrugged.

Miller let them all stew for a bit. "Last night put us on the map. We're set up with product for the next two weeks and users who just got cut off from their regular supplier. So we pick up where Finny's crew was cut off. There's a whole lot of pent-up demand out there. Go find it."

"You getting another shipment?" Kahler asked.

Miller nodded and flashed a satisfied grin. "On the way today. Every two weeks. Here on in, we'll be making it faster than we can spend it."

CHAPTER 24

JESS FOLLOWED EMILIANO AS he raced down the stairs, talking rapidly on his radio to organize the hundred-plus workmen being deprived of the day's pay.

By the time they reached the tenth floor, he'd made an agreement with the construction company about compensation, and conversations got easier.

The descent took almost five minutes. The constant turns at each half floor left Jess feeling dizzy.

The kernmantle rope would have enabled the shooter to exit much faster. Thirty seconds, maybe. A huge advantage if he were racing to evade incoming police after the gunshots started.

Denver PD had arranged the workmen in two lines with an officer at the head of each line taking names and statements.

Two women in one-piece snow suits identified with crime scene designations emblazoned on their backs had cordoned off the area around the construction trailers.

Jess stared at the watchman's body, wondering if the man had family.

"You okay?" Henry asked as he approached.

"The night watchman." She shuddered. "Shot in the face and chest."

Henry gestured to the body. "Doing his job."

"Except his job was to fend off kids and petty theft, not defend the business at gunpoint."

"Yeah." Henry hummed his agreement. "He has a gun but hadn't pulled it. Radio's still on his belt, too. Logic suggests this kill has to be connected to the warehouse murders."

"Yep." Jess nodded. "Thirty-third floor. There's a ten-foot area where it looks like the shooter laid down a blue tarpaulin to collect brass. And a kernmantle rope down the elevator shaft for a rapid exit."

Henry looked at the half-constructed building. "You've been up there?"

She nodded.

He cocked his head and narrowed his eyes as if he could see the rooftop. "Be a long shot."

"Almost straight down. No one would suspect a shooter up there. Wouldn't even think to look up."

"Still a long shot."

"One of the dumpsters has a long streak of bare metal. Like a bullet missed its target and headed down."

"I noticed. And that dumpster is almost straight on from here," Henry mused quietly. "We'd really need forensics to connect the dots."

"That'll take time."

"Always does. But we only get one chance to get it right. Everything we do now will be torn apart in court."

She looked at the two women moving slowly as they photographed the body between the construction trailers, studious in their work. Henry was right. Nothing they could do now would bring the night watchman back, but they were his best chance for justice.

Jess could think of no solid alternative. "Better leave them to their work then."

The drive back to her office passed in a blur. Before she knew it, *Taboo*'s elevator doors opened on the tenth floor.

Several people inquired whether she was okay after the attack at her apartment. It felt odd to be the center of attention in her own office. She had to remind herself that news traveled fast between news teams.

Mandy held out a cup of coffee. "You just walking around?"

Jess frowned. "What else am I supposed to do?"

"Well...you were shot at. Don't you get police protection or something?"

"They offered. I turned it down."

"Shouldn't have," said Carter, striding over. "Reporters have had to move after groups of extremists read their articles."

"No evidence the guy who attacked me was an extremist," Jess replied, shaking her head.

"Do normal people go around attacking reporters in their homes? I think not," Carter said sternly. "And you have family to think of now. What about Peter?"

Carter was right, of course. Reporters were targets too often. Random victims and avengers, organized groups, and state-sponsored terrorists considered reporters like Jess fair game.

She knew the world had become a dangerous place for journalists. "But what have I done lately to make anyone want to kill me? I had two months off with Peter. No way I could have pissed off a killer in less than twenty-four hours without even realizing it."

"True," Carter said slowly, thinking it through. "And the attack can't be connected to the road rage case. Can it?"

She shrugged.

His lips curled down. "You have taken on our most difficult and sometimes dangerous projects. This road rage thing wasn't supposed to be one of them."

Jess nodded. Carter meant well. Perhaps if she'd stuck to his rules, no one would have tried to shoot her. But sticking to rules wasn't her specialty. Far from it.

"Heck of a first day back," said Mandy as the phone on her desk rang. She answered, then cupped her hand over the microphone. "It's for you. Someone named Goodwin?"

Jess hustled into her office and put the call on speaker. "Keshawn. Good to hear from you. I think I caused you some trouble last night. Sorry about that."

"I think you're the one who's in trouble. Morris called you yet?"

Jess leaned forward. "No."

Mandy poked her head into Jess's office. She pointed behind her with her thumb as Henry stepped past her, a briefcase in one hand and a heavy-duty suitcase in the other.

"He's just arrived," Jess said.

"Good."

Henry pointed to the phone. "Goodwin?"

Jess nodded. "What's going on?"

"Tell him video conference," Henry said. "Usual number."

Jess repeated Henry's message and hung up. "I've never been so popular. Care to enlighten me?"

Henry pulled a tablet computer from his briefcase and set it up. "You need to see this."

The tablet buzzed for an incoming call. Moments later Keshawn Goodwin's face filled the screen. Hand-scrawled numbers covered the wall behind him. He wasted no time on pleasantries.

"This is the bullet you found out on 44W." A closeup image of a deformed bullet appeared on the screen, rotating slowly.

"I thought it was taken," Jess said.

"I got plenty of pictures. The big marks are where you dug it out of the tree." Goodwin changed the slide and several circles appeared, highlighting places on the dark metal. "But there's plenty of other tool marks."

"From the rifling," Jess said.

"Yep. Turns out the combination of tree and this type of bullet left us a good sample."

"Do you know the weapon?" Morris asked.

"Can't identify the actual gun yet. Something with a long range, obviously. Sniper rifle or similar. There's some databases might help. I'll have to check."

Jess frowned. "So what does this tell us?"

"Nothing, until seven this morning," Goodwin said. "When I got a batch of the bullets from the Golden's warehouse shooting."

"And?" Jess leaned forward for a closer view.

The image of a second bullet appeared on the screen, rotating in sync with the first. Small circles highlighted tool marks. The second image moved synchronously with the first image.

"They're a match?" Jess asked.

"You could walk them straight into court and I'd testify to that without an ounce of doubt," Goodwin said.

"Rooney's death is connected to the warehouse shootings?" Jess asked, the tone of her voice rising.

"Rooney wasn't shot," said Henry. "He ran off the road and crashed and burned. Not shot."

Jess replied, "True, but the bullets match."

"They aren't the only ones that match, either," Goodwin said.

Two smaller bullets appeared on the screen, rotating as before. Circles highlighted matching marks on both smaller bullets.

Jess leaned closer. "You found more bullets at Rooney's crash site?"

"Nah," Goodwin replied. "The one on the left was recovered from the building site. Near the night watchman's body."

"And the one on the right?"

"That one is from your apartment," Goodwin stated flatly.

Jess rolled her chair backward. "You mean…all three are connected? Rooney, the warehouse shoot-out, *and* whoever shot at me? But why?"

"Well, the same two guns were used, for sure. Who was holding those guns and why?" Goodwin grimaced. "Not my department."

"But someone tried to take me out, and the bullet from Rooney's accident has been stolen."

"Don't I know it," said Goodwin.

"Someone didn't want that link discovered."

"Maybe," Henry said. "Don't get too carried away. Follow the evidence. We'll get there."

"But what other reason could there be?" Jess asked with wide-eyed astonishment.

Henry shrugged. "Can't say. But let's not jump to conclusions. That's not helpful."

"Shooter must have seen me find the Rooney bullet and casing." The idea made Jess shiver.

"Out in the mountains?" Henry asked. "Anyone could have seen you. Lots of traffic out there. Plenty of people around."

Henry was right. With the trees and snow blocking her sight line around the crash site, she could have been watched from a distance and not realized someone was there. "And I visited Naya Bozeck, the woman first on the scene after his crash."

Henry scribbled down the name in a small notebook.

"She said she saw someone walking away immediately after the crash. Saw him in the distance. Guy was dressed in white."

Henry added to his notes.

"There's more," Goodwin said. Two more images appeared on the screen. "Crime scene techs found a cartridge embedded in some polystyrene blocks on that tower roof. Matches the one you found."

"We think the shooter used the polystyrene on the thirty-third floor," Henry said. "Possibly a plastic canvas tarp, too."

"The blue threads in the anchors I found secured to the concrete?"

"Guess he thought the tarp would catch everything, but the hot shell melted into the plastic," Henry said.

"So whoever was atop the tower shot all those people in the warehouse lot?"

"Possibly. Probably, even," Goodwin said. "But multiple weapons were fired. So we still need to sort all of that out."

"Autopsy results should show us who was killed by what," Henry added.

"I have to go," Goodwin said. "Another call coming in."

"Can you send me those pictures?" Jess asked.

"I wouldn't even have shown them to you without Henry's permission." Goodwin shook his head. "This work is on the FBI's dime. Evidence and conclusions belong to them. At least for now. Gotta go."

The screen went dark.

"Now for the news you're not going to like." Henry shut down his tablet. "We got a preliminary ID of one of the warehouse bodies. Charlie Finnegan."

"The guy they call Finny? Didn't he beat some serious charge recently?"

"He and another guy were caught and two kilos of Fentanyl eleven months ago. Should have been enough to lock him up for a while, at least."

"What happened?"

"He denied the drugs were his. The DNA samples proving he'd handled the product got suspiciously contaminated and he walked."

"Serious trouble, then."

"Point is, Finny got shot last night. Along with more bodies we think were his main men."

"By a marksman on the thirty-third floor."

"Looking that way."

"It was a hit. A setup."

"Seems like it," Henry said. "Which brings me to this."

He opened the large case and lifted out what looked like a heavy black jacket.

"Body armor?" she said, frowning.

"Standard issue for high-risk situations. Soft armor all around for handgun protection, hard plates front and back for rifle fire."

Jess stood. "I can't wear that. It's enormous."

"It's not as big as you think. Fits under a coat."

"But—"

"Jess. Listen to me. The warehouse murders were a takedown. Might require months of tedious work to nail everything and everyone. If we ever do," Henry said seriously. "But in the meantime, there's a shooter out there with bullets that are good for a couple of thousand yards."

Jess poked the vest. "And this is going to stop them."

"May not be perfect, but we can't have you wandering around unprotected."

"We?"

Henry sighed. "Okay. I."

She scowled. "And I don't wander around."

"You know what I mean."

Jess hated being told what to do. She'd learned to trust her instincts, and her insight had saved her own life more than once.

She wanted to reject the enormous vest. But Henry was right.

If the shooter who killed the night watchman and probably several more at the warehouse wanted her dead, he could try again to kill her. Why not? She had zero evidence to suggest that he was a quitter.

Henry helped her slip her arms into the vest. Though big, it wasn't too heavy. Henry showed her how to strap herself in and then helped her take it off again.

She kept thinking back to the warehouse. "If Finny and his henchmen got slaughtered, it was drug related."

"No argument here."

"Whoever killed Finny also killed Rooney."

"Except Rooney wasn't shot."

"True, but the bullet in the tree just above Rooney's car is too coincidental to be unrelated."

"Fair enough."

"And where there's drugs, there's money. Lots of it."

Henry cocked his head. "Where are you going with this?"

"Justin Rooney worked at a bank."

CHAPTER 25

HENRY WENT BACK TO work after Jess agreed to wear the body armor anytime she stepped outside.

The warehouse crimes would get plenty of attention, so Jess decided to return to Justin Rooney.

She quickly dealt with her emails, and Mandy helped her adjust the padding and tightened the straps on Jess's bulletproof vest. Her ski jacket didn't fit over the vest, so she dashed into a shop across the street and bought a new waterproof jacket. The saleswoman gave her a full rundown on the jacket's new tech, including how the material didn't swoosh as she moved.

Jess took her vest and her new jacket and drove her Jeep to First Aurora. On the way she called Margo Alvarado, the bank's HR manager.

Jess said, "I'd like to talk some more about Justin Rooney."

"There's not much more I can tell you. He was a good employee, and we're all in shock about what happened." Her tone suggested an easy shrug followed the admission.

"I understand, and I'm not looking to add to anyone's grief, but this is important."

"Okay. I can spare a few minutes," Margo said before she hung up.

A smattering of vehicles occupied the First Aurora Bank parking lot. Inside, a couple of tellers handled an equal number of customers.

Margo waited by the staircase and when Jess arrived, she walked over.

"I mentioned your visit to Jerry," Margo said.

Jess braced herself for rejection, but to her surprise, Margo waved her arm toward Larson's office. "This way. We'll join him. His office is nicer than mine."

The sign proclaimed JERRY LARSON—CHIEF EXECUTIVE OFFICER in large block capitals.

His assistant worked in an outer office. She allowed Jess and Margo to enter. "Jerry's expecting you."

The assistant closed the door behind them. To Jess's surprise, Larson was alone. She'd expected him to want a lawyer in the room.

The office decor might have been plucked from a designer's magazine. Dark wood and leather. Recessed ceiling lights and occasional table lamps gave the room an appealing warm glow. By contrast, the gray scene through the floor-to-ceiling windows behind him seemed even colder.

He closed the two laptops on his desk as they entered. Then he leaned over and shook Jess's hand.

"Should we have legal here?" Margo asked.

"No need to involve anyone else." Larson shook his head and gestured toward the chairs. "I understand you have something important to share with us, Ms. Kimball."

"Actually, I was hoping you could tell me," Jess said.

Larson glanced at Margo, then back at Jess. "Tell you?"

"About Justin Rooney."

"I thought we'd told you all we know about him. Good employee. Not much else." He turned. "Margo?"

Margo shrugged. "No personnel issues. Good reviews and ratings for his work. He was quiet, but that's not a bad thing."

"Exactly what did he do here?" Jess asked.

"Network security."

"Meaning?"

Margo shrugged again. "Specialist stuff to keep us safe."

"The bank is connected to the web, as are all banks," interjected Larson. "You just have to secure the interface. That's what Rooney did here."

"Any reason to suspect him?"

"Of what?" Larson asked, raising an eyebrow.

"Criminal activity."

Margo looked shocked. "Good God, no. At the bank? Here? No, we had complete faith in him."

"Wait," said Larson, holding up a hand to cut Margo off. "What exactly are you implying?"

"I'm just looking at every angle."

"Criminal activity is more than an angle, Miss Kimball. We're a bank. We depend on trust. And to ensure that, we have lots of procedures and checks and balances." Larson paused. "We don't employ criminals here. We don't encourage criminal activity from our employees, either."

"Criminal activity doesn't usually stand out on a routine compliance checklist."

Larson scoffed. "I don't know him personally, but I'm sure he was an upstanding member of the bank's team. Unless…"

Jess waited. "What?"

"Do you have evidence?"

"Just a coincidence."

"So…you're just fishing."

"As I said, a coincidence. An unusual coincidence."

"Concerning what?"

"A possible connection between Justin Rooney and the shooting at the Golden's warehouse last night."

Margo gasped and sat up straighter. "That old place? That can't be. He was such a nice boy. He wasn't…He wouldn't…No, I can't believe it."

"Hang on," said Larson. "Justin was already dead. How can he be involved with whatever happened at Golden's last night?"

"I didn't say he was physically involved. Only that there is a potential connection between the two."

"I can't believe Justin would be involved in a shooting," said Margo. "He wasn't that sort of—"

"Stop," said Larson, leaning forward and holding up his hand again. "We're a bank. We have hundreds of millions under our care. If you have evidence of wrongdoing, you need to tell us."

"I can't."

"I'm sorry if you think your journalistic ethics are being violated, but we need to know," Larson demanded, as if he were rarely thwarted. "Tell us. Now. Right now."

"I'm not discussing rumors and guesses that may turn out to be nothing more than coincidence."

"We're not spreading things all over the internet, for heaven's sake. We're a financial institution. We have standards. Morals. A conscience. People depend on us." Larson's bluster bordered on comic at this point.

Jess didn't argue and kept her voice calm. "I'm sorry. You'll have to wait."

"This is unacceptable. You cannot hold a sword over our heads like this." Larson slapped his palm onto the table to punctuate.

"You will be the third to know when I have proof."

"Third!" Larson scowled.

"The FBI and Denver PD are investigating the same potential coincidence," Jess explained easily. "Of course I'll need to inform the authorities first."

"Really? Good. Because I know the chief of police."

"Are you threatening me?"

"I might ask you the same question." Larson stood.

"You expect me to give you evidence of criminal activity before I give it to the police?"

Larson scoffed. "Margo, show the woman out. I have calls to make."

He picked up his phone and turned around to gaze past the big windows behind his desk.

Margo sprang up and gestured to the door.

"Thank you for your time, Mr. Larson," Jess said and left with Margo.

She hadn't expected Margo or Larson to reveal some deep dark secret about Rooney, but Larson's reaction had been over the top. What was he afraid of?

CHAPTER 26

JERRY LARSON WAITED FOR a minute after Kimball left to punch the cushion in his seat. The thickly padded headrest of his expensive leather chair made a good target. He punched and punched, swearing, grunting, anything to fight off the desire to scream.

He noticed his knuckles grow sore and he quit before the damage became obvious and suspicious.

How could this be happening? Senator MacKrell had promised to stop Jess Kimball. What kind of idiot was he, anyway?

And now Kimball had turned up some link between Rooney and the shooting at the Golden's warehouse? How was that possible? What could he…?

Goosebumps prickled over Larson's skin. He squeezed the headrest hard. Rooney had all that equipment at his apartment. Heaven knows what he'd been up to, but it wasn't normal. Could Rooney have been some criminal mastermind? Larson chuckled. Dumb idea.

Larson walked around his desk, then dropped into his leather chair. No. Rooney didn't have what it took to mastermind anything. Even when he'd stumbled upon patentable projects, Rooney hadn't so much as whimpered when Larson named himself their owner.

So what could connect Rooney's death and the warehouse shooting? Rooney was an IT guy. Not a mobster. As far as Larson knew, Rooney didn't even own a weapon of any kind.

Larson's epiphany slammed into him like a runaway train.

Rooney knew everything about banking security.

People didn't rob banks with guns and masks anymore. At least not if they knew how a bank connected itself to the outside world.

Which Rooney absolutely knew. Better than most.

Larson switched on his computer, his foot tapping nervously as the small blue bar crept slowly across the screen. When the machine finally finished booting, Larson typed as fast as he could. Two fingers, hunting and pecking, stabbing the keys.

The bank management screens came up. Dashboards of information that reflected the health and status of the bank. Inflows, outflows, investments, cash on hand.

He glanced over it all, scrolling through several pages. The numbers weren't great, but the bank was hanging on. Nothing had changed from the day before. Or the day before that.

Larson leaned back and struggled to breathe normally. Whatever Rooney might have been doing, he hadn't hacked into First Aurora and wiped them out. At least not yet.

He looked up the number for the IT department and dialed. Lucy Cranfield answered. He didn't introduce himself. They had caller ID.

"I understand you have taken over IT security?" Larson said without greeting.

"Er…yes. Until we—"

"Are all the systems running normally?"

"Which systems, sir?"

"Domestic and international transactions?"

"You mean are our clearing processes still functioning?"

He frowned, not quite sure what she meant. "Of course."

"Yes. No problems, sir. It's mostly automated."

"And the systems that aren't automated?"

"I've taken those over after…after Justin's accident."

"Right. Yes. Terrible shame." He tried to sound sincere.

"Yes."

"I was devastated."

"We all were."

He hummed. "Anyway. Customers are able to access their accounts okay?"

"Yes, sir."

"And international transactions?"

He heard a keyboard clicking. "No problem. We've had eight so far today. All fine."

"Good. Any glitches at all, I want to know."

"Right, sir."

"Immediately."

"I understand, sir. Any problems and I'll let you know."

He hung up, not quite sure what he felt. It wasn't relief.

If Rooney didn't steal from First Aurora Bank, why was all that equipment in his apartment?

He had to be a hacker. Nothing else was remotely feasible.

If that damned reporter or the police could link the shooting at Golden's to Rooney, First Aurora could be implicated.

Which would be a disaster. No other word for it. The feds would close the bank. Larson could lose everything. In little more than an instant.

He tried to think of alternatives but came up empty. No other viable option. Larson would return to Rooney's apartment and remove all that equipment.

Without Rooney's equipment, the police would have no idea what he might have been up to. If Rooney had been messing with First Aurora's accounts, destroying that equipment was the first step to self-preservation.

The more Larson thought about it, the more sense it made to him.

Why would Rooney have all that equipment in his apartment? The only thing that made sense was that Rooney wanted to keep everything close to him and under his control at all times.

And why? Why would Rooney be so worried?

Larson could think of no harmless answers to that question.

He patted his pockets until he found Rooney's key.

In the cabinet on the far wall, he found the pair of duffel bags he used for his weekly racquetball game. If they weren't big enough to carry everything, he'd make two trips. He returned the bags to the cabinet to wait until he was ready.

His heart raced with anxiety. He told himself not to worry. Chances were that Rooney really wasn't that smart.

Larson needed to take precautions, of course. But Justin Rooney had always been harmless. And now that he was dead, he was even more harmless.

Larson settled in to wait until the bank closed. And then a bit longer. Until after midnight.

No one would see him hanging around Rooney's place in the early hours of the morning.

CHAPTER 27

JESS DROVE ACROSS TOWN to Justin Rooney's apartment. A modern concrete and glass three-story structure that had opened only recently, the building wasn't lavish. Designed to appeal to renters flipping through online brochures rather than living quarters that might last for decades.

A tall girl in her late teens sat behind a desk in the leasing office. A sign on the desk said her name was Kelly. She smiled as Jess approached.

Jess held out her press card and introduced herself.

Kelly took the card. "Nice to meet you. I love *Taboo Magazine*. I read it every month."

"Thank you," Jess said. "I'm hoping you can help me."

Kelly nodded. "Sure. If I can. I'd love to."

"I'm looking into Justin Rooney's accident."

Kelly stood and slipped the card into her pocket. "We were all shocked. We've never lost one of our tenants before. Just terrible."

"I'm trying to make sense of it," Jess said.

Kelly's eyes widened. "He went off the road, didn't he?"

"There may be more to it than that. Which is why I'd like to look at his apartment."

"But you don't have a court order?" Kelly said, as if she were truly sorry to ask.

"I don't."

"Then I can't let you in," Kelly replied. "I can't afford to lose my job."

Jess smiled. "You can be there with me while I look around."

Kelly shook her head. "Company policy. Have to do everything by the book. I let Justin's father in and then got chewed out by my boss."

Jess frowned. "His father? When?"

"Yesterday."

"He was upset, I guess?"

"Oh, yes. Definitely," said Kelly, nodding.

"I haven't met him. What does he look like?"

"Medium height. Fifties. Bushy jet-black hair and a big mustache." Kelly leaned forward and lowered her voice. "To be honest, I think he was probably wearing a wig."

"And he entered the apartment?"

Kelly gave a pained looked. "Which is how I know for sure that I can't let you in."

Jess hummed. "Did you know Justin Rooney?"

"Kind of. He used to get a lot of packages. We keep them here for the residents to collect. And there were the socials. Once a month in the clubroom. He only attended a couple of times, but I remember him. Talked about cars. A lot."

"To whom?"

"Me. Which says something."

Jess frowned.

Kelly patted the top of her head to indicate her height. "I tend to intimidate men."

"Rooney was a confident guy, then?"

"On the subject of cars."

"What about visitors? Anybody come around regularly?"

"Couldn't say. His apartment's at the back of the complex, out of sight. We have security cameras back there, but security isn't my job," Kelly said.

"Did Rooney talk about his work at all?"

Kelly shook her head. "Don't think so. Never seemed to talk about anything but cars when I was around him. He leases a couple of garages here."

"Two?"

"At the back. Near his apartment. For his old cars."

"How old?"

"Ancient. Fifties and sixties kind of things. Took them out on the weekend," Kelly said. "He parked his daily vehicle outside in the uncovered lot like the rest of us."

"Could I see them? The garages?"

"Can't." She shrugged. "Policy."

"Could I?" Detective Norton said, the front door closing behind him as he strode to Kelly's desk. He held out a sheaf of paper and his badge. "Detective Norton. Denver PD. I have a warrant."

Kelly alternated between staring at the badge and the paper. "I...er...will have to check."

She dialed a number and walked away, obviously talking to her manager.

Norton said, "I hear there are a series of matches between the bullet you found and the shootings last night, yours and the one at Golden's."

"So Goodwin said."

"I should have paid more attention to your theories. I was too focused on the crash because…well, you know."

Jess nodded. "You're still calling Rooney's death an accident?"

Norton shrugged. "I interviewed his mother. She said they don't talk often, but according to her, Rooney was a solid citizen. Everybody liked him, she said. No enemies. No reason anyone would want him dead."

"Maybe. But someone else has already searched Rooney's apartment," Jess said. "He told Kelly he was Rooney's father. But he wasn't. Rooney's father died a few years ago."

"I saw that in his profile." Norton nodded toward Kelly. "Does she know?"

"Apparently not."

"I'll get the CCTV video. Must have cameras all over in a place like this." He paused a beat and pointed to her enlarged jacket. "Morris got you fitted."

"After last night."

"Can't say I blame you."

She tapped the hard slabs in the vest. "Doing my best."

"Good. Yesterday I couldn't get anyone interested in the Rooney crash and today it's my number one priority. Only one thing does that."

"Gangs?"

"Yep. And you don't want to be taking risks where they're concerned."

"Anything helpful from forensics at the site of Rooney's crash so far?"

"Nope. At least nothing of use. And I'm not stalling you here. There's just nothing helpful."

"Rooney worked at a bank," she said.

"They're on my list after this."

"What are you expecting to find?" Jess asked. "A connection to Rooney's crash? Or to the warehouse shooting? Or?"

"I never expect anything. But I'm hoping to find all of the above." He breathed loudly for a moment. "Word has it you've helped the FBI in the past."

It was Jess's turn to shrug.

Kelly returned to her desk, searched through a drawer, and pulled out a key. "I can show you around."

"Denver PD appreciates your cooperation," Norton said without a trace of sarcasm. He turned to Jess. "Coming?"

CHAPTER 28

KELLY LED JESS AND Norton past a covered swimming pool and through a maze of apartment blocks. Rooney's place was on the third floor. They climbed an open staircase and walked along a corridor.

Kelly stopped at the last of four doors. Norton stopped her and knelt in front of the lock. "Looks good. Not forced," he said.

Kelly opened the door and stood to one side.

Norton produced a pair of blue nitrile gloves for himself and a pair for Jess, followed by white paper surgical caps.

"Is that normal?" said Kelly.

"Only if you're looking for clues in a potential murder case," said Norton with a straight face.

"Is that...? Do you think...?" Kelly backed away as if something in the apartment might be contagious.

Norton pointed to a video camera in the corner of the breezeway. "I'm going to need all the video from Rooney's father's visit."

"Do you think he was involved?" said Kelly, aghast.

"His father?" said Norton. "No, I don't think his father was involved. Because Rooney's father died several years ago."

Kelly's mouth hung open. "But, but, but…"

"That wig you thought the man might be wearing," said Jess gently. "It was a wig."

The girl's shoulders slumped. She closed her mouth, pressing her lips together.

"Don't sweat it," said Norton. "No way for you to know Rooney's family history. Just get the video, please."

"Right." Kelly turned away to make a phone call.

Norton stepped into the apartment. Jess followed.

"Look, but don't touch," he said.

Jess resisted the temptation to reply.

The apartment consisted of a combined living room, kitchen, and dining area, along with two bedrooms. Large glass sliding doors opened onto a balcony from the living area. The dining table had been pushed up against the kitchen countertop, and both were covered with computers and electronic equipment.

Jess recognized some of the larger manufacturer names, but the array of boxes, small and large, was totally foreign to her.

Plenty of wires crossed the area, going under and over the boxes. Most wires were black or white, but some were yellow or blue.

There didn't seem to be any organization to the whole. The wires were knitted together like a bird's nest.

Bright LEDs covered the collection of electronic boxes. There were greens and blues and yellows. Some were constant, but many blinked in an unsynchronized fashion.

Jess couldn't make anything of the computer equipment. So she moved on.

In the first bedroom, the bed was unmade. A tablet computer lay on the bedside table on top of a stack of thick books about security and encryption. She took a picture of the titles.

The second bedroom had two tables and no bed.

The equipment piled on them was mostly unplugged and stacked in heaps. Wires were curled in loops and secured for storage.

Shipping cartons filled the closet. The main item of interest was a large-format printer. The two-foot-wide paper fed from a large spool. The last printout was still attached to the printer.

"Carburetor," said Norton. He leaned closer. "Looks like a Weber."

"You're into cars?"

"No choice." He laughed. "When I grew up, keeping a car going was an every-free-weekend project. We had to do the work ourselves or go broke. Weber carbs were a big thing back then."

A momentary buzz sounded from the living room. Norton stepped out into the hallway. "What do you make of all this stuff?"

Jess shrugged. "My son's into computers, but most of this is just bewildering to me."

"Rooney was a geek, for sure."

"Looks more like a laboratory than a hobby," Jess said. "He's got a lot of stuff here."

"You think he was a hacker?"

"Possibly. Could have an innocent explanation, though."

"Such as?"

"He was First Aurora Bank's main security guy. Maybe he had to keep up with hacker things as a part of his job." Jess held her hand over the top of the equipment, feeling the heat coming from it. "Hot. Like it's always on."

"Guess he meant to come back and turn it off," Norton said.

Kelly, still standing outside the front door, said, "Everything will go off at noon tomorrow. We notified the electric company a while ago."

"Why?" Jess asked.

"Rooney was one of those absent-minded types. He hadn't paid the rent in a while. We gave him several warnings and a courtesy extension, which ran out yesterday. I told his father when he was here, too. Neither of them paid the rent or the electric bill." Kelly shook her head. "To be honest, I thought he'd decided to move and stiff us for the rent and the electric."

"Can you make an exception? Keep the electricity going?" Norton asked, nodding sympathetically. "There's too much equipment for me to take now. And I don't need a bunch of useless stuff clogging up my evidence lockers, either. I want to get an IT team in here to look things over and take whatever they think is worth further examination."

"Sorry." Kelly shook her head. "The electricity is computer controlled. We gave the company and Rooney notice more than sixty days ago. The schedule is already in place. I couldn't stop it if I wanted to."

"Guess we'd better do all we can right now, then." Norton made a call, requesting an IT forensics person ASAP.

Jess took pictures of everything. Far more than she would need for a story, but she had the feeling she wouldn't get a second chance to photograph anything here.

"Garages," Norton said to Kelly.

"Not mentioned on the paperwork," she replied.

"It's a warrant. Issued by a judge. To search Rooney's property," Norton said, annoyed now.

"But—"

"You rent him the garages?"

Kelly nodded.

"Then he paid the rent and that makes the contents his property. Let's go." Norton stepped into the breezeway and turned Kelly toward the stairs.

"He didn't pay the rent, though. Or the electric bill. That's the issue," Kelly protested.

"You said he was being evicted effective tomorrow. Until then, it's still Rooney's property as far as I'm concerned," Norton said as he moved forward.

Jess closed the door as she left, the lock clicking into place.

Inside the first garage were all manner of tools hung on pegboards on the walls. Several car parts in various stages of disassembly lay on a workbench.

"Presumably where he parked the Plymouth," Norton said.

A long, low cream-colored convertible with a red leather interior sat in the second garage.

"Thunderbird," said Norton. "Early model. Mid-fifties."

Jess squeezed down one sidewall of the garage. She couldn't even find a fingerprint or smudge in the Thunderbird's gleaming paintwork. The leather looked perfect, too. No rips, tears, or split seats. The radio had a period look, but she suspected it was a modern radio made to look authentic.

Norton knelt to look in the wheel arches and underneath the car. "This thing is fantastic. There's no sign of rust, or wear and tear, or anything."

"Like new," Jess said, reaching the rear of the garage.

The second garage had the same pegboards and tools as the first. On the bench was a sheaf of printouts for various car parts, line drawings covered with dimensions.

A large silver refrigerator-like appliance stood in the space beside the workbench. Tucked under a wrench, she found a pile of receipts, the last one from Easy Tire and Oil for fixing a flat.

Norton stood beside her. "He really kept his car in good shape. These things used to dissolve at the first mention of winter. No rust protection at all."

He pointed to the large silver appliance. "What's that?"

"Beats me." Jess held her hand over a door handle. "Want to see?"

Norton nodded.

She pulled on the handle. It didn't move. She pulled harder, but it didn't budge. She ran her fingers around the edge and found a latch. The door sprang open.

The interior glowed brightly, almost blindingly so. The lights illuminated arms and spindles. A large yellow and black sign warned of lasers. She took a picture and closed the door. "It's a 3D printer," she said. "My son has a small one in his bedroom. But this is industrial."

"It's all fascinating," Norton said. "But I don't see anything that might have led to his death."

Jess pursed her lips. "No."

CHAPTER 29

THE NAVIGATION SYSTEM IN Jess's Jeep told her Easy Tire and Oil was a thirty-minute drive. She pressed start and followed the directions, which were, for a change, perfect.

The entrance to the parking lot was marked by a tower of giant tires, the sort that might be used on a tractor or big earth mover.

The building consisted of a line of four roll-up doors and a tiny office on the end. Parking slots faced the roll-up doors.

She found the last free space and walked into the office.

Straight ahead, a receptionist sat behind a counter. Stairs led to an upper floor, probably offices. Windows in the wall to the left looked out onto the car servicing area. Each of the four bays had a car up on ramps with mechanics working underneath.

A woman behind the desk chatted to a customer on the phone. Jess waited. The woman's conversation didn't seem to be wrapping up, so Jess took a door from the office into the service area.

The smell of oil and the clanking of tools filled the air. A man approached, waving his hands. His blue overalls were stamped with his name.

"Can't be in here," Kemp said.

"I'm looking for anyone who might know Justin Rooney."

Kemp's mouth froze open for a moment. A frown flickered across his face as if he were trying to remember something. It disappeared as quickly as it came. "He don't work here."

"He was a customer."

"Nah," said Kemp, shaking his head. "Don't know him."

"Would anyone else—"

He gestured to the door she'd walked through. "You can't be in here."

"Rooney was involved in an accident. This weekend. Route 44W. Up in the mountains."

Kemp offered a sympathetic, "I'm sorry to hear that."

"He didn't survive."

"Damn." Kemp looked at her sideways. "You family?"

"A friend." Jess could tell the man would clam up if she told him her job.

Kemp's expression hardened. "Is there a problem?"

"He had a flat repaired here. Month ago."

"A lot of people do."

"A Plymouth Barracuda. Seventy-seven."

Kemp pursed his lips. "We get a lot of those in."

"Really? Because I'd think they're pretty rare."

Kemp shrugged.

"This one was like new," she said.

"We get all sorts."

Jess glanced around the service area. The other mechanics looked busy, tools in their hands. She wasn't going to get much out of them.

She thanked Kemp and returned to the office. The woman was still busy on the phone. She wasn't going to learn anything here. Jess turned and left.

CHAPTER 30

MILLER PACED AROUND HIS small office. Two of his men sat at his desk, hunched over laptops, busy. Beside them was a stack of pages covered with letters and numbers.

Kahler sat in the only other chair, watching the men work.

"We should have waited to get rid of Rooney," Kahler said.

Miller stopped pacing and glared. "You don't make the decisions."

"But look where your decision got us," Kahler said, gesturing to the men at the desk.

"Don't tell me how to run my business." Miller's tone was menacing, as if he might actually do something about Kahler's impertinence.

"*Our* business," Kahler said, unflappable.

Miller clenched his teeth and hissed through his nose. By taking Finny out, he'd made the giant leap from lowlevel pusher to controlling supply over all of Denver. But Kahler wanted to muscle in on Miller's plan. Which would make a big dent in Miller's share.

He'd built the team he needed by offering them shares if they came aboard. They all had a stake. Everybody wanted a big payday.

And they would end up with a hell of a payday. No ifs, no buts. Mountains of cash. Very soon.

Miller clenched his jaw. "Rooney was about to talk."

"We coulda watched him. Made him understand his risks," Kahler replied reasonably.

"And when he talked to the bank? Or the cops? You going to be there every minute, attached to the guy with Gorilla Glue?" Miller demanded.

Kahler shrugged. "Could have whacked his family. That'd have got his attention."

Miller slapped his forehead as if he'd been an idiot. Then he growled, "Rooney only had his mother and they didn't talk much, he said."

"So he didn't send her a Christmas card. So what? Doesn't mean he didn't care."

"And doesn't mean he did."

"All I'm saying is that Rooney was useful. Now he's dead. Not helpful." Kahler stood and waved toward the men at the desk. "This is what happens on your plan."

"Rooney gave me the instructions. Showed me how to log on. Everything we need to know," Miller replied.

"Well, that's just grand. Because I was beginning to worry. I thought for one awful moment that maybe you didn't know the password." Kahler's sarcasm was obvious even to Miller.

Miller crossed the small space and shoved Kahler back into the chair. "Don't you dare. Don't you even—"

Kahler bounced up like a kid's punching balloon and pushed Miller back. "Dare what? What you gonna do? You screwed up the damned password!"

"I entered it! Last time. It worked. Exactly as it was written," Miller growled.

"Yet here we are." Kahler pointed to the laptops. "Going through every possible combination."

The men at the laptops jumped to their feet, guns drawn.

Miller glowered, but Kahler was right. He had entered the password personally both times. First time, it worked. Second time, it didn't.

He was sure he'd entered the exact characters as written on Rooney's piece of paper both times. Rooney must have made a mistake when he wrote it down. Maybe an uppercase letter that should have been lowercase. Mixed up an I and a 1 or used a G in place of a 6.

Miller had spent the morning writing down every variation he could think of. Then he brought in the two men at the desks and set them to work. They were punching in the long string of characters and digits. Every combination. A hundred and fifty for each man.

"We're cool. We'll get there." Miller shrugged and waved the men to return to their laptops.

Kahler shook his head. "Really. Because I'm watching failure here."

"Once we hit the right combination, we'll be fine."

"How d'you know it's not one of those websites that finds you trying to break in and just gives you an error message every time?" Kahler said.

"I don't. No one does. But we keep trying. Because I, for one, am not going to give up on the first attempt."

"But eventually? If the typing pool here can't get into our money?"

"I am not giving up."

Kahler exhaled. "You know if we can't get another shipment, people will be pissed. You'll leave a vacuum where the product should be. And nature don't like no vacuum. Someone else will step in. Sure as hell."

"You threatening me?" Miller said, his hand on his pistol, challenging demeanor on full display.

Kahler shrugged. "We had the sweetest gig ever until you loused up the password."

"I did not louse up the password," Miller said, pulling his weapon and brandishing it like he knew where to aim.

"Yeah, right." Kahler turned his back to Miller's threats and left the room, sneering at the two men working the laptops.

Miller plopped into the chair, mulling over what Kahler had to say. Taking Rooney off the board had been the right thing to do. Rooney had been one of those dumb smart guys. He knew a lot about some stuff and almost nothing about how the world works.

The little nerd had been happy enough to demonstrate the process of transferring money online. Big mistake. Miller didn't need Rooney after that. Made the nerd expendable.

Then he started asking too many questions. Like he was fishing for private stuff he had no need to know about the Finny operation.

Rooney crossed the line when he started to hint that he could close down Miller's operation. Not something he should have dropped into casual conversation.

Like lobbing a hand grenade. Damned idea was rolling around. Clattering and bouncing. Waiting to go off with a blinding flash and bang.

Yep. That was the moment Rooney became a serious liability and he acted like he didn't even know it.

Miller couldn't wait around to be hit by shrapnel. The plan was already in motion. With Finny out of the way, Miller's crew would make another thirty mil every week. He was too close now to give up.

But he'd known from the start that if the plan went south, Miller and Rooney and all the rest would go down, too. Territory had to be claimed, defended, serviced, funded. Absorbing Finny's territory was a full-time operation and, as Finny found out, things could change in a moment.

Other distributors would notice Finny's death and try to acquire the territory.

There were probably men from Chicago or Vegas on the ground already. Trusted henchmen. Midlevel. Sizing up the growth potential and the competition.

They would have big networks. Dealers, pushers, sellers. More importantly, they would have the muscle to protect their business interests.

Miller didn't have any of that. Only a dozen people right now. Large enough to operate the territory but small enough to control information leaks. A compromise he settled on, planning to expand as the cash rolled in.

He'd never expected Finny's business to run long term, but— he glanced at the men working the laptops—he'd expected to get farther than this.

CHAPTER 31

JESS MADE IT HOME in time to meet the building contractor to arrange repairs to her apartment. The man whistled at every bullet hole he found, but he took copious measurements, made a long list of supplies he needed, and left.

Goodwin called. "Got some results on that bullet and cartridge you brought in. Thought you ought to know, since I'm charging your magazine for the work."

"Seems totally fair. What's the news?"

"The bullet and cartridge definitely came from the same gun. Marks line up on both. And they're from a .338."

"Didn't we already know that?"

"Yeah. But the marks were pretty good. Couple were kind of strange. Like the gun was out of alignment. Firing pin strike was slightly off and the bullet has a slight widening of one of the rifling marks."

"Meaning?"

"You don't ever see that unless the gun is worn out or just plain built wrong," Goodwin said. "Point is, there's several ATF databases with some slick software that can match that sort of thing up, and I found a match."

"Goodwin, you're killing me. Where? What?"

"Kalabar K10 Precision Rifle .338. Big gun. Four feet long. Sniper rifle. Only this one's kind of unique. Early development model. Had a problem with the twist. Fixed it for production, of course. Otherwise they wouldn't have been selected."

Jess felt as bewildered as if he were speaking an alien language. "Selected by whom? For what?"

"US Army. They ran a competition out of Fort Cavazos a couple of years ago. Several companies were involved in the testing, but they selected the Kalabar."

"You sure about this?" Jess asked.

"One thousand percent." Goodwin chuckled. "Computer found the match, but I've checked it with my own eyes. They're identical."

"I guess this isn't the first time government property has ended up in civilian hands."

"Sadly, no."

Jess thanked Goodwin and hung up. Finding a match between the bullet, cartridge, and gun was one thing. Finding the shooter was another whole problem.

She called Norton and left a message to pass on the news. A few minutes later, he called back.

"Fort Cavazos is in Killeen PD's area. They'll see what they can get through their MP liaisons. Didn't sound hopeful. Apparently, army tends to take the lead."

"That legal?"

"Fort Cavazos could swallow Killeen for breakfast. And if an investigation involves one of their own."

"This is a gun, not a person."

"Someone had to hold it."

"Yeah, but that someone didn't necessarily have to be a soldier. Did you try the stolen government property angle? They might be more forthcoming if they thought you weren't trying to call a soldier a thief," Jess suggested.

Norton wasn't impressed with her suggestion. "I did and we'll have to see what we can get."

"We? We're a team now?"

"Turn of phrase. But we're on the same side, aren't we?"

Jess thanked him and hung up. Then she called Mandy and explained about the gun.

"See if you can find a contact at Fort Cavazos."

"Fort Cavazos. Right. That's in…" Mandy said, floundering.

"Texas. Big place. The state and the base."

Mandy's keyboard clicked fast as lightning. "They have a publicity office. I can give you the number."

"No. We don't want statistics and a nice picture. Look for surplus equipment. Tell them we're doing a piece on how the government can recoup money through selling the excess."

Mandy said, "You think the gun was sold off as surplus?"

"Dunno. But I'm sure someone in the army knows everything about the way surplus stuff can end up in civilian hands. Legally and illegally," Jess said.

Ten minutes later, Mandy texted a number with the words "fairly helpful."

Jess called the number.

The guy on the other end picked up on the second ring. "Yo."

She introduced herself.

"Got ya. Deets on surplus sales, right?"

"Yes. Specifically guns." She saw no need for subterfuge here.

The guy on the other end of the phone went quiet.

"Hello?" she said.

He came back, stiff and formal. "You need to pass your inquiry through the appropriate liaison office for weapons, ma'am."

"I just—"

"Sorry, ma'am. I can give you their number."

"Can I have your name?"

He ignored her question. "Do you need the liaison's number?"

"What if I told you that an army gun has been linked to a multiple-fatality shooting."

"I have the liaison number for you. Got a pen?"

"A Kalabar K10 Precision Rifle."

No reply.

Jess waited, listening to the guy's breathing. Fifteen seconds passed before he came back. "Hold the line."

Three minutes later she was ready to hang up when a different man asked, "Miss Kimball?"

"Yes."

"A reporter?"

"Yes. *Taboo Magazine.*"

"You told one of my staff an army rifle may be linked to a shooting with multiple fatalities."

"It's early in our investigation, but that's what we have so far," Jess replied. "Who am I talking to?"

"Major Mifflin. You know you should be dealing with the liaison office?"

"It was a Kalabar K10 Precision Rifle."

"The new standard sniper rifle. Yes, I heard," he said. "The army's procuring a considerable number of them."

"This was an early development model. There was a problem with the twist," Jess said, as if she had a clue what a twist was or how it might have been a problem.

"Interesting. I remember there were improvements required to meet army requirements."

"Can you trace those early models?"

"One moment."

Jess heard a lot of typing before Mifflin came back on the line. "Kalabar originally submitted six rifles for testing. Improved versions were received. The prototypes were sent to be scrapped three months ago."

"We found bullets from one of those guns," Jess said. "No doubt about it."

"Not possible, though," Mifflin said. "They were shipped to the Holston Army Ammunition Plant for disposal. They recycle the metal and anything else they can. Environmentally friendly and all that. The rest goes in the crusher."

"You don't think ballistics matched up with the wrong gun, surely."

"Wouldn't be the first time a mistake was made." Mifflin hummed. "But I can't say what happened here. Haven't seen the evidence."

"Could you check to confirm the prototypes were destroyed?"

Mifflin said, "We got a certificate from Holston saying they did the work."

"Are you sure?" Jess pressed.

Mifflin chuckled. "Sure as I can be. I'm looking at the certificate right now."

Jess sighed and thanked him for his help. "Let me give you my number. Just in case you turn up anything helpful."

"I never refuse the offer of a woman's phone number," Mifflin joked. "But I won't know any more about this subject. Holston said they did the work. The guns were destroyed. End of story."

CHAPTER 32

JERRY LARSON SCHEDULED A meeting with his chief financial officer, Hiromi Tsui. She arrived two minutes early and sat opposite his desk. Of mixed Chinese and European descent, she had left college in Spain and visited Colorado for a winter's skiing. Twenty years later it seemed she would never leave.

Tsui tapped her pen on the small notebook she always carried, a habit that irritated Larson.

"I want to sell my vacation house," he said.

"Sell it?" she said.

"Yes. Is there a problem?"

"No, but it's an asset. An appreciating asset."

"More of a liability."

"But it's a beautiful place," she said.

"I haven't been there in months."

"Your wife has. Twice. With your kids."

Larson huffed. "Melissa? She complains about having to clean the place every time she goes there."

"Then get a cleaning service," Tsui suggested.

"Look, I've made up my mind," Larson replied flatly.

"What about Melissa?"

"You're forgetting whose name is on the deed."

Tsui stopped tapping her notebook. "Yours. I know. I arranged the financing."

"So it should be easy for you to unarrange."

"I'm just trying to offer the sound financial advice you pay me for," Tsui said.

"Sounds like you're trying to stop me."

She held on to her patience. "You want to sell beachfront property, Jerry? Big as the coastline of Florida is, there's only so much beachfront. People are flocking to the state. That house has already appreciated substantially and there's no indication of any kind of slowdown. You're printing money like crazy with that place."

"How much can I sell it for?"

Tsui cocked her head. "I'd have to get an expert in there. Someone local. He can give us a price range for homes in the area."

"How long will that take?"

"Tomorrow, I guess. If you're really determined to sell."

"I am. I need to know the equity after the loan's paid off. Check with one of those places that specializes in discounted cash in exchange for a deed."

"Jerry." Tsui shook her head. "Are you short of money? Because there are other ways—"

"I'm not short. Just sick of the weight around my neck."

She laid her pen down on her notebook. "You want to talk about it? We've been friends since this bank started."

"And you know how it's going."

"The banking business isn't a get-rich-quick scheme. We've just got to ride this slow period out and business will pick up," she said. "You'll see."

"No." Larson shook his head. "I'll be lucky to avoid bankruptcy."

She shrugged. "The Colombia bank wasn't the best deal, but we've trimmed the poor-performing branches. Couple of years and it'll dig its way out of the red. Once that's—"

"I know, I know. You don't have to snow me."

"Don't let work get to you, Jerry. This is just a job at the end of the—"

"You know what business is like these days. Some teller ticks off a customer and we get a bad tweet. Next day the whole company's toast."

"That's not going to happen."

Larson thumped his desk with his palm. "Look, get the place in Florida sold. Now."

Tsui leaned forward. "You have discussed this with Melissa, right?"

Larson glowered. "I'll tell her. When the time's right. She'll understand."

"Jerry—"

"Don't lecture me on my marriage. The Florida place is in my name. I'm the only person who you can discuss this with. You tell her anything at all about any of this and I'll damned well see you never work in finance again."

"Jerry!" Tsui stood. She closed her eyes for a moment.

Larson gave her a hard, blank glare. Tsui needed to understand her position. They weren't friends. Theirs was a professional relationship. A large financial transaction with all the legalities was on the table. He waited for her to recognize the truth.

After a moment, Tsui picked up her pad and pen. "All right. I'll see what I can do."

CHAPTER 33

JESS'S PHONE RANG. THE area code showed 254, Fort Cavazos. She picked up. "Jess Kimball."

"Major Mifflin."

The continuous roar of background machinery made it difficult to hear him. Was he in a factory? Jess covered her left ear with her palm to block out competing sounds from her end.

"I did some digging into the records," Mifflin said. "Those particular rifles are big and heavy. Seventeen pounds just for one rifle. Paperwork says forty-one pounds per unit inside the shipping container. We shipped all six for disposal, as I told you before. Thing is, one of the cartons weighed only thirty pounds."

"Can you be sure?"

"Definitely. We pay on size and weight. Army's very careful not to overpay."

"But you said Holston sent you a scrap certificate."

"They scrapped something all right. But here's the thing, standard-issue M4 carbine is six pounds. Put that in a twenty-four-pound Kalabar box and—"

"Thirty pounds."

"Can't be sure of course, but…" Mifflin allowed his voice to trail off into the land of possibility.

"So you're saying Holston scrapped a lighter M4 and someone skipped out with the K10?"

"It's a possibility."

"Who could do that?"

"Don't think it'd be anyone in transportation. We ship a ton of stuff. If they were looking to rip us off, they could take things worth millions."

"So who?"

Mifflin chuckled sardonically. "It's logical to assume the thief knew what he was stealing."

"Meaning the soldiers who tested the K10? Can you give me their names?"

Mifflin whistled. "Sorry. I've stuck my neck out too far already. You'll have to go through proper channels."

"Which will take forever."

"That's the army way," Mifflin confirmed.

Jess sighed. "So if you won't give me names, why tell me at all?"

"Quartermasters get our fair share of flak. But we manage millions of pieces of equipment. Track, trace, maintain, prep, ship, and so on. We do everything but use it all." Mifflin was wound up, passionate, and sincere. "The job's not glamorous, but when our guys need something, I want them to have it. Every time. No shortages, no bad gear. So any light-fingered guy thinks Uncle Sam owes them extra? I'm glad to put the smackdown on that."

Jess said, "But the K10s were sent to the crusher. Nobody was going to use them. It's like stealing scrap, isn't it?"

"Yeah, well." Mifflin paused a beat, as if he were having some sort of internal argument. "Have you asked why the tool marks and rifling signature of an army development rifle are found in the civilian law enforcement databases?"

Jess's eyes widened. "This gun has been involved in a crime before."

"Major Herman Horatio Oppenheimer," Mifflin said. "Look it up."

He disconnected the call and Jess was holding dead air.

Jess searched the name. A string of hits came up. Six months prior, Oppenheimer was shot outside the Mad Hatter Bar in Killeen, Texas. He'd been decorated during multiple tours in Iraq and Afghanistan. No suspects or motive for the shooting and the case remained open.

The *Fort Cavazos Post*, the newspaper for the base, added that Oppenheimer had been working on the army's new sniper rifle in a project called Long Shot.

Searching for Long Shot brought up thousands of irrelevant hits before she found a reference to the effort to improve the effectiveness of army snipers in combat zones.

There were no further details. But she found a picture from a year earlier showing six men selected to test the new weapon. Beneath the picture, the names were listed. Oppenheimer was second from the left.

She copied the article into an email and sent it to both Henry and Norton along with a summary of what she'd discovered.

A cold shiver ran down her spine as she listed the names. All were top snipers. Oppenheimer had been killed by a prototype K10. The same type of weapon that was stolen and used to kill several people at the Golden's warehouse.

No one would know more about the prototype than the five remaining men.

Which meant one of the other five men in the picture could be guilty of murder.

She took a deep, shaky breath. Had one of the remaining snipers tried to kill her?

CHAPTER 34

JESS'S PHONE RANG AGAIN. This time Henry's number appeared on the display. She picked up.

"I read your email," he said. "You've been busy. Goodwin gave us the link to the army, too. We sent a request for details through official channels. Which will take a while."

"Forever, I'm told." Jess smiled.

"Our request was hand carried by a liaison guy. Ex-Ranger. Should bump us up on the waiting list. We're hoping for information tomorrow," Henry replied. "But the picture of the test team you found is a real bonus. We've started comparing the photo to CCTV around the Golden's warehouse."

"Anything good?"

"In short, no. The warehouse cameras were taken offline the day before. So we've only got peripheral views from nearby businesses," Henry said wearily.

"Goodwin said only the military takes planning seriously. He might be right." Jess suggested the possibility she'd been mulling over since she'd learned about the scrapped K10s.

"Just got the details for the other five snipers in that picture," Henry mumbled as he skimmed the email. "Two still stationed at Fort Cavazos. One at Fort Benning. The last two took honorable discharges a few months ago. We have no details for them yet."

"Nothing?" Jess asked incredulously. "I didn't think it was possible to live off the grid in America anymore."

"Believe me, it's not easy to pull off. He's gotta be determined," Henry said. "No credit cards, no vehicle registrations, no housing that we can find. Neither one is collecting an army pension. So far, no records of health care at the VA, either."

"We need to run them all down if only to eliminate them," Jess said.

"I'll put them on our to-do list. Please stay away from these guys. If they were involved with the Golden's warehouse murders, they won't stop at hurting a reporter."

Jess was nodding, although Henry couldn't see her. "They won't stop for an FBI agent, either."

"Agreed," Henry said emphatically. "Which is why we'll be there in force when we find these guys."

"The two snipers who are still at Fort Cavazos. Did they fly to Denver recently?"

"No records of air travel for the three snipers in the photo who are still serving Uncle Sam."

"So probably not involved," Jess affirmed.

"Probably," Henry said. "When the army confirms their whereabouts, we'll take them off the list."

"I'll check them out. Informally. People are more likely to talk to a reporter than the FBI."

Henry sighed. "I'd be happier if we got a response from the army first."

"You said you'd get an answer from your guy tomorrow."

"I said we're hoping for something tomorrow."

"And he'll be talking to the two still on base?"

"Standard practice."

"So I'll meet them off base. Conversation flows better in a bar."

Henry was silent a moment. "I can't tell you what to do, Jess, but I'd be happier if we could bird-dog you."

"Me too. The last flight to Fort Cavazos leaves in ninety minutes. I won't have time to get my weapon through proper channels," Jess said. "So I can use the backup."

By the time Henry wished her a safe journey, she had grabbed her bag and headed for her Jeep.

CHAPTER 35

LUCY CRANFIELD RETURNED TO a dark studio apartment. Taking over network security at the bank after Rooney's death had been like drinking from a firehose. It wasn't that she couldn't answer the questions or do the work. The problem was that Rooney had kept so much to himself that she couldn't do the work fast enough.

The clock on her microwave read seven when she closed and locked her front door. Her cat roused from Lucy's bed and hovered around her feet as she changed clothes.

"Ready for dinner, Bella?" she said.

Bella curled her tail around Lucy's leg and purred.

Taking a small can from a pile in the cabinet by the kitchen sink, she emptied the food onto a clean plate and placed it on the floor. Bella stopped purring and buried her face in her dinner.

Lucy looked through a freezer full of frozen meals for her own dinner. She heard a hard knock on the door. She put her eye to the peephole but couldn't see through the grime.

Engaging the security chain, she opened the door about three inches. A man wearing a ski mask shoved a pair of bolt cutters through the gap.

Lucy slammed her full body weight against the door, but the bolt cutters prevented her from closing it.

One click later, the intruder cut through the chain.

He shoved the door inward, pounding the wood against her head. She stumbled aside.

Two men raced inside. One closed the door. The other grabbed her neck with one hand and shoved the barrel of a large handgun into her stomach.

"Make trouble and you'll never walk again," he said as he gave the gun a second shove.

"Assuming you don't bleed out before help arrives," the second man said casually.

Lucy's heart raced and she breathed in short panting gasps. The man with his hand around her neck towered over her. His gaze bored into hers. Every cell in her body urged her to scream, but she knew he'd pull the trigger without hesitation.

"Wh—" she tried to ask.

The tall man tightened his grip on her neck and shook her hard. "What don't you get? Talk and you die. Simple stuff."

Lucy closed her mouth. Sweat trickled down the side of her face. Her arms remained rigid at her sides.

The second man walked into her bedroom and returned with a coat. "Put it on," he said, tossing it toward her.

She could barely move her arms to take the coat. She grunted and blubbered. The man shoved the coat harder against her. She bent her arm behind her and fumbled for the arm holes as the first man kept up his grip on her neck. Her heart slammed so hard she felt as if it would burst from her chest. The coat flapped as she panted, but eventually she shrugged it on.

172 | DIANE CAPRI

"Good," said the first man. "Now, my friend is going to put a gun to your back. One wrong move and he will blow a hole in your spine. Understand?"

She panted. Small gasping breaths as if she didn't dare exhale fully. "Yes," she whispered.

"Gun that size makes a real mess," he said.

She nodded. "I...I understand."

"Good. Now comes the easy part. We're going to walk out of here and you're going to help us."

"Help?" She tried unsuccessfully to swallow. "With what?"

The man laughed. "An internet problem."

"I...I can't help with that."

"You're the security geek at the bank. We know what you can do."

She gasped, "I...I—"

"Save it. Let's go."

The second gunman walked behind her. He gripped her upper arm hard and wedged the gun painfully into her back.

The first gunman kept close to her side to hide the gun. He opened the rear door of an old Toyota. She and the second gunman climbed in.

They drove out of the apartment complex and onto the highway. The gunman sitting next to her wedged a black cloth bag over her head. Her heart rate climbed higher. The air under the hood grew hot and suffocating.

"Chill," the driver said. "We're all wearing hoods for good reason. If you don't see us, no reason for anything bad to happen to you. Understand?"

Lucy nodded and they drove on in silence. The words made sense, but the gun didn't move from her side.

Streetlights glowed through the dark fabric hood, pulsing as if she might use them to count the distance. After fifteen minutes the lights stopped. Which meant the vehicle had traveled out of the city.

The driver took frequent turns, rolling left and right, but the gunman kept his pistol wedged firmly in her side.

The road sloped upward, and the frequent turns continued. Eventually the vehicle slowed, and gravel crunched under the wheels. They were off-road. The car bounced and slithered.

The crunching continued for ten minutes before they came to a stop.

The driver turned off the engine.

The gunman dragged her out of the Toyota. She tried to shuffle and guide herself with her arms, but his iron grip never relented.

The air was fresh and the wind brutally cold. She could smell the scent of pine trees and in the gaps around the bottom of the hood she glimpsed the remnants of snow on gravel.

They were in the mountains.

"Steps." The gunman shoved her forward.

She staggered up two wooden steps and into warmer air. A door closed behind her with a wooden thump.

The gunman pushed her. "Sit."

She felt behind her with her hands, found a chair, and lowered herself into it.

The gunman pulled off her hood.

She was in a single-room wood cabin. Windows on both sides of the room had been covered with butcher paper. A bed was placed in one corner.

In front of her, a laptop and wireless modem rested on a small table.

There was another man in the room on the opposite side of the table. He wore a ski mask that exposed his eyes and one of them was only half-open.

"Call me Vlad," he said.

She made a small sound. Breathed out. A huff of air, her lungs too paralyzed for more.

The first gunman stepped to one side, covering the pair of them with his pistol.

Vlad pointed to his ski mask and to the men wearing ski masks. "We're hidden. You can't tell who we are. It's protection. For you. You know why?"

Lucy knew why. One of the gunmen had already told her. But she shook her head. The dumber she looked, the more her captors might relax.

"Because if you can't identify us, we can let you go after you help us out," Vlad said reasonably.

She nodded.

"You want us to let you go, right? Back to your apartment and your cat?"

She nodded again.

"Good. Just do what we say," Vlad said easily. "You knew Justin Rooney."

She frowned, then took a deep breath. "A little. At work."

"More than a little. You were both at the bank for several years. And you took over his job after his unfortunate accident."

Her mind raced. There was no point in denying anything. They'd been checking up on her.

"We were very sorry to hear about Rooney," Vlad said. "He was a good guy."

She didn't respond. She realized now that this was all about Rooney.

"He found a way to transfer money through the bank's computers without recording the transactions."

"What bank?"

"First Aurora."

"I don't think that's possible," she whispered, shaking her head.

"Totally possible. Rooney did it. Several times." Vlad gestured to the men in the room. "For us."

Lucy remained silent.

"There's a web page with a password." Vlad pushed a sheet of paper with an internet address in front of her. "We need to know why it's stopped working."

Her heart rate picked up again. "I can't...I mean there could be—"

He leaned across the table. "I have faith in your abilities."

She looked at the paper. The web address was written in numbers, the bare format that underlay the words people usually used to identify websites. The password was a long string of special characters.

She pointed to the website. "You just put this into a browser. It should come up."

"It does. Afterward there's a second password required. A random number."

"Random?" She frowned. There was no way to make a random number a password. Both the user and the website had to agree to the password in advance. She kept quiet. The less she said, the better.

"Lots of letters and numbers." Vlad took another sheet of paper from an inside pocket in his jacket, unfolded it, and smoothed it out on the table. "This was the last one. It no longer works."

She recognized the format of the password.

It was the type used for heavy-duty encryption. A one-time password.

Clocks used a complex algorithm to roll over to a new, equally arcane password every thirty seconds.

It was a type of protection used at First Aurora to communicate with other banks.

"I can't just come up with another password like that."

"We know it won't be easy. That's why we're here." He gestured to the cabin. "So you have time to concentrate."

"It's not just me or time to concentrate. It's not humanly possible."

"No?" Vlad leaned closer. "But what about your mom?"

Vlad held his phone with a picture of Lucy's mother's house, the kind of slightly grainy picture produced by companies that make internet mapping software.

"Nice house," he said. "Well kept. Even has one of those little camera things on the front door. A caring, considerate daughter might have installed it. The sort of daughter who knows plenty about IT and security. You, probably."

Vlad put his phone back in his pocket. "Thing is, all that security doesn't help when she goes out. Shopping. Church. Meeting friends. All those times she's very exposed. Very... unsecure." He gestured to the two men in the room. "Especially if my friends happened to take an interest in her."

Vlad walked around the table and leaned down close to Lucy's ear. "So get to work. Then we won't take our uncomfortable masks off. Or drop in on your mom. Does that sound like a good deal to you?"

Lucy lowered her head to concentrate on the problem.

CHAPTER 36

LUCY SHIVERED. THE SINGLE bare bulb in the hut gave everything a cold, blue-white industrial look. The small electric heater in the middle of the room created so little heat that she kept her hands on the laptop simply to keep them warm.

Vlad sat on the bed, facing her, gun resting in his lap. Occasionally, he paced the small room, staring over her shoulder.

She ignored him as best she could. Her assailants still wore their ski masks. A good sign, she reasoned. They *could* let her go when she found what they wanted. Though whether they would release her was an entirely different question.

The work hadn't proven too difficult. The web page held scripts that interrogated network links and sent a report to a server. By mimicking the report, she tricked the server into showing her the second page.

The second page was encrypted. But if it was connected with Rooney and the bank, she guessed it might require passwords that were used at the bank.

After several tries, she found the right password and a mass of complex code appeared on the screen.

Hours of work later, she determined that the code injected itself into the bank's servers and sent a transaction to an obscure network address.

She looked up the address and found the physical location was in Denver, just two streets away from her apartment. The record didn't show the actual snail mail address, but she didn't need it.

Lucy knew who lived on that street. Justin Rooney. The last piece of the puzzle could only be found on a server located in his apartment. Which was what she told Vlad.

Vlad sent his men to break into Justin's apartment to retrieve the server. She wasn't allowed to leave the cabin, so they planned to video call so she could point out what she needed.

Ninety minutes later, Vlad shoved his phone in front of her. The screen showed Justin's cluttered apartment by flashlight.

Laptops and desktops lay all over the place. Wires snaked around and over everything. In one corner a stack of old disk drives looked as if it were about to topple over.

Lucy began to sweat. With so much equipment, how could she tell which was important? Should she tell them she needed it all? Would they believe her? Or would they think she wasn't capable? Or worse, lying?

She swallowed hard. She knew she was relatively safe as long as they considered her valuable. If they thought she was stupid, or useless, they'd have no incentive to keep her alive.

Lucy told the guy to show her around the apartment again. She saw several modems that were plugged in, yet they showed no lights or flashing LEDs.

"Is the power out?" she asked.

"No, but it's too risky to turn the lights on," Vlad said.

She pressed her lips together. Those individual modems with no lights or flashing LEDs must be turned off.

There were any number of reasons why Rooney might not want to run multiple modems constantly, particularly given all the equipment he had in the apartment. His electric bill must have been substantial, for one thing.

Lucy suspected the transaction Vlad had tried to process didn't go through for a simple reason. Because somewhere in the apartment, Rooney had simply turned the power off on the last necessary link.

To be sure, she rechecked the phone's screen.

Any of the laptops could be vital, but which ones?

"Stop there and move closer to that large metal device," she said, pointing as if he could fathom what she wanted him to see. "There. The wide one with the screw holes at either side."

It was designed to fit into an industrystandard nineteen-inch rack. The front bore the swooping letters *RXP*. Which was not only the world leader in banking encryption systems but also the very equipment used at First Aurora.

Lucy frowned. Such devices weren't commercially available. Rooney must have taken this one from work. Given the amount of dust she could see on top of the unit even in bad lighting on a phone screen, she guessed he'd taken it several weeks ago.

"Please get closer and show me the back of the box," Lucy asked.

The bank didn't use wireless systems in the back office. As expected, Rooney's RXP box had ethernet cables coming out of it.

The cables meant Rooney had been using the device.

And there was only one possible reason.

To communicate with other banks.

Lucy nodded. "Okay. I know what this is. Bring the RXP box and everything connected to it."

The two men set about tracing the wires and collecting modems and laptops.

"A lot of stuff," one of them said.

"Find a suitcase," Vlad replied.

The man moved around the apartment until he found a closet. Lucy glimpsed hair and a face before the picture became a blur.

She heard cries and punches and grunts. The camera tumbled to the floor until it stopped to reveal a view of the ceiling.

"Stop," Vlad said. He glanced at Lucy. "Stop. Who is that?"

The man picked up the phone and focused on a figure facedown on the floor beside two crumpled duffel bags. He rolled the figure over. Lucy gasped.

Vlad glowered through the eyeholes in his mask. "What?"

"I…"

Vlad shook her by the arm. "Who? Who is it?"

Lucy knew her reaction had betrayed her. She couldn't feign ignorance. "Larson. Mr. Jerry Larson."

"Who the hell's Larson?"

She stared at the picture on the phone; her mouth hung open. "The CEO. Our CEO. First Aurora."

"What?"

Vlad put his hand to his forehead. "I don't believe this."

"What'd you want me to do with him?" said the cameraman.

Vlad exhaled. Seconds passed.

"Boss?"

"Take him to Toppers," Vlad said. "The back room. Lock him up until this is over." He looked Lucy in the eye. "We're not murderers."

Lucy didn't believe him for a minute, but she closed her mouth. She had no idea what Larson was doing at Rooney's place. But she felt certain that Vlad didn't intend to let either of them get away with their lives.

Three hours later, one of the men arrived carrying the equipment and a heap of wires. The other one must have taken Larson to Toppers, whatever that was.

Lucy reassembled the connections and switched on the RXP device. The computer would expect it to be powered and ready when the laptop booted.

Gooseflesh prickled on her arms and legs as she reached for the switch at the rear of the unit.

She had all the necessary equipment now, but could she get it to work?

CHAPTER 37

JESS WOKE AT 6:00 a.m. in her hotel. She had showered, dressed, and finished breakfast in the small restaurant before seven. Killeen, Texas, was in the middle of one of its brief cold spells, so her Colorado ski jacket was suitable attire outdoors. She'd peeled it off before she came inside.

Henry had sent the addresses of Bret Martini and Tyrus Butler, the two members of the K10 test team still working at Fort Cavazos. They lived a few streets apart in an area of Killeen that housed primarily base personnel.

The FBI liaison called at five minutes past seven. She told him where to find her.

Shortly after the call, he entered the restaurant, poured himself a coffee, and walked over. He had an unhurried gait, turning his head casually to scan the room before sitting across from her at the small table.

His fair complexion came along with thick ginger curls. Jess doubted they'd look any neater even when combed. He sat upright, shoulders filling every inch of his dark tailored suit.

"Jess Kimball?" he asked, offering a firm handshake, not a death-match grip. "Hugh Loughrey."

A man with nothing to prove. Jess preferred to work with competent people who knew they were competent. So much easier.

He pushed a business card across the table.

"It's pronounced lock-rey," he said, pointing to the printed name. "Irish, via Liverpool, thanks to my grandfather."

Jess picked up the card. "You have a slight Irish accent."

"If only I had the Irish luck, too." Loughrey grinned briefly before turning serious. "You have friends in high places."

She shrugged. She had nothing to prove to him, either.

When she added nothing more, he said, "I'm told we're looking for a missing gun connected to Fort Cavazos."

"That's what we know so far," Jess explained. "The gun was used in a multiple-fatality shooting at a warehouse."

"I read that in the report. But why are you involved?"

"The same someone tried to use that gun to kill me."

"My report failed to mention that bit." Loughrey pursed his lips and frowned. "You think two of the snipers, Butler and Martini, were involved?"

Jess shook her head. "I'm hoping they'll prove they're not."

"Any chance a meeting with them could go sideways?" Loughrey asked.

"Not likely. They were part of a team testing the K10 sniper rifle. Two members of that team have gone rogue. I expect Butler and Martini to be as outraged by that as we are."

Loughrey said, "You think the two rogues are Kahler and Jones."

She nodded. "When will we hear about our meeting with Butler and Martini?"

"About eight-oh-two. I have a friend in the MPs who's just started his shift."

Jess glanced at her watch when Loughrey's phone rang. A couple of minutes past eight.

Loughrey had a brief conversation and hung up. "We're scheduled to meet. Eleven thirty. Pizza place on base."

"On base? I was hoping to see them in a more casual environment."

"No dice." He shook his head. "Unless you want to knock on their front doors at home. Which I wouldn't recommend. Press tries to talk to them without approval and the chain of command will put the hammer down in a heartbeat. Cooperation between the army and the FBI is a two-way street."

Jess shrugged. No reason to argue the logistics now. The decision had been made. "You have a formal interview scheduled with them?"

Loughrey shook his head. "No reason to at this point. Pizza place will give us a free-speech zone and some flexibility. No recordings."

"But—" Jess said.

Loughrey interjected. "Besides, these two are not suspects. They've been on base the past four days, every day. Confirmed."

Jess replied, "So we can cross these two off the list of possible snipers."

"Roger that. Three to go."

"Right." She paused a moment. "What are the chances we might meet Major Mifflin?"

Loughrey cocked his head. "I don't know who Mifflin is. What's the connection?"

"Quartermaster. He's the one who uncovered the fact that one of the development rifles had gone missing."

Loughrey paused a long moment. "Let me check."

He sent a message and sipped his coffee. A minute later he received a call. He stood as he listened and walked toward the exit, motioning Jess to follow.

He led the way to his car, hanging up as he walked. "Mifflin can give us ten minutes at nine. We need to hustle."

Loughrey drove fast, weaving through traffic on the freeway and braking only as he exited for the visitor center. He guided Jess through the paperwork to obtain a visitor's pass and minutes later they were at the six-lane entrance to the base.

On base, Loughrey drove the speed limit. He grinned as he pointed out Tank Destroyer Boulevard, Old Ironsides, and Hell on Wheels Avenue.

They parked on K Avenue, beside an almost windowless five-story building.

Inside, a woman with a friendly smile named Kathy met them. She led them up three flights of stairs and through a warren of corridors and cube farms until they reached a small room with a wall of filing cabinets behind a desk.

"My office," Kathy said.

Two doors led off the sidewalls, one labeled MAJ. MIFFLIN. Kathy checked her watch before knocking.

"Come in."

Kathy opened the door, allowed them to enter, and closed the door behind them.

Jess and Loughrey took seats in front of Mifflin's desk.

He was typing furiously. He spoke without looking up. "I remember your call, ma'am. I don't see how I can help you further."

"We know the names of the K10 test team members," Jess said.

Mifflin looked up, frowning. His typing slowed but didn't stop. "I don't follow."

"We suspect one of them stole a K10 and used it in a recent shooting."

Mifflin stopped typing. "I told you. Those early K10s were scrapped."

"No," Jess replied. "You told me one of the boxes was light. Like the K10 had been replaced by something else. An M4 perhaps."

Mifflin's forehead wrinkled and his mouth slacked. "What are you talking about?"

Damn. Was Mifflin recanting what he'd told her? Should she have left Loughrey outside? "Major Mifflin, you called me back. Told me—"

"Ma'am, I did not call you back," Mifflin insisted more firmly.

"You discovered that one of the boxes you shipped was eleven pounds lighter than it should have been."

Mifflin scowled. "I have no idea what you mean."

"I assure you…Wait." Jess frowned as the truth dawned. "Are you saying you didn't call me back?"

"That's exactly what I'm saying."

"Then…"

"We can clear this up pretty quickly," Loughrey said, turning to Jess. "Do you have the callback number?"

She found the number on her phone and showed it to Loughrey and then Mifflin.

Mifflin looked it up in the base directory. "Eleven pounds light you say?"

Jess nodded.

He kept looking until he found it. "This number is a general-purpose phone in one of our warehouses."

"Does the name Oppenheimer mean anything to you?" said Jess.

He looked up. "Oh yes."

He walked out of the office, closing the door behind him. A minute later he returned to his desk and put his hands together.

"I can't confirm who you talked to, and it's against regulations to release information outside proper channels." He paused. "However, the information you were given could well be correct."

"*Could* be?" Loughrey asked.

"That's as far as I am prepared to go." Mifflin stood and extended his hand. "If you need anything further, you'll have to go through official channels. It's been a pleasure meeting you, ma'am."

Jess hesitated before standing. Mifflin would say nothing more. He'd made that plain.

They shook hands and he showed them to the door. Kathy was waiting to walk them back through the labyrinth to the entrance.

A soldier sat on a chair against the wall. He looked directly ahead, not making eye contact.

As they exited Kathy's office and turned to walk down the corridor, Jess winced with pain. She leaned against the corridor wall and removed her shoe. She checked inside it, shaking it as if looking for a stone.

Mifflin's voice was muted by distance, but his words and tone were quite clear. "Oppenheimer."

The soldier hurried off to the major's office.

"Herman Oppenheimer?" Jess asked, the fake stone now forgotten.

"Karl, his brother." Kathy leaned close and lowered her voice. "Herman died in a shooting. Six months ago."

"Here on the base? What happened?" Jess put her shoe on.

"Shooting accident during training. That's the official word, anyway," Kathy replied.

"Karl isn't satisfied with that answer?"

Kathy shook her head. "Not even a little bit."

CHAPTER 38

LOUGHREY SPENT THE HOURS before their meeting at the pizza place showing Jess the base museum and a bewildering array of tanks, helicopters, and other vehicles.

"So it was Oppenheimer's brother that found out about your call and fed you the information," he said.

Jess nodded. "And he'll get some sort of discipline because I walked in and told Mifflin."

"Don't sweat it. Neither Mifflin nor Oppenheimer expected something like that to stay undiscovered forever. The army looks after its own. Mifflin will want to know what happened to his soldiers just as much as we do."

"How do you know?" Jess asked.

"Experience."

They were seated in the pizza place with two large pizzas on the table. The restaurant had rows of tables, mostly empty, and walls of historic army pictures, mostly filled.

Two men walked in, both broad-shouldered, rigid posture, and the same unhurried gait as Loughrey. They headed straight for the table and introduced themselves.

Tyrus Butler sat on the left and Bret Martini, on the right.

"Ranger, right?" said Tyrus.

Loughrey nodded. "Iraq, Uganda, Somalia. Usual places. FBI for three years now."

"Sweet."

Jess pushed the pizzas closer to the men.

"Before we eat," Martini said, "we've been cleared to talk, but only off the record."

Jess replied, "At this point, we're just looking for insight into the team that evaluated the early K10."

"Unless you want to get a whole army butt-covering team in here now, you print anything we say, and we'll deny ever meeting you."

Loughrey said, "We understand."

"Good," said Martini, sliding three pieces of pizza onto his paper plate, "'cause I hate to see good pizza going cold."

Butler loaded his plate, too.

"Who was on the K10 team?" said Jess.

"Whole cast and crew," said Martini. "Mechanical engineers, systems engineers, weapons specialists, illities, bean counters, you name it. Start an army program and they appear out of the woodwork like termites."

"Illities?" Jess asked.

"Maintainability, reliability, affordability, yada yada. There's a neverending list of illities."

Butler finished a mouthful of pizza. "But I'm guessing you want to know who was actually using the K10s?"

Jess nodded.

"Us, plus Sandy Jackson, Randy Bailey, Theo Kahler, and HH Oppenheimer."

"You all know each other beforehand?"

"Army snipers? Sure. It's a small world."

"And what did the six of you do for the K10 team?"

"Evaluate how well the average sniper could handle the rifle and what accuracy they'd be able to achieve."

Jess was awash in terms she didn't want to misunderstand. "Average sniper?"

"No one on this particular K10 team was anything close to average, but that's what you have to assume. So we did plenty of time on a range and training missions," Butler explained between bites. "Can the average guy handle the weapon in the dark, under pressure, stay concealed. Strip down. Reassemble. Clear jams. That sort of stuff."

"And then we'd do the reviews," Martini said.

"Endless arguments about whether the handling was good enough or the accuracy was good enough." Butler rolled his eyes. "What would make it better. What if they took ten grams off the weight. Made this or that a fraction bigger. Or smaller. It takes a lot of patience."

"Everyone on the team was a damned good sniper. But that doesn't naturally make them the best communicator," Martini explained.

"Were there arguments among members of the team?" said Jess.

"Are you kidding?" Butler laughed. "Always."

"What about HH Oppenheimer?"

"Yeah, he got into some disagreements." Martini took another mouthful of pizza and chewed.

"Like what?" said Jess.

Butler and Martini looked at each other a moment before Butler spoke. "The manufacturer sent flawed rifles. HH wanted to wait until they corrected the problems before we did any testing."

"And?" Loughrey wanted to know.

Butler shrugged. "I didn't mind either way. The guns worked. Maybe short a hundred yards on what they were supposed to do. But others on the team weren't so easygoing."

"Who?" Loughrey demanded.

"You have to understand. It takes balls to put on the uniform and face an enemy. Doesn't matter if you're in the jungle, clearing a building, or a sniper laid up for days in a hideout," Martini said for Jess's benefit. "The difference is, snipers are competitive. Very. Longest shot matters. And some guys won't ever say they can't do it. No matter what."

Jess asked, "And someone on the team was like that?"

Butler held up three fingers. "Sandy Jackson, Theo Kahler, and, to a lesser extent, Randy Bailey."

"They argued with Oppenheimer?" Loughrey asked.

"Big-time. HH had the most experience on the team and the longest kill. Kind of gave him the lead. Professional standing, that sort of thing," Martini said, swallowing more pizza as he talked, as if he had only a brief time to eat. "Jackson and Bailey thought HH was wasting time. Kahler just thought he was better than everyone else and had no patience for guys who couldn't keep up."

Butler said, "Things got pretty heated."

"Enough for one of the snipers to kill Oppenheimer?" Jess asked.

"We've all asked that question." Butler took a deep breath and offered a solid stare around the table.

"We're trained killers, but one of our own?" Martini sucked air between his teeth. "That's a long stretch. Hard to believe."

"Yet Oppenheimer was killed with a K10, wasn't he?" Jess pressed.

Butler nodded. "And believe me, we got grilled about it. Local cops, MPs, top brass. We all had alibis. None of us took HH out."

"And the army just let that go?" Loughrey said incredulously.

Martini shook his head. "Let's just say the incident put a dent in our promotion prospects. We'll be working it off for a while."

"Even if you were not at fault?" Jess asked.

"The army way." Martini shrugged. Butler and Loughrey nodded. "It's not policy, but…"

Jess moved on to a different question. "How would one of those K10s get off base?"

Butler winced. "We all used all the rifles. We all had access. Put one in your car and drive out, I guess."

"How about people not in your sniper group? Could anyone else access the K10s?"

Martini shook his head and reached for the last slice of pizza. "They'd have to have the code to access the room where the K10s were stored. When HH's death was investigated, all of us denied sharing the code."

"And it was a week before the connection to the K10s was made, anyway. Kind of wiped out the chance of finding evidence," Butler said.

"So no one else came into contact with the K10s?" Loughrey asked.

Butler shook his head. "Can't see it. We lived with the K10s, day in, day out. Even storing them was part of the evaluation. No one else touched those guns but us."

Martini wiped the grease off his hands. "Even so, you reckon one of the guns was used in that warehouse shooting in Denver?"

"Seems so." Loughlin confirmed with a nod.

"We swapped the guns between us. Everyone used everything. Sample the manufacturing tolerances. Make sure we experienced the good and the bad, as it were," Butler said.

"Was there any special knowledge required to use these particular guns?" Jess asked.

Martini shrugged. "Not for a sniper. Set up and load up and figure out when to pull the trigger. Pretty much the same process as others."

"In Denver, the shooter was maybe six to eight hundred yards away."

"Cinch for any of us," Martini said. "Or a well-practiced civilian."

"Moving target?" Butler asked.

Jess nodded. "In the middle of a gunfight."

"Six to eight hundred yards? Is that possible in a built-up city area?"

"The shooter was thirty floors up," Jess said.

"Ah." Butler and Martini stared at each other.

"What?" said Jess.

Butler glanced at Martini and then took a deep breath. "Afghanistan. Tribal leader causing all sorts of problems. He and five others. In a compound. Six shots and six kills. Shooter was located at a cell phone tower on the side of a mountain eight hundred yards away. They were moving targets. Shots placed in rapid succession. Not a great distance. Didn't get a lot of recognition at the time. But still quite an accomplishment."

"We certainly heard about it often enough," Martini said.

"That sniper was a member of the K10 team?" Jess asked.

Butler nodded. "Theo Kahler."

CHAPTER 33

JESS LANDED IN DENVER midafternoon. As the pilot taxied
to the gate, she listened to her messages. Among them, Armando
asked her to call him back.

Jess sorted through the people she'd met on the Rooney case.
She finally remembered that Armando was the taller of two men
she'd met at the gathering after Rooney died. Armando and Darrin
worked in the IT department with Rooney at First Aurora Bank.

Jess redialed his number.

He answered after a couple of rings with a lighthearted, "Yo!"

"It's Jessica Kimball, Armando," she said.

His voice changed. "Right. Thanks for calling. I was…I
mean…well, given the circumstances, it seems odd."

Jess blinked. "I'm sorry. I'm lost. What are you talking
about?"

"Lucy."

"Who's Lucy?"

"Justin's replacement at the bank. Lucy Cranfield," Armando
said, as if Jess might not be the sharpest knife in the drawer.

After a minute, Jess remembered. "Lucy? The girl I met at the Mellon Tree after Rooney died?"

"Yeah. She didn't come into work today." Armando's concern was plain.

"People get sick, take time off, have a holiday," Jess said reasonably.

"Not Lucy." Armando disagreed. "Don't think she's missed a day for any reason for years."

"Did you try to call her?"

"No reply. And I knocked on her door at lunchtime. Nothing."

"What door? At home, you mean?"

"*Yeah*," Armando stressed, as if Jess should know exactly what he meant. "I couldn't get inside. I mean, she's got heavy shades on her windows, and I don't have a key. Sorry."

Jess was running out of suggestions. "Okay. Have you checked social media?"

"Zip since four o'clock yesterday afternoon. She's not addicted to socials or anything, but it's not normal for her to miss that much time," Armando said.

"Have you checked with folks around the bank?"

"Of course," Armando replied. "No one's seen or heard from her since she left last night. After the thing with Rooney, I'm just a bit worried."

"Sure. That makes sense," Jess said. "Have you talked to the police?"

"Don't they say to wait for a missing person forty-eight hours or something?"

There were probably a million reasons why Lucy might skip a day's work, but like he said, under the circumstances Armando's worries seemed appropriate.

"Send me Lucy's address. I'll check around. And this isn't a normal situation. So call the police. They have better ideas and a lot more resources."

As soon as they hung up, Armando sent the address. Jess looked it up on her phone while she was waiting to deplane at the gate.

Lucy lived two streets away from Justin Rooney's apartment. Hers was a ground-floor unit on an average apartment block. Not new but not old. Pictures showed a pool and a fitness room.

The same company owned Rooney's building. Which meant Jess would encounter the same "no cooperation if you're not family and don't have a warrant" policies if she tried to inquire about one of their residents.

She was off the plane and behind the wheel of her Jeep soon after landing. A thirty-minute drive brought her to Lucy's apartment.

From her position on the street, Jess saw the building was three stories. According to the layout map she'd found on her phone, four apartments on each floor were arranged around a central open-air stairwell.

Jess shrugged on her bulletproof vest under her new ski jacket before she stepped out of the Jeep. She walked purposefully toward Lucy's front door in case the neighbors were watching.

Knocking and listening at Lucy's door produced no response. Maybe one of the neighbors was home. Jess approached the other apartments on the ground floor, but no one answered the doorbells. Not surprising, probably. It was the middle of the workday.

Jess stepped back and texted Armando a request for Lucy's license plate number and what kind of vehicle she owned. Jess expected him to look it up, but he responded immediately.

She walked around the building to the resident parking. There were only a few vehicles in the lot. Lucy's bright orange Beetle was easy to spot.

Finding Lucy's car was unnerving. There were few businesses nearby. Unless Lucy caught a ride or something, finding her Beetle here was more concerning.

The apartment had four windows. The drapes were tightly closed on three. The last window in the back had a two-inch gap between the panels, which was wide enough to see inside.

Cupping her hands on either side of her eyes, Jess pressed her face close to the glass to see inside.

The open-plan apartment looked normal enough. A small kitchen. Dishes in the drying rack. A table with a flowerpot. A cat sleeping on the sofa. Books on a coffee table in the living room area. One throw pillow on the floor close to the sofa. It could have been placed there intentionally, not dropped after a struggle.

Jess sighed and stepped back from the window.

Unexplained disappearances of anyone within the sphere of an investigation were never good. And with Lucy's role at the bank, there were plenty of reasons to be concerned. But to achieve any more, she would probably have to enlist law enforcement.

She raised her phone to the window and fired off a photo burst, panning the space. She thumbed through the pictures.

Dim light in the room produced grainy images. She zoomed in and out, hoping to spot something useful as she selected the ones she would forward to Detective Norton.

The last image required a closer look. She returned her phone to the glass and snapped two more photos, holding the camera as still as possible and zooming closer this time.

The new images were clear enough to confirm that the security chain on the front door had been severed.

She sent the pictures to Norton. He texted back. "Wait for me."

Jess returned to her Jeep to wait. Norton arrived twenty minutes later with an unhappy woman holding a bundle of keys and protesting about policies and procedures.

Norton ignored her complaints and took the keys from her to unlock the door. He eased the door open and peered around inside.

"You're right. The chain was cut," he said. "Good strong chain, too. Must have used bolt cutters to do it. Not the sort of thing most people have in their pockets."

Norton locked the door and handed the keys back to the woman. "No one goes in or out of here as of now. We'll have a warrant and a crime scene team here within the hour. Meanwhile, I'll need a list of residents and access to your CCTV."

The lady left, muttering about calling the boss, but she didn't refuse.

When she was out of hearing distance, Norton reported Lucy Cranfield as missing, possibly abducted. He answered a couple of questions, requested the warrant, and disconnected the call to wait.

Which was when he turned to Jess. "Guess I shouldn't be surprised to find you here. We got a call reporting Lucy Cranfield missing thirty minutes ago."

"Yeah, I told Armando to call you. Glad he did," Jess replied. "Lucy and Justin Rooney worked at First Aurora Bank. In the same IT department. She could be in danger."

"Absolutely."

CHAPTER 40

JESS DROVE HER JEEP, following Norton's vehicle two streets over to Justin Rooney's apartment.

Jess answered Henry's call along the way. "Hey."

"Loughrey filled me in on what happened at Fort Cavazos," he said.

"Yeah. The guy who told me about the guns wasn't Major Mifflin after all. Turned out to be HH Oppenheimer's younger brother."

"I heard," Henry replied. "Kurt Oppenheimer. Local police have a thick file on him. He's been strident about trying to solve his brother's murder. Not everyone appreciates his efforts."

"Can't blame him for that," Jess replied.

"No, we can't. Looking at the other five snipers on the K10 team, Randy Bailey was definitely on base at Fort Benning. Which means he's got a solid alibi. With HH dead and Martini and Butler accounted for, that leaves us two options. Sandy Jackson and Theo Kahler."

Jess nodded, thinking back to the pizza place interview. "Kahler did an op during the war very similar to the hit at the Golden's warehouse."

"I heard. We're running that down now," Henry replied.

"Have you identified the victims at the warehouse shooting?"

"Yeah. Several had criminal records. Some extensive. We're working it. Interviews going on now. Background, acquaintances, so on," Henry told her. "Looks like a drug gang. Plenty of evidence to conclude they were midlevel dealers. Not pushing hits on street corners."

Jess tapped her index finger on the phone. "So we think this was a turf war?"

"Yeah. And they might have been expecting to get hit. They were heavily armed, and they definitely returned fire. But most of the kills were made by the man on the tower's thirty-third floor."

"Could there have been two men up there instead of one?" Jess asked.

"No. The .338 bullets all came from the same gun. Goodwin is certain about that."

Jess nodded and wrapped up with conclusions. "So we're thinking one man, excellent skills, very quick. A man like Theo Kahler."

"That's the working theory. We still need a lot more evidence before we can convict him, though," Henry reminded her.

Jess remained silent.

After a moment, Henry said, "One of the victims was unusual. Found him on the edge of the parking lot. Lenny Maw."

"Bystander?"

"Probably not, but we can't rule it out yet. Maw was armed. He stood a good distance from the others, suggesting he might not have been involved. But his gun was fired, which muddies the waters," Henry replied. "All we can find on him is a couple of parking tickets, but there's no known association with the other victims."

"You think he was part of the attack team, then?" Jess asked.

"Can't rule that out yet, either. He could have been hanging back. Not enough intel yet to say for sure."

"Friendly fire, then? Shot by his own team?"

"Unlikely. Maw was hit by the shooter on the thirty-third floor."

"Deliberate." Jess whistled. She felt her skin tingle. "One of the snipers, Butler, said Kahler thought he was better than everyone else. Had no patience for anyone who couldn't keep up. Maybe Maw was not doing the job to Kahler's satisfaction and Kahler took him out."

Henry sighed. "That's a reasonable theory, too. I've gotta go. Keep me in the loop, okay?"

"You bet," Jess said as she ended the call and approached Rooney's apartment.

The door opened as she climbed the steps. Two men walked out, oversize briefcases in either hand. Norton gave them Lucy Cranfield's address and they set off.

Norton pointed to two lines of tape on the carpet. "We're allowed to be between these two lines. Only. No touching."

Jess nodded and stepped into the designated space.

Two men in white overalls were hunched over the mass of equipment piled in the dining area. Yellow fingerprint dust covered the mainly black boxes.

They'd brought a generator along to power the equipment now that the power had been turned off. LED lights flashed everywhere, and a nest of wires connected the devices.

"IT," said Norton. "Nothing much yet."

The IT people had brought laptops and several boxes with antennas. "Tons of Wi-Fi networks in this place," said Norton. "One of them has to link to this stuff, they tell me."

"You think all this equipment and how it's connected is significant to Rooney's death? Or the warehouse shooting?" Jess asked.

"Can't say what it's all related to, one way or another. But got to be a reason for having so much of this stuff in his apartment," Norton said, thinking out loud. "If Lucy Cranfield's actually missing, that suggests a connection between Rooney and Cranfield. Banks mean money and lots of it. Seems wiser to consider everything together at this point."

"Except all these machines have been erased," the IT guy with KHALIL embroidered on his coveralls said. "We're recovering the data. The erasing wasn't done by an expert. Which means we can probably get it all back."

Jess pulled out her phone.

"No photographs," Khalil said.

"Okay." She flipped through her saved picture files to find the photos from her last visit to Rooney's. "You've moved some things around."

Khalil shrugged. "To connect the cables."

"No." Jess shook her head. She pointed to a bare circuit card on top of a desktop computer on the floor. "That was on the table."

Khalil glanced at his colleague and back to Jess. "When?"

"Yesterday." She held up her phone. Khalil looked back and forth, comparing the equipment to the picture.

"Lots of things have moved," he said, swiveling his gaze from the photos to current conditions.

Norton stood beside Jess and did the same comparison with the pictures he'd stored on his phone. He glowered at Khalil. "Are you sure you didn't move this stuff?"

"Positive. The fingerprint guy could have done it. He was in here before us." Khalil swept a wide arc with his arm to indicate the entire collection. "And it doesn't matter who moved things around. It's all networked."

Norton shook his head. "I was here. The fingerprint guy didn't move this equipment."

Jess was still comparing her pictures to Rooney's apartment. "Something's missing."

She compared and counted painstakingly, identifying each piece of equipment. Finally, she settled on a black box, a laptop, and a bundle of cables.

She pointed them out to Khalil, who frowned and zoomed in on the black box's label until he could read it. "RXP? What's that?"

He and his colleague spent a minute searching the internet on their phones.

Khalil said, "Remote Exchange Protocol Inc. Looks like a model nineteen."

"Meaning?" said Jess.

"An encryption server, it says. But they only sell them to financial institutions."

"Banks." Jess met Norton's gaze. "You think someone from First Aurora Bank took it?"

"I'm sure as hell going to find out," Norton replied tersely on his way out.

CHAPTER 41

JESS FOLLOWED NORTON ACROSS the parking lot as she scrolled through her recent phone calls. She quickly found the number Karl Oppenheimer had used to impersonate Major Mifflin.

She made the call from her Jeep. The call rang several times but never switched to voicemail.

After a couple of minutes, a man finally answered. "Bullets, bombs, boots, an' beans. You want 'em, we got 'em. Whatcha need?"

"Karl Oppenheimer," Jess said abruptly.

"Wait up," the man replied.

The phone's receiver clanked as if he'd left it swinging on the cord, knocking against a hard surface. The same industrial noises she'd heard on Oppenheimer's first call filled the background. Finally, a new voice came on the line.

"Oppenheimer," he said flatly.

"This is Jess Kimball. Sorry I got you in trouble."

Karl's tone changed a fraction. "I didn't expect you to come down here."

"I can't research everything over the internet." Jess paused. "Did you receive some sort of reprimand for talking to me?"

Oppenheimer grunted. "Got chewed out. Working weekends for the next month. Coulda been worse."

"Everyone deserves justice, Karl," Jess said.

"Maybe. He's just got a stick up his…you know."

"Look, I may or may not be able to help you find your brother's killer, but finding out more about that gun would help with the investigation in Denver."

Oppenheimer paused a moment. "Mifflin made it clear. I'm to butt out. If you want the specs for the K10, you can look them up online."

"The shipment to Holston. Who on your staff handled that?"

Oppenheimer scoffed. "Well, you know it ain't my staff…but I might be able to see who packed and shipped. Should be on the paperwork."

"Anything you can find might be helpful."

"You think whoever kept the K10 from the scrap heap did the Denver shooting?" Oppenheimer asked.

"We don't know yet."

The line went quiet for a moment. "You think it's the same person who shot my brother?"

Jess said nothing.

"You know, I don't care if they get charged for my brother's murder, long as they get put away. For a long time. Like life."

"I'll do everything I can," Jess promised.

"You ain't police though, are you? You can't charge anyone."

"Any evidence I get goes straight to Denver PD and the FBI."

"Yeah." Oppenheimer struggled to control his breathing. "HH survived two tours in Iraq, two in Afghanistan, and deployments to places he couldn't even tell me about. Served our country more than most people can imagine. He didn't deserve to die the way he did."

Jess swallowed. "No."

"It would be good to know someone cared enough to find my brother's killer," Oppenheimer said quietly.

"I'm working on it."

Jess waited through a very long silence.

Finally, he said, "I'll get you everything I can."

CHAPTER 42

JESS PULLED INTO THE First Aurora Bank parking lot right behind Norton. At four thirty, daylight was fading fast, the heavy overcast sky ushered in the darkness earlier than usual.

Norton had left Rooney's apartment like a man possessed, infuriated by the idea the bank might have broken in and stolen evidence.

Though not technically a crime scene, Rooney's apartment had been secured like one because of Norton's growing concerns. When he arrived at the bank, Norton stomped straight into the building, his badge already drawn from his pocket.

Jess raced to join him.

Norton must have called ahead because Margo Alvarado waited in the lobby with her best welcoming smile.

He skipped unnecessary introductions. "Found your CEO yet?"

"Mr. Larson is not here, I'm afraid," Margo replied.

"So where is he?"

"I haven't been able to reach him."

"Tried his cell phone?"

"Obviously, but no reply."

"How about Mr. Larson's assistant?" Jess asked.

Margo shook her head. "Nothing on his calendar."

"Nothing? At all? For a CEO?" Norton pressed.

Margo shifted her weight. "Well, nothing that would cause him to be off-site."

"Does he have meetings scheduled here?" Jess asked.

She nodded.

"And he's missing them? Is that normal for Mr. Larson?"

"Well...sometimes he invites people as a courtesy, but he doesn't actually expect them to show up. So it could be normal. Or not." Margo's welcoming smile evaporated. "Look, let's get to the point. What do you need to know?"

"Right now, who's next in line under Larson?" Norton asked.

"His deputy, Hiromi Tsui, chief financial officer."

Norton nodded firmly. "I'd like to see Tsui now. Assuming she hasn't mysteriously gone AWOL."

"I'll see if she's available."

"Tell her if she isn't, I'll call in for a warrant and wait right here until it arrives," Norton replied sternly. "And the head of security. I want to see him, too."

"Right." Margo walked over to a house phone, dialed, and talked in hushed tones. A moment later she hung up. "This way, please."

She waved them upstairs and led the way to a large conference room.

Seconds later, a slim Asian woman with jet-black hair entered. She shook Norton's and Jess's hands and gestured toward the chairs.

"We need to see Jerry Larson. Do you know where he is?" Norton asked.

Tsui shook her head. "He's not answering his phone at the moment."

"Text messages?"

She shook her head again. "CEO isn't a desk job. He meets with a lot of people in a lot of places."

Norton frowned, but before he could say more, a uniformed man walked in.

"Kevin Upshaw, head of security," he said and sat opposite Jess.

Tsui cleared her throat. "What's this about, Detective?"

"You're familiar with Justin Rooney?"

"Of course," Tsui replied.

"Did the bank remove anything from Rooney's apartment?"

Upshaw leaned forward. "What things?"

"Anything at all," Norton replied.

Upshaw shook his head. "Not that I'm aware of. We're not in the habit of removing anything from our employees' homes."

Jess asked, "Even equipment that might be owned by the bank?"

"Sure, if it's a laptop or something. We'd request that back from the family. In due course."

Norton grunted and Upshaw leaned forward to ask, "What have you found at his place that is owned by the bank?"

"Let's just say a computer."

"We all take laptops home with us. We have tight security on everything. No one will be able to access the laptop contents without special sign-in credentials," Upshaw explained.

"What about the IT department? Rooney worked in IT. What else might he have taken home from the bank?" Norton asked.

Tsui leaned forward. "Detective, please be clear. We want to help you find out what happened to Justin Rooney. We could be more helpful if you tell us what you want."

Jess brought up a picture of the RXP device on her phone and held it out.

"I have no idea what that is," Upshaw said, passing the photo to Tsui, who shook her head as if she was also clueless.

"Maybe we should talk to Armando," Jess said.

Tsui frowned. "Who?"

"He works with Rooney in your IT department," Jess explained.

Tsui checked the staff contact list on her phone. "Armando Castillo. Network specialist. How's he involved with this?"

"He worked with Rooney. He might know what this equipment is and what it does," Jess said.

Tsui called Armando. Two minutes later he knocked on the door and entered.

Looking around nervously, he took a seat beside Jess. "Is this about Lucy?"

"Detective Norton's team is searching her apartment," Jess said. "She's not there and the security chain on the door has been cut."

Armando's eyes widened. "Is she okay?"

Tsui interrupted. "Lucy Cranfield?"

"One and the same," Armando replied.

"Her car is still parked outside her apartment," Norton replied. "We're checking hospitals and put out a BOLO. We'll find her."

Tsui leaned forward, hands twisting. "What's going on here, Detective?"

"You tell me."

"You think Larson's involved in whatever's happening here?" Tsui asked.

"I think he should be using every resource at his disposal at this bank to figure this out. Instead, he's off somewhere, drinking martinis," Norton said.

"Jerry isn't that kind of person. I'm sure he has a good reason not to be here at the moment," Tsui replied coldly while squaring her shoulders.

"But since he isn't here, we can't ask him, can we?" Norton snapped.

The room went silent.

Jess held out her phone to Armando. "Do you know what this is?"

He nodded. "Encryption server. Model nineteen. For SWIFT transactions. We use them in all our branches."

"What's SWIFT?" Norton asked.

"Society for Worldwide Interbank Financial Telecommunications," Armando recited as if he'd memorized the name in grade school.

"What does it do?" Jess asked.

"Realtime multifactor encryption. Dedicated vector—"

Jess held up a hand. "Wait, wait. In layman's terms."

Armando shrugged. "It encrypts data. Basically, allows money to be transferred."

"Between banks."

"Between most financial institutions in most countries."

Tsui shuffled in her seat. "What countries?"

"There's a few embargoed places, but basically any country," Armando replied.

"So anyone could have one of those boxes?" Upshaw said, as if he were preparing to broaden the subject and get the spotlight off First Aurora.

Armando shook his head. "RXP only sells to financial institutions."

"But the equipment could have been stolen," Upshaw said.

"Anything can be stolen," Armando said. "They have some protections. There's a complex set of passwords. Setup isn't easy.

And if you open the unit, it will erase itself, which disconnects it from the SWIFT system."

"Has this one been opened?" Upshaw demanded, still looking for a way to avoid police involvement.

Armando took Jess's phone and looked at the picture, zooming in and out. "Can't tell. If it has, they screwed it back together and replaced the tamper seals. Where was this picture taken?"

Jess looked to Norton, unsure of what details he wanted to reveal.

Norton cleared his throat. "Justin Rooney's apartment."

Armando's expression froze. "Justin's?"

"Yep."

Armando bit his lip. "I hadn't heard Justin was doing any work with RXP."

"Is it ours?" said Tsui.

Armando zoomed in on the photo again. He wrote the serial number on a sticky note and then used his phone to access the company database.

A few moments later, he said, "Yes. We sent it to our Cali bank. It stopped functioning after six months. They sent it in for repairs."

"Where'd they send it?" Tsui asked.

"San Francisco. Where they're made." He tapped his phone. "It's still there, according to this."

Jess retrieved her phone. "I saw it in Justin Rooney's apartment yesterday."

Armando whistled. "There could be a legitimate reason for that. I mean, Justin worked with these things every day."

"At home?"

He paused. "That wouldn't be easy to do from home, no."

"Why not?" Norton demanded.

"Well, there are other layers of security. This piece of equipment can't really be used without all the supporting infrastructure," Armando explained.

Norton pushed the point. "But it's not impossible to do the work from home, is it?"

"Not impossible, no," Armando replied. "A majority of the financial institutions in the world use SWIFT. But you do need to know how to do it."

Jess found another shot of Rooney's apartment showing the table filled with equipment. "Could this stuff be the supporting infrastructure for the RXP?"

Armando shrugged. "Can't tell without firing it up and checking the software."

Tsui leaned forward. "Would Rooney know how to set up this infrastructure?"

Armando nodded slowly. "He set up ours and the ones in Cali, too."

"So what could he be doing with this equipment in his home?" Jess asked.

Armando shrugged again. "I don't know. Maybe if I can connect to the encryptor..."

"That's why we're here," said Norton. "It's gone."

Armando's eyebrows went up. "Gone?"

"Gone where?" said Tsui.

"We thought you took it," said Norton.

Upshaw shook his head. "We didn't take anything from Rooney's apartment. Like I said."

Tsui looked at Armando. "Are we at any risk from this?"

"The RXP is usually kept in a secure environment with—"

"Yes or no," Tsui demanded. "Are we at any risk if someone has stolen that box?"

Armando swallowed. "Yes."

CHAPTER 43

AS THE MEETING DRONED on, First Aurora Bank's conference room became too warm. Jess unzipped her jacket.

Kevin Upshaw and Margo Alvarado had made excuses and left.

"We've got three people involved here. Justin, Lucy, and Larson," Jess said.

Tsui shook her head, refusing to lump them all together. "I'm sure Jerry is just caught up with work. Maybe he turned his phone off and forgot to turn it back on. He does that sometimes."

Norton said, "Finding Miss Cranfield is my top priority at the moment."

"Maybe we should look at the laptops at Justin's place," Armando suggested. "Might be something on there that could help."

"We have our people on it," Norton replied.

"I could help," Armando said.

Norton pondered the offer a moment. "Okay."

Armando looked toward Tsui. She nodded, and he hurried out of the room.

Jess sent a message to Mandy to look up Larson's home address since First Aurora had refused to provide it. Mandy responded a moment later.

Norton called to report what little they'd learned to his boss and to tell him Armando was on the way.

Armando soon returned with a bulging bag of equipment and cables. "I'm off to Justin's apartment."

"My guys are expecting you. Keep us informed all the way," Norton insisted.

"Will do," Armando said on his way out.

Tsui had moved to a quiet corner to call several numbers in a luckless search for Larson.

"You haven't called his wife," Jess said.

"I have," Tsui replied. "Went to voicemail."

"When did he answer his last email?" Norton asked.

"Yesterday."

"I'm going to visit his home," Jess said.

"Why? He's not there," Norton said.

"I'll find out."

"I'm coming, too," Tsui said. "Our business is at risk. He needs to know that. I need to talk to him."

While Tsui went to grab her coat, Norton spoke quietly to Jess. "We'll follow up with Rooney's equipment. And we'll find Larson and Cranfield, too. We have a whole police department to do this job, you know."

"Right. But I have a job to do, too. And I can take liberties that you can't," Jess replied. "I'll keep you posted all the way. I'm not interested in another gunfight."

"See that you do," Norton growled and turned to answer his phone.

While he was distracted, Jess went down to meet Tsui in the lobby. They took her Jeep.

"Do you know Lucy Cranfield well?" Jess asked as she followed the GPS directions toward Larson's address.

"I know who she is. We have a lot of employees. I don't know Cranfield personally." Tsui's tone was a little huffy.

Jess absorbed the words and the vibes. "Any big changes coming up at the bank?"

"Such as?" Tsui arched her eyebrows.

"Is the business up for sale? Hostile takeovers in the wings?" Jess listed the first two ideas that came to mind.

"No. Nothing big like that in our immediate future."

"But First Aurora's business is doing well?"

"I can't discuss the bank's internal operations with you," Tsui said. "What makes you think the bank's business is relevant here, anyway?"

Jess wondered briefly if Tsui was just thick or if she was being deliberately obtuse. Could go either way. Tsui wouldn't be the first CFO to have no frigging clue what was going on under her nose.

"Justin Rooney died under suspicious circumstances. Lucy Cranfield has disappeared." Jess listed the top-of-mind answers to Tsui's question. "Rooney's apartment was full of the bank's equipment. Which should not have been there at all and has now been stolen. And your CEO is missing."

Jess glanced toward Tsui. "Shall I keep going?"

"Okay, okay." Tsui took a deep breath, shaking her head. "But it's still highly sensitive private information. Publish anything you learn, and we'll sue you off the map."

"Keep relevant information about a criminal enterprise from the police and you'll be the one off the map. For a good long time, too," Jess replied flatly.

Tsui fell quiet as she seemed to be working things through in her head. Finally, she said, "There was a bank for sale. In

Colombia. It was listed at a good price. Heck, it was a great price. A whole bunch of companies were competing to buy it."

"Yeah, I heard."

Tsui frowned. "Jerry, being Jerry, developed a good relationship with the owner. He could have sold the bank for more. But they went with us because of Jerry."

"A single owner?"

"Yeah, the Colombia bank was personally owned," Tsui said. "Unusual, but it still happens. Jerry started First Aurora with his own money."

Jess frowned. "Really?"

"Really. But he's sold off shares over the past couple of years to raise capital."

"To buy the Colombia bank?"

"Yeah. And our expansion hasn't worked out as we planned. The big chains have been working their way into our markets. And we overextended ourselves to buy the bank in Colombia."

"How badly?"

"We're still afloat, but we have to manage our cashflow and debt day by day," Tsui said. "We have a big payment due in two months. Jerry's trying to liquidate what he can. So we'll be ready."

"Sounds like a lot of stress," Jess said.

Tsui insisted, "It's entirely manageable. First Aurora will be fine."

Jess didn't reply. They completed the drive in silence. When the Jeep arrived at the gated entrance to an affluent neighborhood, a security guard came out to meet them.

Tsui rattled off Larson's address and told the guard to use her name when he checked with Larson. The guard returned a minute later, opened the gate, and wished them a good day as Jess drove past.

Larson lived in a spacious community of individually designed homes on oversize lots of at least an acre. The houses varied from ornate French châteaus to monstrously large log homes.

Trees dotted a landscape unmarred by fences. A row of pines bordered Larson's Colonial-era two-story home near the end of a cul-de-sac. The gravel driveway looped around an oversized fountain. Giant pillars supported a full-width balcony across the upper floor. Plants and bushes broke up the expanse and a separate four-car garage was set back from the house.

Jess circled the fountain and parked directly in front of a double-width front door.

She climbed out of the Jeep to see the front door had opened. A blond woman at least a decade younger than Jerry Lawson stepped out onto the porch wearing skinny jeans and a shirt that cost more than Jess's entire paycheck. Her vivid blue eyes flicked from Jess to Tsui.

"Hiromi. This is unexpected," she said.

"Hi, Melissa. Sorry for the intrusion," Tsui replied.

"No problem." Melissa Larson moved with the easy grace of an athlete, leading them into the house.

They entered a cavernous foyer with a soaring ceiling. A pair of staircases curved down from the upper floor, flanking a large stone and metal abstract sculpture across from the entry door.

Jess introduced herself.

"I know your magazine," Melissa said, leading them across the parquet flooring to a living room. One of several, Jess suspected.

A fireplace with a roaring log fire dominated one side of the room. Three dark leather Chesterfield love seats were arranged around a large, square coffee table. Oil paintings dotted the walls and large plants filled the gaps between them. A giant wrought-iron chandelier hung from a fifteenfoot ceiling.

Melissa gestured toward one of the seating groups.

"We're looking for your husband," Jess explained after they were settled.

"Jerry?" Melissa looked at Tsui. "He's at work, of course."

"He's not at the office," Tsui said. "And he's not answering his cell phone."

Melissa shrugged. "Out of range? Low battery? He told me he would be late last night and must have left early this morning. He might have forgotten to charge it."

"You didn't see him?"

"He uses a guest room when he comes in really late. Doesn't want to disturb me. I'm a very light sleeper."

"Any idea where he might have gone today?" Jess asked.

Melissa shook her head. "Are you...? Should I be concerned? I mean, he often doesn't return my calls for a few hours, but you're beginning to worry me."

"No reason to worry. We just haven't seen him today," Tsui replied.

"Is he answering texts or emails? He's usually better with that," Melissa said.

Jess said, "Not since yesterday."

Melissa fell silent.

"Is there somewhere he likes to go? Coffee shop? Restaurant? Bar?" Jess asked.

"Tina's Perk-Up. Park Hill. On the weekend he can stretch one coffee out for hours there." Melissa's face relaxed. "He's probably just hiding out to get some work done. He does that sometimes, too."

Jess texted Norton to ask him to check the coffee shop.

A tall, thin teenage boy with a shock of blond hair appeared at the doorway with a game controller in his hand. Melissa waved him over and put her arm around his shoulder. "This is Tom. My son."

The boy smiled. He stood an inch taller than his mother. He turned his back to the room and whispered to her.

"Show us," she said.

Tom picked up a remote control from the coffee table and pressed various buttons. A screen appeared on the wall over the fireplace. He clicked through a couple of menu options and a map appeared.

"Location services. I heard you talking about my dad. We share family locations. So…" Tom gestured to the screen. A blue dot labeled DAD pulsated on the location of the First Aurora head office.

"I don't understand," Tsui said. "I looked all over. I mean, he'd have to be hidden somewhere."

"In a quiet corner with his phone on silent, probably," Melissa offered with an indulgent smile.

"Maybe." Tsui drew out the word like she didn't believe it.

Jess held out her hand. "May I?"

Tom handed her the remote.

She navigated the cursor to a small box marked DETAILS and clicked. The screen listed technical details for the location such as latitude, longitude, and altitude. But it was the time that interested her.

"That was his position at seven p.m. yesterday," Jess said.

Melissa waved at the screen. "No. He's always on the phone. That thing must be wrong."

Tom pointed to two dots superimposed on an image of their house. "It's got us both updated, showing that we're here. And we've been out today."

"I don't care," Melissa said. "I…"

"Does he have another phone?" Jess asked.

Melissa shook her head.

"Social media?"

"Dad hates it," Tom replied.

Melissa wrapped her arms around herself. "This is beginning to…I mean, there's a logical explanation, isn't there? I mean… there must be, right?"

"There could very well be an entirely logical explanation," Tsui said. "But I really need to talk to him about some business issues. Urgently."

Jess's phone vibrated with a reply text from Norton. She read it out to the room. "Confirmed Larson not at Tina's Perk-Up today."

Melissa took a deep breath and let it out with a worried sigh. "I'm not sure I can help any more."

"Does he have family in the area? Parents, siblings?" Jess asked.

"No. He's from upstate New York. It's just the three of us here in Colorado."

"Friends?"

"Plenty. But I can't imagine him hanging out with them on a workday and not letting anyone know," Melissa said. "Especially me."

"I understand he's been under a lot of pressure lately."

Melissa shrugged. "He keeps it to himself. Doesn't want to worry us. I was thinking we might go to Florida. We have a house there and he likes the water. But he wouldn't go without us."

"Melissa," Tsui said. "Did Jerry talk to you about selling your place in Florida?"

Melissa frowned. "No. Why would he do that? We love the house."

Tsui shook her head. "He asked me to get it valued. He wants to sell the place."

"What?" Tom asked.

"He told me yesterday," Tsui said. "Apparently, he hasn't been there in ages, and he didn't want the hassle."

"But I went with the kids a month ago."

"He said the place always needs cleaning."

Melissa frowned. "We have a service. The house is spotless."

"He was determined," Tsui said. "Made me get a valuation yesterday. One of those 'buy anything' places. He signed the papers already. It'll take a couple of weeks, but the sale is going through."

It was Melissa's turn to take a deep breath. She blew it out slowly. "I don't know what to say. We loved that house. He loved it."

"I tried to talk him out of it," Tsui said.

"It was an investment as well. We bought it really cheap and renovated." Melissa continued to mumble. "Has great views and…"

Melissa put her hands together. She looked down at the coffee table, breathing loudly.

"I've been very lucky." Melissa reached for her son's hand. "We've been very lucky. As you can tell. He bought this house with cash when I got pregnant, and I've never thought about money a moment since."

Tsui closed her eyes.

"What?" said Melissa.

The CFO shook her head. "Jerry didn't tell you, did he?"

"What?"

"He mortgaged this house a month ago."

Melissa went white. "What do you mean?"

"He had me get an appraiser in. They valued the house, and he took out the loan the next day." Tsui looked down at the floor. "I'm sorry. I thought he told you."

"But, but…why didn't *you* tell me?"

"He asked me not to," Tsui said quietly. "But the house is in his name only. Legally, he could do what he wanted with it. And he told me he would talk to you."

"But…I…Oh God." Melissa sagged back against the cushions and her jaw hung open. "I didn't know things were so bad."

She reached for Tom and pulled him down next to her, squeezing him tight.

Jess waited a few moments before she asked, "Mrs. Larson, does your husband have any other interests?"

Melissa frowned. "Not golf or anything like that. But sailing our boat. He loves that. He's a natural on the water. We joked that he must have been a fish in a prior life."

"I meant, outside your marriage."

Melissa exhaled sharply. "You mean another woman? No. There's no…I haven't seen any signs."

"Late-night calls or messages?" Jess asked.

"He's a CEO. He gets messages at all hours. But nothing suspicious like that. Not that I've noticed, anyway." She pursed her lips and shook her head. "No. No. I don't think there's another woman involved."

"Okay."

After a moment, Melissa asked, "Should I call the police?"

"They're already aware, but yes, making a formal missing person record would be a good idea," Jess said.

Melissa looked numb. "I can't believe this."

"There might still be a logical explanation," Jess said, offering Melissa a business card. "But we need to find your husband as soon as possible. If you hear from him, please give us a call right away."

CHAPTER 44

JESS DROVE BACK TO First Aurora. Tsui didn't speak until they reach the highway.

"Why did you have to do that?"

"What?" said Jess.

"The other woman thing."

"A man is cashing in his assets and disappears. It's an obvious question."

"In front of her son?"

"He was a lot more worldly than you're giving him credit for. Besides, a man and a woman are unaccounted for from your bank."

Tsui's mouth hung open. "You think Jerry and Lucy are involved?"

"Why not? It's a possibility."

"She's thirty years younger. And Jerry hardly knew her."

"What if Jerry had a breakdown? Drove off with Lucy stuffed in the trunk of a car. You think we should wait to ask that question?"

Tsui scoffed. "You're making things up."

"Maybe. But Jerry obviously needs money and lots of it. Why? We need to find out what's going on here. Fast," Jess said. "I've got a bad feeling about this. Time is not on our side."

Tsui's shoulders drooped and she exhaled. "I've worked with Jerry every day for years. I trusted him. In fact, I still trust him."

Jess cocked her head. "You really think his disappearance has nothing to do with either Lucy or Rooney?"

"Yes," Tsui said emphatically. "Until we have something more concrete than his phone being turned off, yes, I do think so."

A tractor trailer roared past, sending up blinding spray. Jess gripped the steering wheel with both hands and waited for visibility to improve. "Why didn't you tell me about selling the houses?"

"Just because we can't get ahold of Jerry for a while doesn't mean I should tell a reporter his personal business."

"He's liquidating assets. Surely that's a red flag for you?" Jess passed an eighteenwheeler. "Did you process Larson's personal loans to First Aurora after he mortgaged the two properties?"

"No."

"How much cash did Larson clear from the two properties?"

Tsui didn't respond.

Jess made a note to look up the property records and trace the equity.

"Where did the money go?"

Tsui failed to answer.

"Did he hide the money from his wife?"

Tsui said, "Jerry has a broker he works with. Bensons. I don't have any contact there. Melissa may well know all about it. You'd need to ask her."

"He didn't put the money in an account at First Aurora?" said Jess.

Tsui shrugged. "If anything happens to the bank, that money will be safe. Common sense."

Jess realized Tsui either didn't know or wouldn't say more, so she asked, "How did Larson seem the last time you saw him?"

"He's been demanding recently. But he's got plenty of reasons to be stressed, as you know."

Tsui's phone rang. She pulled it from her bag and *uh-huh*'d her way through the call, ending with "Not a word to anyone. Meet me back at the office."

"News?" said Jess.

Tsui sat, lips pursed for a moment before she said, "Armando's at Rooney's place. He's found evidence of communication with the bank's servers. Could be innocuous, but without the missing RXP gizmo, he doesn't know what the communications actually were."

"Surely the bank can look at its records and sort that all out?"

Tsui nodded. "Which is why we're meeting at the office."

Jess drove the remainder of the route in silence. The bank's main entrance had been locked when the branch closed. They walked around to the rear and Tsui buzzed them through a secure door with a keycard and PIN.

She returned Jess to the conference room.

"Wait here," Tsui said on her way out. "I'll see what Armando's found."

Jess called Norton and reported the conversation with Larson's wife. Norton told her that his IT team had witnessed Armando's results. All agreed nothing more could be done without the RXP device.

"Selling two houses and disappearing is one heck of a red flag," Norton said thoughtfully. "I'll follow up with his broker."

"Bensons has a place in town."

"I'll also get to work on a warrant, just in case they want to play hardball."

Satisfied, Jess asked, "Any news on Lucy Cranfield?"

"Nothing yet. No signs of struggle or blood in her apartment, which is a good thing. She doesn't have any of the sort of equipment we found in Rooney's apartment."

"You don't think the two things are connected, then?"

"We're pulling phone records now, but so far we haven't found any reason to believe so. They weren't even friends on social media," Norton said before he hung up.

Jess slid her phone into her pocket and paced the conference room until Armando appeared.

"It's going to take some time to figure out what Justin was accessing here," he said.

"I thought banking stuff was mostly automated," Jess replied.

"Totally automated for routine operations," Armando confirmed. "But this isn't normal."

Jess nodded. "So how did Rooney acquire the RXP device since they don't sell to individuals?"

"The company repaired this one and shipped it back to the bank, but it wasn't logged into our system. So we had no record of it."

"Rooney took it from the bank, then?" Jess asked.

"I guess. You think you know a guy," Armando said slowly, shaking his head. "I still can't quite believe it."

"Did Rooney know Lucy?"

"Sure. There are twelve of us in IT. We all know each other."

"Were they a couple?" Jess asked.

"No chance," he scoffed. "Justin had no life apart from work and his cars. But Lucy was, well, normal. She went to see bands in town. Kept up with old college friends. Organized the office party at the end of the year. That sort of thing."

"So, no social or romantic connections." Jess bit her lip as she tried to think what other connections the two could have. "Someone must have known what Rooney was up to. When he died, they took Lucy as a replacement."

"Come on," Armando said with disbelief.

"Let's just use it as a working hypothesis. Do we know what Rooney was actually doing with the RXP?"

Armando stood. "I'll go back to look through the server logs again. There has to be something. Maybe Rooney made a mistake."

"Yeah," said Jess. "All we need is one."

CHAPTER 45

THEO KAHLER PULLED UP the hood of his old parka. The waterproofing had worn off, but the hood was large enough to protect his face from cameras.

He pulled a rolling suitcase from the rear of his hatchback. With the zips and expansion section open, the rifle case fit perfectly inside.

The car was the opposite of a perfect fit.

He'd stolen the keys from a guy in a supermarket. The idiot had the keys hanging off his belt. One bump, a murmured apology, and Kahler had a new set of wheels.

Turned out the Volkswagen hatchback was way too small. He had to fold himself double just to fit behind the wheel. He'd ditch the hatchback as soon as he had the chance.

Meanwhile, he strolled to the entrance of an upscale parking garage. He took the ramp to the lower level and waited behind a concrete pillar. A large blue Mercedes pulled in and parked. Once the owner exited the car, Kahler walked toward the elevator.

The Mercedes owner was in his fifties. He wore an expensive wool coat and leather gloves. Kahler timed his pace to arrive just as the man swiped his keycard to unlock the elevator doors.

"Damned flight delays," muttered Kahler as he stepped into the elevator.

The man grunted without making eye contact and pressed the button for fifteen. Kahler pressed seven. They rode seven floors in silence. Kahler stepped off, and the elevator continued upward.

The corridor was quiet. Four doors to the left and six to the right.

At both ends of the corridor, fire doors led to stairwells.

Kahler headed to the closest stairwell. The door opened and closed smoothly and quietly.

He took the stairs upward, two at a time. It was tempting to dispose of the large suitcase, but he'd need it on the way out. At the top of the stairwell, the exit door also opened smoothly and silently. He walked through and onto the roof.

The wind blew hard, so hard he stepped back into the protection of the stairwell to assemble his gun, tripod, and scope. When he was ready, he stepped out again.

The night sky was clear. He scanned to confirm he'd selected the highest building in the vicinity. Air-conditioning units and various electrical units dotted the roof.

Kahler worked his way through the heavy wind to the front of the building.

The view to the ground looked good. There were no cables or flags fluttering in the wind to distract him, and he was high enough to see over tall-sided vehicles. The buildings were blocking the wind at street level, which meant the wind should not interfere with his shot.

He unfolded a small stool designed for fishermen. Not the most comfortable, but not the worst either. He perched on the seat and positioned his gun. The tripod allowed just enough height to see over the guardrail to the entrance of the building across the intersection.

Jessica Kimball's apartment building.

He had calculated the range and set up the scope earlier, working from previous test shots. No time for a dry run, which always added risk. But he could compensate after his first shot if he needed to.

An SUV arrived at the entrance to Kimball's parking gate. An arm reached out and waved a card in front of a small box. Nothing happened. He'd sawed through its power cables, which had effectively stopped the gate from functioning. The gate blocked entry and exit.

The SUV's driver waved the card at the box until she gave up and stepped out of the vehicle.

Kahler started a timer on his watch.

The driver was a woman with blond hair, tottering on high heels. Wearing a fitted blouse and a short, tight skirt, she wasn't dressed for the cold, but the outfit admirably emphasized her figure.

She leaned forward to the intercom. Kahler guessed she'd be complaining about the blocked entrance and having to stand out in the cold.

Kahler lined up the rifle. It would be an easy shot to hit the woman's back. She'd never know what hit her.

He should have done this the first time. Kimball would be dead and gone now.

Which was history. He'd rushed that first attempt. He'd planned the attack, but he hadn't evaluated all his options. A bad decision and he knew it. No one else to blame.

But this time would be different.

The woman leaned away from the box. The barrier rose. She slid back into the SUV, closed the door, and drove into the parking garage.

Kahler stopped the timer on his watch. Nineteen seconds. Not a long time. But plenty long enough for a bullet traveling at nearly two thousand miles an hour.

He continued to survey the traffic, watching for Kimball's white Jeep. The wind died down, which was good. If for some reason his first shot missed, he would make a small correction and the second shot would be perfect.

An hour later, the light had faded. Streetlights came on, bathing everything with a colorsucking yellow glow.

A Jeep turned onto the far end of the street. He angled the gun to use the scope. The colors were hard to distinguish. The Jeep approached. It had a roof rack. Did Kimball's Jeep have one?

The Jeep slowed and approached the parking garage barrier arm. A light over the entrance showed the Jeep's silver color, but he kept his gun on the driver's door just in case.

After a moment of waving his card around, a male driver got out and talked into the box.

"Pow," he said quietly.

"Pow," someone behind him said, louder.

Kahler jerked his head around. Miller and his new number two, Kemp, stood right behind him, six feet apart, machine pistols leveled at his back.

"What the hell is this?" Kahler asked.

"Put the gun down," Miller said.

Kahler paused. Two against one. Them standing and him perched on a tiny stool. Their light and maneuverable machine pistols against his fifteen-pound, four-foot-long rifle. Their broad automatic and burst fire against his perfectly placed shots.

He took another breath and raised his hands.

Kemp gestured for him to stand. Miller pointed his pistol into Kahler's face. Kemp stood to one side, patted Kahler down, taking his knife and handgun. Kahler's weapons were dumped in a pile, fifteen feet away, along with his K10 rifle.

Miller gestured for Kahler to sit.

"What the hell's this about?" said Kahler.

"I might ask you the same thing," said Miller.

Kahler's mind raced. Caught. It was the situation they prepared for in the army. Prep. Get your story straight. Learn it. He took a deep breath, but he didn't speak.

Kemp stood to one side with his gun aimed at Kahler's head. "He asked you a question."

Kahler turned to look at Kemp. "What do you think I'm doing? Baking cookies?"

"I told you to keep a low profile," said Miller. "Taking over Finny's business ain't something we want to advertise. No unwanted attention. Stealth in all things. Something you army punks are supposed to understand."

"This is important," said Kahler.

"To us? Or you?"

"To all of us."

"Yeah, right," Kemp said. "Ain't no us in your mind."

Kahler scowled. "Without my steady hand, you'd have been creamed at the warehouse."

"Don't overestimate your value—" Kemp growled, aiming the pistol at Kahler's head.

Miller raised a hand. "Enough."

"Only one man had eyes on Snout," Kemp said, gesturing toward Kahler with his gun.

Kahler shrugged. "Ricochet. Happens all the time."

"I said *enough*." Miller spoke sternly, as if he had control over them. Which he did not.

Kahler and Kemp fell silent because it was prudent to be quiet. No other reason.

"I told you no moonlighting," said Miller. "And now I find you here. Explain yourself."

Kahler sighed. "The woman from Rooney's accident site."

Miller stared, silent, gun leveled at Kahler's face.

"The one I told you about," said Kahler. "She was checking out the accident scene with the cop."

"The woman I told you to watch."

"Exactly," Kahler said. "She's a loose end we need to silence."

Kemp said, "She looked at a burnt patch of ground two days after a car crash. How does that make her a loose end?"

"She's hanging out with Detective Norton, the cop on the case."

"Hanging out? Like married? Shacked up?"

Kahler shook his head. More likely a relationship with some FBI agent, but now wasn't the time to bring that up.

"Then what?" Miller asked. "Why put our whole operation at risk?"

"She's a reporter."

"Seriously?" Miller dove forward and jammed his gun against the side of Kahler's head. "And you didn't tell me?"

"I can handle it."

"Handle it? She's a reporter. Makes a living digging things up. And she's hooked up with some cop. You can't handle nothing." Miller drove his gun into the side of Kahler's head, pushing him sideways off the stool.

Kahler scrambled to stand. "Reporters always hang around cops. That's how they get their stories."

"What makes this one special?" said Miller, stepping away, gun still trained on Kahler.

"She went to the crash site."

"So what? Some kid lost his life driving too fast. Boo-hoo. Accidents happen all the time. Back-page news." Miller waved his gun at Kahler. "But you're set up to take her out."

"She's a loose end." Kahler insisted, providing no further information.

"If she's uncovered anything, the cop already knows. You going to whack him, too?"

"If we need to."

Miller groaned. "You don't get it, do you? FBI is all over the party at the warehouse. We got heat scaring buyers off already."

Kahler stayed silent.

Kemp held his gun steady, but Miller holstered his. "Question is, are you with us or against us?"

Kahler straightened up. "I froze my ass off to make sure Rooney went down, and I took out Finny's mob. I'd say that's a pretty clear statement of intent."

Miller stared a long moment. "Pack up your gear. From now on, you don't do squat unless I tell you. In triplicate. Get it?"

Kahler forced his facial muscles to relax. He kept eye contact and gave a single nod. "Got it."

Miller stared a good long time, as if he wasn't convinced. Finally, he said, "Good. More deliveries tomorrow. Show up at two p.m. Sharp."

Kahler nodded again. "Got it."

Miller walked to the stairwell. Kemp backed away, gun still leveled on Kahler until he closed the door between them.

Kahler exhaled. He collected his gun and knife and checked the rifle. Apart from some scratches on the tripod, it looked intact. He'd test it later to make sure no real damage had been done.

As he broke down the tripod, a white Jeep arrived at the parking garage entrance. Kimball's Jeep. She unsuccessfully tried her keycard before stepping out and talking into the speaker box. Moments later the barrier rose, and she was back in the vehicle and driving underground.

Six or seven seconds. She didn't have the high heels and short skirt the previous woman had to slow her down. But he could have done it.

The temptation to take the shot was strong, even now. Anger burned in his veins and his trigger finger twitched at the thought.

But she was no longer important. No plan survives first contact with the enemy, he remembered.

Now he had bigger problems. Kemp and Miller suspected he'd killed Snout. Which meant they'd be looking to get rid of Kahler soon. Maybe as soon as tomorrow, when he reported for more deliveries.

He needed a new plan.

CHAPTER 46

JESS CLEARED A SPACE on her dining room table. Though she had the urge to clean the whole apartment, she would wait until the workmen finished rebuilding the wall between her hallway and kitchen. They'd be back tomorrow to generate more dust.

She ate lentil soup and toast. The heat from the liquid felt good in her throat. She surfed a couple of news channels, then switched off the television. The warehouse shooting was still getting coverage, but there was nothing new to report.

As she placed the bowl in the dishwasher, her phone rang. The call was from the Fort Cavazos area code, but she didn't recognize the number.

"Jess Kimball," she said when she picked up.

"Karl Oppenheimer here. I found the guy who shipped the rifles. He's in the system."

"That's good news. What's his name?"

"Charles Brantley. I remember him well. Miserable SOB. Always complaining. Mainly about money," Oppenheimer said. "I ignored him at the time. He was retiring. No reason to get drawn into his misery, you know?"

"I do. I'll go talk to him. Do we know where he is?" Jess asked.

"The pension group has an address on file," Oppenheimer replied. "So yeah, I can give you that."

Jess bit her lip. Was he fishing for money? She could offer a tip reward in an instant. But that wouldn't bring his brother back to life.

"The guy's in Denver."

"Karl. Listen. Do you need money? How much do you owe?"

He ignored her questions. "I'll text you the address when we hang up."

"Karl. Come on. Let me help you."

He went silent. "It doesn't matter. It's just a bit more."

"What do you mean?"

He was silent longer this time. "Local cops wanted to hand the problem to the army. Army was like 'Happens every day, son. Move on.' That's what they told me. But I can't, you know."

His voice cracked at the end of the sentence.

She waited while he regained his composure.

"I followed my brother into the army," he said quietly.

Jess listened.

"Good job, HH told me. And it is. I love the army. Always have."

"Seems like there might be more to this, though," Jess said.

"Definitely. Your only brother doesn't get killed every day. Not on American soil. Not on his day off. Not by some..." He sighed. "So I hired a PI. Charged a lot of money and didn't learn much."

Jess pressed the phone closer to her ear. "What did the PI actually find out?"

"Nothing I didn't already have from the police reports."

"They must have found something?"

"Nothing. A total waste."

"Why didn't you tell me?"

"Because he didn't find anything. And I...I felt conned. So much money, and nothing."

He wouldn't be the first person conned after the violent death of a loved one. The desire to bring the killers to justice was too strong to ignore.

"There's no shame in trying to find your brother's killer," Jess said kindly.

He grunted.

"Email me his report and I'll try to follow up," Jess said.

"I don't have an electronic copy and it's pretty long. Lots of pages, not many answers."

"Right. So overnight a copy to me. And include the PI bills with it," Jess said.

"Okay." he replied. "You'll have it in the morning."

She took a deep breath. "I can't promise you I will find your brother's killer. But I do promise I won't give up. I never give up. Okay?"

"Uh-huh."

"And if that PI conned you in any way, I can expose that, too."

He went quiet. "I'll send you Brantley's address now. He definitely shipped the K10s. And he probably side hustled the one you're looking for. But I don't think he pulled the trigger to kill HH. Brantley is a weasel, but he's not a killer."

"Every lead helps."

"Yeah." He paused. "Thanks."

Jess ended the call and sat thinking about the case.

Karl Oppenheimer had come up against the same bureaucratic indifference so many people encountered. Sometimes it was because the organizations were overloaded. Sometimes there was a question about jurisdiction. And sometimes the bureaucracy simply didn't want to know the answer. Whatever the case, Karl Oppenheimer deserved to know what happened to his brother. No question about that much.

Oppenheimer texted Charles Brantley's address to her cell phone. No phone number was included, and she couldn't find it on the web.

The address was twenty minutes away. A short drive. If she went this evening, she might have a better chance of finding him at home.

She grabbed her keys and headed for her Jeep.

CHAPTER 47

JESS TOOK THE FREEWAY exit for Brantley's apartment. The complex looked new. Front gates were access controlled, but she arrived immediately behind a large SUV and followed it inside.

The navigation route led her around a large swimming pool that was covered for the winter. Parking spaces were numbered, and a few were labeled for visitors. The building numbers were hard to read from the drive, so she parked and finished her search on foot.

Brantley's apartment was two blocks away on the second floor. She climbed the steps, knocked on his door, and waited.

"What?" a man's voice demanded from behind the door.

She held out her press card so it could be seen through the peephole. "Jessica Kimball. *Taboo Magazine*."

The door cracked open. Cigarette smoke wafted out. A man scowled through the gap, a few days' growth on his chin. He looked Jess up and down.

"I don't want no subscription," he said, his voice hoarse.

"I'm not selling anything."

He grunted. The tension relaxed from his face. He opened the door wider, but he didn't invite her inside.

He was not much taller than her. His dark brown hair was gray around the ears. He wore a ragged dark blue jacket with bright yellow trim outlining the sleeves and pockets. His jeans and sweatshirt had seen better days.

"You were at Fort Cavazos, right?" she said.

"My last five years, yeah." He stood a little straighter.

"The army has been telling me about shipments." She had the feeling she'd get further with him if she used the army's name.

"What shipments?"

"Guns that were sent from Fort Cavazos to the Holston plant to be destroyed."

He shrugged. "We shipped tons of things every day. Literally."

"There were six of these rifles. Early prototype K10s."

He shook his head as if he had no memory. "We shipped so much stuff. It's all a blur."

"One of the K10s got swapped for an M4."

"Mix-ups happen. We're only human."

"The M4 was put in the wrong gun case. Which means the mistake would have been obvious," Jess said, making it plain that she didn't believe his feigned ignorance.

"We could have shipped a nuke and not remember it. Like I said, so much stuff. Every damned day."

"But someone had to swap out the K10 for the M4 in this case."

He closed the door an inch. "You trying to accuse me of something?"

"I'm just trying to find out what happened."

"You kidding me? About one mix-up in tons and tons of shipping over how many years?"

Jess stepped back and squared her shoulders. "The K10 rifle that didn't get destroyed was actually used in two shootings earlier this week. People were killed."

Brantley stepped back, closing the door even further. "I don't know nothing about that. I just did my job. If something got mixed up, well, I'm very sorry. But I don't remember squat about no mixed-up rifles."

He put his hand on the door to close it. "I got a job to go to now. Gotta work."

"The army told me you were retired," Jess said.

"On my pension? No chance. Need some part-time work just to get by."

"You're working part-time in the evenings?"

"What is this? Twenty questions? I gotta go." Brantley closed the door.

Jess walked back to her Jeep. Brantley was lying. She'd bet money on it. But lying about what, exactly? And why?

She sat in her Jeep and picked up the phone to call Henry. Brantley hustled from his apartment to a silver Honda Accord, still wearing his blue jacket with its yellow trim. Quickly, he fired up the sedan and drove away.

Jess dropped the phone and followed.

Brantley tore through the streets, twenty or thirty miles an hour above the speed limit. Jess kept well back, trying to anticipate his lane changes and stay unnoticed.

After fifteen minutes, he braked hard and turned left into an auto repair lot.

Jess cruised past the entrance and pulled into the next parking lot, a one-time resale shop that had closed down.

The clock on her dash read 7:47. Brantley said he had a job. But he seemed to be in a panic to get to work at such an odd start time.

Jess pulled on a fleece hat and stepped out of the Jeep. Brantley might have a reason for being in a rush. Maybe he was supposed to have clocked in at seven thirty. Maybe his boss was a stickler for timekeeping. His pension probably wasn't great. Maybe he was worried about losing the job.

As she crossed the parking lot, Brantley's Honda raced around from the back of the garage. She hurried to her Jeep and started the engine as he barreled out onto the main road.

She followed as closely as she dared.

He slowed his pace to take the freeway. She hung behind an eighteen-wheeler, moving out from time to time to keep Brantley in view.

Brantley took the exit for Cherry Hills Village. He slowed further when he reached the surface streets.

They passed illuminated mansions with manicured lawns. Fences and automatic gates ringed each home. Range Rovers, Escalades, and Lincolns seemed to be parked in every drive.

Brantley took his Honda through a couple of rapid turns and entered a narrow lane along the back of a line of houses. Jess drove past the lane, which was too narrow to allow her to follow Brantley without being observed.

She did a quick U-turn, parked behind a large tree, and checked the map on her phone. The lane Brantley drove deadended at an enormous estate featuring a Queen Anne mansion.

Brantley's terse and false responses back at his apartment might have been motivated by his desire to remain uninvolved. But what was the link between a small auto repair garage and a multimilliondollar home in Cherry Hills?

Before she could find out, the Honda emerged from the lane. Jess followed as he retraced his route to the freeway.

This time the Accord exited the freeway for the Sunshine Park area. The contrast was dramatic. A whole street in this area costs less than one Cherry Hills mansion.

Most Sunshine Park houses had bars across the windows and broken lights above their front doors. Pickup trucks squeezed onto driveways built when vehicles were far smaller.

Jess hung well back, and the Honda was barely visible ahead as it navigated twists and turns.

On Redwood Drive, brake lights flared, and Brantley stopped. Jess switched off her headlights, rolled to a halt behind a pickup parked on the side of the road, and waited in the dark.

She noticed movement around the Honda. Maybe two people. She inched her window down and heard indistinct male voices.

Moments later, the garage door opened. Brantley drove in and the door closed. She waited, still listening intently, but only the sound of the freeway filled the night air.

She tried to make sense of Brantley's movements. After considering several scenarios, the only conclusion she reached was that something felt off. She couldn't identify the problem with the limited information she'd collected so far.

She took her Glock from her glove compartment, exited the Jeep, and locked it behind her.

The night air was colder than ever. The temperature and the humidity combined to steal her body heat. Her new jacket's pockets were big enough for her to keep her hand on the Glock as she walked.

She skirted around a couple of badly parked cars as she covered the hundred yards to the place where Brantley entered. Some of the houses seemed occupied and some didn't. Like every neighborhood everywhere.

She checked behind her. The Jeep was a good distance away. Perhaps too far. She should have moved it closer. But she was committed now. No going back.

The garage where Brantley parked had lights burning in both the front and rear. Two lights on the house lit up as she walked past. Infrared sensors, she assumed.

The house Brantley entered was the single-story ranch style of all the others on the street. The front door was solid steel. Across the windows, heavy drapes blocked all but a tiny sliver of light. Fence panels and overgrown weeds blocked access along the sides of the building.

Two black, late-model Cadillacs were parked in front of what Jess assumed was the living room. Polished chrome and metallic paint glittered in the faint light, an extravagant contrast to the neighborhood.

The situation frightened her. The house and cars fairly screamed criminal activities of some kind.

CHAPTER 48

JESS KEPT WALKING, HOPING for a side road to loop around behind the building and return to her Jeep without being seen. After two minutes, the road dead-ended.

She slowed her pace as she turned around and walked back on the opposite side of the narrow street as if she were out for a casual stroll. But no one walked around in this neighborhood and definitely not at night.

The nearest streetlamp was on the opposite side of her Jeep. Moonlight cast a faint glow. Approaching the house and the Cadillacs, she kept her head forward, straining her eyes to look sideways.

"Wait up," a man called out.

She kept walking.

"Wait up," he repeated, a hard edge to his voice.

She looked back toward the house. The man stepped from behind a tree and crossed the road, rapidly blocking her path.

She sidestepped, but he countered her move.

"What are you doing here?" he asked, menace unmistakable.

"Walking."

"Just enjoying the scenery, huh?"

She didn't respond.

"It's a deadend street," he said.

"So I found."

"Not a great place for walking, either."

She shrugged.

"What's your name?"

"What's yours?"

He handed her a card. "Neighborhood watch."

Jess glanced at the card for the briefest instant, not wanting to take her eyes off him. NEIGHBORHOOD WATCH was printed in bold letters with unreadable text beneath. No picture.

"How do I know this is real?" she asked.

"Who else would be out here at night watching for people like you sizing the place up?"

Jess opened her mouth to reply. Before she had a chance, she heard a male voice she recognized. Charles Brantley.

Calling urgently from the front door without shouting, Brantley said, "She's the one. The woman at my place."

The first man clicked open a switchblade, which had been concealed in his left hand. "That so?"

She whipped the Glock from her pocket and pointed it at the man's chest. "Move. Back inside."

She nodded toward the house.

He didn't move. He didn't drop the switchblade.

She took two rapid steps back and fired at the man's feet. He jerked sideways involuntarily.

Jess capitalized on the opportunity, diving forward and elbowing him into the weeds at the side of the road. Then she ran for the Jeep.

Following behind her, she heard the first man shouting as he batted bushes and plants and trash aside. A second man hurtled diagonally across the weeds, turning to face her just as she reached him.

Jess tucked down, ramming her shoulder low into his rib cage.

"Ooof!" he said as he grabbed her, and they tumbled onto the road.

He turned her around to face the houses on the street. She had momentum and managed to pry herself out of his grasp and jump up to run.

Gunfire chased her as she ran along a driveway midway between Brantley's house and her Jeep. Dull thuds landed too close as their bullets hit the trees.

A low chain-link fence ran along the side of the building. Jess scissored over the fence to the house in the back.

Angry dogs barked terrifyingly loud enough to wake the dead. She glanced in every direction, attempting to locate the dogs, but didn't see them. All she could do was hope she wasn't trapped inside their fences.

Jess hurdled another chain-link fence. They saw her and shouted her location. She could run for miles, but all they needed was one clear shot to bring her down.

The next house had a detached garage. The door was open, and a car was backing out. For half a second, Jess tried to catch a ride. Only to give up when she realized she'd be putting an innocent stranger in jeopardy.

Jess ran from the front yard toward the end of the driveway. The car paused at the road briefly to confirm traffic had cleared. Just before the car drove away, Jess yelled, "Wait!" She pitched her voice loud enough to be heard in the open air but not inside the car.

Then she doubled back around the far side of the house and pressed herself between two garbage cans, pistol ready at her side. She fought to quiet her breathing.

The car pulled away from the drive into the street.

Chain-link fences rattled, and heavy footsteps pounded across the front lawn and driveway.

The car's engine slowed a moment at the end of the street. The pursuers ran after it, shouting for the driver to stop. He didn't.

Jess heard the engine speed away even as her heartbeat sounded in her ears.

Indistinct voices snapped off short sentences nearby. Her pursuers were coming back, talking on the phone. They struggled to recall the car's license plate.

Then they were arguing and making excuses. Were they calling for backup? After a few moments, they disconnected and stood in the street in front of the house. One of their phones dinged with a message. They took off down the street at a full-out run.

Jess didn't move. Vehicles drove by and dogs barked occasionally, but the men chasing her were gone.

She swapped the Glock from hand to hand in her cold-numbed fingers. She regulated her deep breathing to keep her crouched body oxygen charged.

Jess scanned the darkened streets looking for her Jeep.

She eased herself from between the garbage cans, checking for movement in all directions. Satisfied no one was observing her, she stood and stretched the cold from her joints.

There was only one possible way back to her Jeep, so she walked along the road parallel to it. Reaching the crossroad, she waited on the corner. She heard a ping like a phone receiving a message, followed by another.

Someone was there. More than one, probably.

They might have found her Jeep and believed she would be stupid enough to walk straight to it. They'd be disappointed.

Keeping to the shadows, Jess turned and walked a mile in the opposite direction. She found a street with a gas station and access to the freeway. She called a ride-sharing service. Ten minutes later an SUV arrived, and she climbed in.

In the backseat, she called Henry with a rundown of her evening following Brantley and the address at the house he'd entered. To his credit, he didn't admonish her for anything.

"I've been worried. I'm glad you're okay," he said with obvious relief. "I'll have your Jeep collected and returned to you in the morning."

As the SUV merged onto the freeway, she saw a flickering yellow glow behind her. Had they set fire to her Jeep? A warning, a threat, or simply retaliation?

A few minutes later, Henry called back. Denver PD had arrived on the scene. Her Jeep was untouched, and he'd return it in the morning, but the fire department was tackling a blaze at the house Brantley entered. The occupants were already gone.

"Thanks for the help, Henry," Jess said. "Let's have breakfast in the morning. We've got a lot to talk about."

CHAPTER 49

KAHLER SAT IN THE stolen Volkswagen eating a burger and fries. He'd been careless and he was angry about it.

Miller had tailed him and Kahler hadn't noticed. How long had Miller been following? Minutes? An hour? Surely not much more. He would have noticed.

Or at least, he liked to think so.

His burger tasted like vinegar. He lifted the bun. The jackasses had added pickles. What the hell?

He threw the offending vegetables out the window and took another bite. The faint taste of vinegar was still there, which pissed him off. But he was cold and hungry, so he ate the burger anyway.

What should he do now that Miller knew about the reporter?

He hadn't taken any action against Kahler, and he probably wouldn't. Not right away, at least.

Miller repeatedly insisted that the whole plan to take over distribution in Denver depended on drawing no unwanted attention. As if they might actually fly under the radar on this.

Stupid idea. Zero chance this thing would go unnoticed, regardless of how Miller's crew handled themselves.

Miller was a drug dealer. Finny, too. The Denver territory came with plenty of attention. Most of it negative.

The gunfight at the Golden's warehouse was all over the news. Every pusher and middleman knew about the change in distribution.

What difference could killing that reporter possibly make? Zero. Zip. Nada.

Kahler shook his head, finished his burger, and fisted the fries into his mouth.

He'd joined Miller's crew for the money. Uncle Sam's soldiers weren't well paid, and he'd served the army long enough to dig himself into a significant financial hole.

It started with poker. He'd play with other soldiers to pass the time during deployments. Soon his gambling became an addiction he couldn't shake. Casinos, private parties, tournaments. He didn't dwell on his debts. But he needed to find a way to pay them off.

When he was on a bender one night, a guy he met in a dive bar off base near Fort Cavazos offered to help him out. Turned out the guy was an army shipping clerk with only a few months left before retirement. He'd been looking for a big payday, and he said he'd found it.

He told Kahler about Miller.

Miller was already in the drug distribution business. He had a crew. He had a network. Neither the shipping clerk nor Kahler had those elements in place and no desire to build them.

Kahler agreed with the shipping clerk that partnering with Miller was the best option.

Instantly, Kahler realized the shipping clerk's idea had the potential to make him rich. Really rich. Rich beyond his current needs, at least.

Right away Miller was keen to make it work. He saw the potential as clearly as Kahler and the shipping clerk had.

Miller's experience was working with thieves and killers. He trusted no one. Which was how he held on to power as well as how he stayed alive.

Like any big business deal, the three unlikely entrepreneurs needed start-up cash to make it happen. Which was the second piece Miller could bring to the table.

Miller lined up the kid working at First Aurora Bank to steal enough money to buy large quantities of drugs. Kahler had asked several times, but Miller kept the kid's exact methods to himself.

Of course, not all of Miller's decisions were stupid. He'd stayed alive in a dangerous game for a while now. He'd found the kid at the bank. He'd kept the method of stealing the bank's money secret. He'd also kept his gang of thieves and killers in line.

Miller understood his people in a visceral way. He knew they were loyal to money and no other master. So he divided the first day's take instantly. All twelve gang members. Two hundred thousand each for one day's work. Cash. Right there and then.

Kahler grinned. Money. The glue that binds.

Miller's crew was reassured and determined to move forward. All except Kahler.

Kahler was pissed.

Hanging around to deliver drugs and earn his share had never been Kahler's plan. He'd expected to wait a couple of weeks maybe. Until the cash mountain got big enough. Everyone would be comfortable, feeling good.

Then he'd make his move. Easy to walk in, pop a few of Miller's guys to show he meant business, and walk out with the whole stash.

All the money, all at once.

But with Miller passing out the profits after every job, Kahler saw he'd need to take the money sooner than he'd expected. Might have to take some inventory to sell later, too.

Kahler finished the french fries and placed his hand on the suitcase with the K10 inside. Miller didn't have a clue. He thought Kahler was as satisfied as the rest of the crew to get a measly $200K.

He felt his anger rise in his chest. Without him, Miller would still be a two-bit dealer taking scraps from Finny's table. What a fool.

Miller was right, though. Kahler wouldn't bite the hand that fed him. That would be too little, too late.

He planned to rip Miller's whole damned body apart.

CHAPTER 50

KAHLER CRAWLED FROM HIS bunk bed in the attic half-asleep. The tiny unheated room shocked his eyes open as soon as his bare feet touched the floor.

He picked up a loaded MP9 submachine gun from beside the bed. Without the stock, it was small enough to fit in an improvised holster, which he looped over his shoulder and cinched tight. He pulled on a loose-fitting hoodie to conceal the bulge.

Kahler's watch showed 4:00 a.m. He crawled to the window because the pitched ceiling was too low at that point. A small single-pane window revealed the overcast sky.

An industrial area sprawled four floors below him. Workshops were mixed in with larger warehouses. Plumes of steam drifted from vents in flat rooftops.

Eighteenwheelers and delivery vans sat silent at the loading docks, waiting for cargo and drivers.

A few blocks away, the city was waking. Traffic noises sounded muffled through the single pane of glass. Office workers on the freeway, Kahler assumed.

Everything he could see and hear out there showed life and movement.

Except the sedan at the corner of the street. It was parked on the cross street, uncomfortably close to the intersection.

Only the front half of the car was visible from the attic window. The hood, the windshield, and the driver's door.

Not the same car as the night before. That was a Chevy. This one was an older-model Honda Accord. Same color, same location, same sedan shape as the Chevy. But definitely different.

Kahler slid back onto his bunk. No question. They were watching him. He'd expected it. In fact, he'd expected worse.

Which was why he'd moved from the relative comfort of his bed a floor below to the attic storage closet directly above his studio apartment. He'd left wineglasses by the doors and windows, which would shatter and alert him if they broke in.

Miller must have settled for keeping an eye on him for now instead of a more aggressive approach. Kahler took that as a good sign. Both drivers would report that he had returned to his place and stayed all night. No moonlighting, as Miller had insisted.

The watcher in the Honda, stuck down there on the early shift, must occupy one of the lower rungs of Miller's crew. Probably one of the thugs who used his bulk for intimidation. Guns and close-quarters combat were not his wheelhouse. Good to know.

Kahler crawled from the storage closet above his room down into a corridor. A single bare bulb illuminated the far end of the hallway, but the apartment doors along both walls remained closed.

Kahler moved into his apartment. He twisted and turned, rotating his arms and stretching his hamstrings to warm his muscles. He pulled his jacket and the suitcase containing the K10 from his closet.

He still had the Volkswagen's key in his pocket. He'd parked the car across the street. The watcher had a clear sight line to the Volkswagen. Which was probably the point.

Kahler donned his jacket, tightened his boot laces, and carried the suitcase down the stairs to the ground floor.

"Showtime," he murmured as he pushed the front door open and stepped into the frosty morning air.

He aimed straight for the Volkswagen, keeping his head pointed forward while he watched the Honda in his periphery.

The Honda's windows were heavily tinted, but he could see the dark, rectangular outline of the headrests above the rounder shape of the seats. The driver was shrouded in darkness. His shoulders weren't broad enough to be Kemp or one of the other muscled enforcers.

Kahler's confidence expanded as he unlocked the Volkswagen, stowed the suitcase, and slipped behind the steering wheel.

The Volkswagen coughed to life in the frigid cold. Kahler flipped the heater to max. He'd trained in everything from sweating jungles to the frozen wastelands in Alaska. But the last thing he wanted today was his body slowed by the cold.

As he drove away, the Honda pulled out to follow. The driver's headlights were so close, Kahler could easily keep track of the car. Which was not okay. The area offered plenty of options to lose the Honda, but they required a wider gap between the two vehicles.

He'd need to improvise.

Kahler increased his speed and took a couple of left turns, looping around the block toward an unoccupied workshop. The gate to its potholed parking lot hung off its hinges.

A half-open roll-up door was the only way in. The door had long ago seized in place. Kahler made a quick visual assessment and pulled straight into the space.

The Volkswagen barely scraped underneath the door. The rusted metal dragged across the Volkswagen's roof with a loud, squealing noise that made Kahler cringe.

Inside and to the left, several open doorways admitted the weak morning light. Kahler gunned it to the first doorway. He braked hard, jumped out, and ran for the opening with his MP9 in hand.

He'd left the Volkswagen running and the driver's door open.

Kahler heard the Honda approach and stop on the main road, just past the entrance. Seconds ticked by, but the driver didn't leave his vehicle.

Kahler intended the warehouse to be a killing zone away from witnesses. But the trap only worked if his prey came inside. Which, so far, the driver had not.

"Time to change things up," Kahler said as he switched the MP9 to single shot.

He moved to a broken window to allow the Honda driver to see the muzzle flash. He fired three shots as if he were executing a target. One shot for the kill. Two more to be sure.

The driver dashed out of the car with a small pistol in his hand. He kept to the edge of the parking lot and approached the far end of the building.

Kahler lost sight of him, but he could hear the man's shoes crunching on the frozen ground as he approached the empty Volkswagen with its engine running.

The man was close. Kahler heard metallic clicks as if he were fidgeting nervously with his gun. The guy was a total amateur.

Glass crunched under his feet. The sound reverberated around the empty warehouse. Kahler centered himself in the doorway, half-in, half-out.

A shot rang out. Kahler's jacket twitched, and the fabric pulled on his back. He twisted to see the driver waiting on the outside of the building near the roll-up door. He had his gun leveled on Kahler.

Charles Brantley. The shipping department guy. The one who first introduced Kahler to Miller. The one who helped Kahler steal the K10.

A frown crossed Brantley's face. Something bothered him.

Perhaps he'd seen the Volkswagen's door open and the engine running and expected to find Kahler dead on the ground. Whatever its cause, Brantley's hesitation was all Kahler needed.

The first shot hit Brantley's chest. The impact was off-center, turning him sideways.

As he closed the distance between them, Kahler fired the second and third shots to be sure. The second hit Brantley's throat and the third, his head.

The result was a pulpy, bloody mess.

Kahler grabbed Brantley's coat collar, dragged him under the roll-up door, and dumped the body into the shadows inside the building. Kahler had no qualms about leaving Brantley behind.

The shots would have drawn unwanted attention. He needed to leave.

There were CCTV cameras in the area. He couldn't leave the Volkswagen here. He'd dump it first chance and steal something better.

CHAPTER 51

MILLER SAT AT HIS desk, thumb tapping the metal while he waited. The desk was government surplus. Probably dated from World War II. The drawers squealed on runners long since seized whenever he struggled to open them.

His burner phone buzzed. He recognized Kemp's number and took the call. "What?"

"We've lost Kahler but found Brantley."

"What d'you mean?"

"Kahler's gone. Brantley's dead," Kemp said. "No cops here yet. Don't know about witnesses."

Miller thought about things for a moment. "Can you hide the body?"

"Not well enough."

"Okay. Get his ID and his weapons. He had a car from our pool. Don't leave the car."

"We're on it," Kemp said.

Miller terminated the call, already working on a plan for damage control.

Planning was Miller's greatest skill. Moving his organization to the top spot in Denver's drug supply chain required careful planning of the covert operation and then bringing it down with a heavy, unbeatable hammer.

That hammer was Theo Kahler. But Kahler was not a member of Miller's team. He'd become a straight-up problem. A big one.

Miller managed his team. Organized and motivated them. Applied pressure or dodged problems as necessary. He knew his guys. Knew them well enough to predict and persuade. But, obviously, not Kahler.

What was going on with that guy, anyway? Miller had been ignoring Kahler's issues and now realized his mistake. Losing Brantley was okay. He'd served his purpose when he brought Kahler and the K10 into the mix. At this point Brantley was just another mouth to feed.

But Kahler was another matter entirely. Kahler could blow the whole operation. Miller wouldn't allow it. His sniper skills had been essential to the plan to take over Finny's territory. With that accomplished, Miller didn't need Kahler anymore.

Having made the decision to terminate Kahler, the next question was how and when to do it to avoid blowback.

Kahler had more issues than he'd admitted. Starting with that reporter. He'd been sitting on a rooftop, planning to take her out. She must know something Kahler wanted to conceal.

Made sense. Whatever she knew, it had to be personal to Kahler specifically. Otherwise, he'd have told Miller and brought the whole team down on her head.

Miller bit his lip. He didn't care about Kahler, but he did care about himself. He wanted to preserve his team, too. It'd taken years to get to the top, and regardless of what Kahler thought, Miller wasn't stupid.

He knew one day he'd find himself in Finny's shoes, dead in the mud somewhere. But not yet.

Kemp called again. "We're clear. Nothing left on Brantley to identify him or point to us. But they'll figure it out eventually."

"They got nothing to link Brantley to us."

"Except Kahler," Kemp said flatly.

Miller replied with cold anger. "Think I don't know that?"

"I shoulda shot him in the back when I had the chance," Kemp said. "We gotta do something."

"Agreed. Take two men. Find Kahler and get rid of him. Somewhere quiet where you can hide the body," Miller replied.

"You know that ain't gonna be easy." Kemp grunted. "What if he turns up at Easy Tire?"

"He'll be outmanned if he sets foot near here. He's got no backup," Miller said, attempting to calm Kemp's bad instincts. "Even if Kahler finds backup, he ain't got enough cash to buy quick loyalty."

"He could attack at night. Army trained him for that," Kemp said, but his tone was calmer.

"We have cameras. We can double our guards."

"And if he goes to the cops?"

"What would be the point of that? Nah. Ain't his style. He came to us for the money. Pure and simple," Miller said. "And he won't give it up easily."

"We could get more muscle. I know some guys."

"We don't want to draw more heat here. So we're going to move. You and me. Right now. Up to the hut. Kahler don't know about that place," Miller said, making his plan as he worked it through. "Then, if we have to clear out of town, we can take the goods with us."

Kemp whistled. "Guys won't like hearing that. Some are already asking when they're getting paid again."

"Enough!" Miller slammed his fist angrily against the metal desk. "They just got a year's worth of money already. Next payment's in seven days. That's what we agreed. Anybody got a problem with the schedule, you send them straight to me and I'll deal with it."

"They just—"

"Just nothing. You make damned sure they're being careful. No new cars, Rolexes, expensive women. Like we said."

Kemp sighed. "No one's partying behind our backs. They're a solid crew. Disciplined. We can count on them."

"Good. We got enough trouble with Kahler." Miller glanced out the window. The sky was still darker than it should have been. "Bad weather's coming. Who's watching the girl?"

"Dayton."

"We need to get up there. Encourage her. She's taking too long. One more transfer would double our money. Then you and Dayton can eliminate Kahler, and we can get back to business."

CHAPTER 52

JESS WOKE EARLIER THAN usual, set coffee to brew, and checked her phone.

Henry had sent several text messages. Her Jeep had been cleared from the scene at the drug dealer's house and parked outside her apartment building. Henry kept the keys, so she'd have to use her spare.

The owner of the dealer's house had been out of the country for six months. The neighbors thought new people had bought it, but they were squatting. The owner claimed to know nothing about them.

A patrol car had been sent to Brantley's place, but he'd cleared out his apartment and disappeared. He was on watch lists with the buses, trains, and airlines.

Henry's last text apologized for missing breakfast. He had meetings back at the office.

Jess poured a second cup of hot, black coffee, ate a bagel, and stared through the hole in the kitchen wall into the hallway. The repairs wouldn't start tomorrow. Her home would be disrupted for a few more days.

She glanced outside at the growing traffic. To the west, dark gray clouds covered the sky as far as she could see. Ski resorts in Utah had been hoping for snow. Humid air was mixing with a northwestern cold front. But the timing hadn't worked out. Colorado resorts were a more likely spot for the conditions to combine and produce about two feet of fresh snow.

Jess's phone rang. She glanced at the local number she didn't recognize, but she picked up. "Hello."

"This is Melissa Larson," the caller said in a hushed voice.

"Good morning. Is Mr. Larson back home?" Jess asked.

"No. I called to ask you if you had any news."

"Sorry, no."

"You would tell me. No matter what. Right?" Melissa said, her voice still low.

"Of course." Jess frowned. "You okay?"

"Worried," Melissa said. She took a deep breath. "I just…I'm in Jerry's study. I couldn't talk in front of Tom."

"Your son?" Jess asked.

"He doesn't know and"—Melissa's voice hardened—"he doesn't need to know."

"Know what?" Jess said slowly.

"I don't go into Jerry's study often. But I did now. I mean, anything that might help explain what happened, right?"

Jess frowned, unsure where this conversation was going. "Sure. Of course."

"He has a desk calendar. Big thing with notes all over. And phone numbers," Melissa said. "I've been calling them. They're mostly banks, businesspeople, and such. But one had no area code."

"Denver?" Jess said.

"I tried that, but the number is out of service. So I thought, what would Jerry want to hide? So I tried 212."

"Manhattan?"

Melissa nodded. "It rang and I recognized the voice. Kirsten Ottoman."

"Who's she?" Jess asked, puzzled.

"When we first got married, Jerry worked on Wall Street. He had an affair with her. We argued, but we got over it. It was one of the reasons we moved out West. To get away from her."

"You think he's been in touch with her?"

Melissa sighed. "The desk calendar was open to this month. He must have written her number there recently."

"Did you talk to her when you called?"

"I hung up. I mean, hearing her voice again..."

"I can check on her," Jess said. "Give me the number."

"She's still a partner at the finance company. Married again. Doing pretty well by the looks of it."

"You tracked her down?"

"The internet can be an amazing thing," Melissa said. "Let me know what you learn."

She sent a message to the office to request a full background on Mr. and Mrs. Larson and Kirsten Ottoman. Mandy replied in a moment confirming.

Henry called. "Meeting's over."

"Progress?"

He gave a short laugh. "On what? The person who attacked you? Justin Rooney? The shoot-out at the warehouse? The sniper? Or the people disappearing from First Aurora Bank? Have I missed anything?"

"A drug dealer's house and Brantley's visit to Cherry Hills Village?"

"Okay, okay."

She bit her lip. "Yeah, it's a list all right."

"We've called in evidence response teams from Kansas City and Salt Lake, forensics is stacked up with work, and Denver PD has several teams chasing leads. No one believes all these things are unrelated. But the firearms evidence is all we have to actually link them."

"What about Lucy Cranfield?"

"She's in the mix. And there's a lot of consternation about First Aurora as well."

"Okay. Well, I learned something new." Jess finished her coffee and refilled the mug. "Jerry Larson had an affair the year he got married. Woman's name is Kirsten Ottoman. Partner at a finance company in New York. Mrs. Larson was snooping and found her number on her husband's calendar. She thinks he might have renewed the affair."

"Interesting. I'll have someone check her out."

Jess nodded. Henry was one of the FBI's most patient and detail-oriented agents. When he finished a case, his work was a big reason the prosecutions were successful. But the work took its toll on him, too.

They ended the call with some casual banter, and she promised to meet him for lunch at his office.

Mandy sent ten pages of information on the Larsons gleaned from the internet and the many databases to which the magazine subscribed. Jess thumbed through the material, but the Larsons seemed to be a normal family. If they had skeletons in their closets, none had made it all the way to *Taboo*'s sources.

But Mandy's research on Kirsten Ottoman was more fruitful. First, Ottoman had worked for Bensons since college.

During that time, Ottoman had been cleared in three separate federal investigations. No charges were ever filed against her or Bensons.

Hiromi Tsui had identified Bensons as the company funding Jerry Larson's home liquidations.

Jess moved Kirsten Ottoman up on her list of priorities. She wriggled into her bulletproof vest and donned her jacket over the top before she headed out.

Her Jeep started up easily despite the cold. The heavy snow clouds made the morning seem darker than usual. If it snowed, she'd be okay in her Jeep.

As she put the transmission in gear, her phone vibrated. A message from Mandy. A developing story. Shots fired on the outskirts of the city.

Jess was tempted to ignore it. But the shooting happened at an abandoned warehouse, which felt like a strange echo of the Golden's warehouse shooting.

She decided to stop by on her way to First Aurora Bank. She could see the warehouse from a significant distance because of the number of official vehicles out front.

The police presence was substantial for a single-victim shooting. Two television vans and a smattering of onlookers clogged the street parking.

She found a parking spot directly behind the warehouse. She walked around the block to a small crowd clustered around yellow crime scene tape bordering the warehouse entrance.

Jess didn't recognize any of the officers on duty, so she waited on the sidewalk with the others.

The place looked old. The walls were covered with years of thick black grime. Windows were cracked and broken. Tiles were missing from the roof. An ambulance, two squad cars, and a crime scene van were parked close to the front entrance.

Bright lights, powered by a thick cable running from the crime scene van, illuminated the interior of the building. Techs in white coveralls studied the ground around a half-open roll-up door. Small cones marked the location of evidence they found.

A white tarp had been hung between two poles to block what Jess presumed was a body from public view. A man in a suit and heavy coat was talking to a detective. Jess saw his badge around his neck.

A few moments later, the ambulance crew emerged with a body zipped into a black bag on a stretcher.

Jess watched them lift the stretcher into the rear of the ambulance.

As the ambulance pulled away, she texted Henry. He called back.

"You okay?" he asked.

"Yeah. They removed a body from the warehouse here. Any idea who the victim is?"

"Got word through Norton that Denver PD is pretty sure it's Brantley," Henry said. "Shot multiple times. Close range. That's the judgment of the detective on the scene. We'll know more later."

Jess nodded, thinking about the timing. "Do they know when he was shot?"

"Can't be a big-time window since you saw him alive and moving the night before."

"What about his visit to that garage?" Jess asked.

"Denver PD is running that down."

They talked a few moments more, said their goodbyes, and hung up.

Jess stared at the warehouse as if she could decipher answers to her questions in the grime.

Why was Brantley there? Didn't he have anywhere better to go? Friends? Colleagues?

Hiding in an abandoned warehouse seemed desperate. But why hadn't he cleared out of Denver, then?

She glanced around the parking lot. Brantley was driving a silver Honda the night before and it wasn't parked in the lot now.

Had Brantley been killed elsewhere and dumped at the warehouse?

Casual observers drifted away after the body was removed and the on-air television presenters departed. The media support crews packed up their gear and followed a few minutes later.

Denver PD crime scene techs were still busy and the officers watching the thinning crowd seemed bored. The onlookers filtered back into a building on the opposite side of the street until only two men remained, both older, one with a full beard and one, a goatee. They argued in hushed voices.

She had to walk past them to reach her Jeep. They went quiet as she approached. She smiled, nodded, and kept walking.

"Hey," one of them called after her.

She turned. The bearded man had his arm up.

"Hey," he said again.

There were police in view and neither of the men looked threatening, but she didn't close the gap.

"What?" she called.

"You that reporter woman?"

The man with a goatee grabbed the bearded man's arm and pulled it down. "Don't do it, man. Don't get involved."

"Involved with what?" Jess asked.

"Well, is it you?" the bearded guy asked.

Jess nodded. "What have you got to say?"

"I'm Juan," the bearded man said as he walked closer. He jerked his thumb toward the second man. "He's Rodrigo."

"Do you know something about this?" She pointed to the warehouse.

"Is there like…I mean…a reward or something?"

"Possibly."

Rodrigo pulled on Juan's arm. "Ain't worth it, man. I'm telling you."

"If it's about what happened over there." Jess tilted her head toward the warehouse. "You need to tell the police."

Juan shook his head.

Rodrigo looked back and forth between Jess and the police at the warehouse. "Look, we don't want no trouble."

Jess waited. Nothing she could offer him without knowing more. Experience had taught her that people either volunteered or they didn't.

Juan grimaced, like he was grinding his teeth. "Okay. Fine. We got here early for work. Everything's quiet-like. Some man scoots in an' out of that place. Kept his head down. Didn't hear no shots nor nothing."

"He takes off in a Honda parked over there." Rodrigo pointed along the street. "Real fast-like."

"What time?"

"Six. Five past maybe."

"And you didn't hear any gunshots?"

Juan shook his head.

"Ever seen other people go into the warehouse?"

"Just kids hang out there sometimes." Juan continued to shake his head. "Place has been empty for years."

"Did you call the police?"

Rodrigo pulled Juan's arm. "We need to go, man."

Juan ignored his friend. "Got no phone."

"What model Honda?"

"Saloon. Silver." He nodded to Rodrigo. "He thinks the plate was like 5273."

Rodrigo stopped pulling. "Maybe. But I don't want my name in no paper. No way."

"Just 5273? That's all you can remember?" Jess asked.

"Those was the last four. That's all I'm saying."

"Why? What are you afraid of?" Jess said, suspecting there might be more that they weren't revealing.

"A guy got shot. Over there." He tilted his head toward the warehouse. "I ain't putting the finger on no drug dealer."

"Why do you think he's a drug dealer?"

"Look at the place. Only reason somebody goes in there is like drugs and stuff. Maybe a deal gone south."

"That's a big assumption."

Juan said, "We share a place up Folsom Ave. There's a lane behind. People in that car meet up with another car. Tuesday night. Wednesday sometimes. Swap a couple of bags. One car to the other, you know? No question what they're up to. That's how we got the plate number. Or part of it anyway."

"There are a lot of Hondas on the road," Jess replied, testing Juan's confidence.

"Yeah. But that one has a dent in the roof. On the passenger side." Juan stared at Jess. "That's all we know."

"Okay. I'll look into it. How can I contact you later?" Jess asked.

Juan shook his head, eyes widening with alarm.

"And don't go printing our names or nothing," Rodrigo said as they walked away.

She watched until they entered a building farther down the street and noted the location.

Jess understood their reluctance to get involved. She didn't blame them.

She texted the Honda's license plate details to Henry, Norton, and Mandy as she walked to the parking spot Rodrigo had pointed out.

She stood in the empty space and scanned the area. Brantley, sitting in his Honda, could have seen the parking lot easily, but his view of the warehouse was blocked.

Was Brantley alone? Or had he arrived with someone else in the Honda? Had he been lured, or maybe forced, into the warehouse?

She turned back to the Honda's parking spot. What if Brantley and his killer arrived separately? There would have been another vehicle. If he took the Honda when he left, the second vehicle might still be parked nearby.

Jess climbed into her Jeep and circled the neighborhood. She photographed the rear of every parked vehicle, including the license plates. Assembling the pictures, she sent them to Norton and Henry along with a brief summary of her conversation with Juan and Rodrigo.

After that, she drove toward First Aurora Bank to probe the connection between Jerry Larson and Kirsten Ottoman.

CHAPTER 53

JESS CALLED TSUI WHILE walking into the building. Tsui appeared at the top of the stairs and beckoned. She was wearing yesterday's clothes. She looked tired and anxious, as if the past twenty-four hours had battered her.

Jess ignored a buzzing message on her phone and followed Tsui into a conference room. A large, highly polished dark wood table filled the center of the space.

Armando sat in the middle seat, fingers on a keyboard and a stack of equipment and wires in front of him. He was wearing yesterday's clothes, too. He sported a day's beard on his face. His eyes were bloodshot and red-rimmed.

"Good morning, Armando."

He grunted in return.

Jess scanned the equipment Armando had piled on the table. Jess recognized the RXP logo on one of the black boxes.

"Who told you?" Tsui said.

"Told me what?" Jess said, glancing toward Armando and back.

Tsui paced around the table. She stood behind Armando, which made him fidget.

"We know what Rooney was doing," Tsui said.

"Partly," added Armando.

"He found a way to instigate a foreign transfer through the bank's SWIFT system."

Jess frowned. "Isn't that how all foreign transfers happen?"

"That's the trick Rooney discovered," Armando said. "Rooney's transfers used First Aurora's codes and security protocols. But his RXP box was registered as a separate system. Like a bank within a bank. A Trojan horse inside our own corral, so to speak."

Jess nodded, slowly grasping what he'd said. "How much did he transfer that way?"

Armando cleared his throat. "Millions."

Tsui nudged him.

"What?" said Armando. "We have to tell people."

She glared at him and exhaled slowly. She walked around the table closer to Jess and said quietly, "Hundred million and change over the past month."

Jess whistled.

"Quite a lot of change, actually," Armando said. "And there were a bunch of smaller transfers over the preceding weeks. I think he was experimenting. Seeing if it worked. If he could get away with it, maybe."

"Can the bank withstand that kind of loss?" Jess said.

Armando raised his eyebrows and shrugged.

"Is that a no?" said Jess.

He shook his head. "Rooney's transfers didn't affect the bank's finances."

"So where did he get the money?"

"Made it."

She frowned. "Stocks? Investments? Drugs? Human trafficking? Art theft?"

Armando shook his head. "He literally created it from nothing. If you know the appropriate encryption keys, you can create money on one computer and send it to another. The receiving computer believes the money's real."

"But money has to be real, actual cash at some point," Jess said.

"Not really." Tsui sighed. "The comptroller of currency, the Fed, and the FDIC oversee transactions as best they can. But even so, a degree of trust is required. We can't count every penny at the end of the night. The value and existence of money has always been based on trust."

"Where did Rooney send the money?"

"Colombia."

"First Aurora's Cali?" Jess asked.

"How did you ever guess," Armando replied sarcastically.

"Is the money Rooney transferred still in the bank at Cali?"

"No." Tsui shook her head. "The deposits were split up and transferred out within minutes. Some transfers stayed in Colombia, and some went international."

"You must know the accounts and where the transfers went?" Jess asked.

"After working on this for the past twenty-four hours, we know the accounts. But we haven't traced where the money went."

Jess said, "But you can trace it, can't you?"

"If we get cooperation from the receiving banks," Tsui said. "But that's not a given. And there's the question of reputation."

"Yours or the bank's?" Jess snapped.

"The country's reputation," Tsui explained. "Will our government tell the world that US banks have been forging money on such a large scale?"

"A hundred million."

"That we know about at the moment. There may have been more," Tsui said.

"Aren't we going to want to track that money down? Find out where it went? Counterfeiting is criminal activity," Jess declared. "Don't we care about that?"

"Sure. But the US dollar is the most forged currency in the world. And the guy who did this is already dead," Tsui said. "We'll never be able to reclaim that money without admitting the crime, even if we do find it. On some level, what's another hundred million fake dollars?"

"It's a hundred million!"

Tsui shrugged. "We called the Fed and FDIC and FBI and a bunch of other agencies right before you arrived. Representatives will be here midmorning. Most likely they'll kick the situation upstairs until a politician gets involved. At which point one of two things will happen. We'll either be exploited during the next election cycle as an example of disastrous consequences requiring even more regulation. Or we'll be ignored and the whole issue will quickly fade away."

"And if I print a story about all this?" Jess asked.

Tsui and Armando shook their heads in unison. "To what end?"

Jess sighed. She pulled out her phone and saw a bunch of messages from Henry, briefly laying out what Tsui had just told her.

She shoved her phone back into her pocket. "Did Larson know anything about all this?"

Armando laughed. "He knew something. Server logs show he logged into Rooney's laptop twenty-four hours ago."

"Doesn't mean he was involved in the scam," Tsui said.

"He logged in to six different computers at Rooney's apartment. Every link requires a separate, complicated password."

"That doesn't mean he was involved. Rooney might have recorded the passwords somewhere and Larson could simply have found them," Tsui said.

"No. These are rolling passwords that are synced to the receiving computer." He held up a small plastic card with a string of digits on the display. "He'd need a one-time password generator, like this."

Jess said, "Have you found Larson's card?"

Tsui shrugged. "Haven't had time to look yet."

"Can we search his office?"

"No," Tsui said.

"We should," Armando said. "If we had the right password, we might be able to find out more about the money."

"No," Tsui repeated.

Jess said, "Look, whatever has been going on, it's criminal and First Aurora Bank is right in the middle of it. The more you can tell the FBI now, the more forgiving they will be. Possibly."

Tsui took a deep breath and gestured toward Larson's office. "Very well. We'll need the FBI's help to find Jerry, too."

Armando sat at Larson's big desk and rummaged through the drawers while Jess checked the bookshelves. Tsui stood in the middle of the room, bewildered.

Armando finished the last desk drawer. "Nothing."

"Me neither," Jess said. "So he took the card with him."

"Or it's been lost or stolen," Tsui said.

"You said the transfers happened over the last month. Wouldn't Larson have noticed if he didn't have a secure link into the bank's systems for a month?"

Tsui didn't answer.

Larson's desk phone rang.

"Two-one-two area code," Armando said, glancing at the screen.

"New York," Tsui said reflexively. "Jerry's broker."

"Bensons? In New York?" Jess punched the speaker button without waiting for an answer.

"Jerry?" a woman's voice asked.

"He's out. Can I help?"

Tsui stepped forward, mouth open to speak. Jess held up a hand, silencing her.

The woman on the phone said, "I've been trying his cell."

"His battery died."

Jess waited a good long time before the woman finally said, "Just tell him he was too late last night, but it will go through tonight."

"Uh-huh. I'm writing this down. What will go through tonight?" Jess asked.

"It's personal. Sorry. You understand."

"Who should I say is calling?"

"Kirsten at Bensons."

"Kirsten," said Jess, slowly, as if she were writing it down. "Jerry hasn't been in today. Have you heard from him?"

"Look, I have to go." The line went dead.

Jess pressed the off button on the desk phone.

"Kirsten Tate, previously Ottoman," Tsui said.

"You know her?"

Tsui nodded. "Jerry's broker."

"You've talked before?"

"Couple of times. When Jerry remortgaged, he deposited the money to his brokerage account at Bensons."

Jess asked, "Any idea what she's talking about going through tonight?"

"Money is the obvious answer. They must have spoken late yesterday. Brokerage firms settle accounts at the end of the day," Tsui explained. "If Jerry spoke to her after the markets closed yesterday, the transfer will go through today."

Jess scoffed. "Not likely, I'd bet."

CHAPTER 54

TSUI, JESS, AND ARMANDO returned to the conference room.
A moment later, the doors to the conference room swung open.
Henry and another agent stepped in, holding out their badges.

Henry saw Jess seated at the table and raised his eyebrows.
"You got here fast."

"Could say the same about you."

"I have news on the missing snipers," Henry said. "Sandy
Jackson's been found. Broke his arm two weeks ago. He's still in
a cast."

"So the sniper at the warehouse was Theo Kahler," Jess said
flatly.

"Likely. Although it's still possible someone else ended up
with that gun."

Jess nodded agreement. "Larson had a call from Kirsten
Ottoman. She called Larson's office expecting him to answer."

"Mrs. Larson gives us a name and right away she calls?"
Henry said.

"Turns out she's Larson's broker, works for Bensons in New
York. She called to say some kind of transfer is going through
tonight."

"Fake money transfers like the ones Rooney made from his apartment?"

Jess shrugged. "That would be my guess."

"I'll see if I can find an agent to talk to her in New York."

"Can you get her phone records?"

Henry shrugged, refusing to promise.

"Rooney was literally creating money using the computer equipment we found," Jess explained. "The fake transfers went to First Aurora's bank in Cali, Colombia."

"We've alerted the federal banking authorities. They're already investigating," Henry said. "We're trying to connect with our counterparts in Cali. But don't get your hopes up. Colombia exports drugs to the US and this case has drug money all over it."

"Larson didn't strike me as a drug dealer." Jess cocked her head, thinking about the idea. "You?"

"Not at all," Henry agreed. "Dealer's got to have contacts. A distribution network. Security. It's a full-time business. Larson's got more than he can handle with the banks. I'd bet my last nickel that Larson's not running a drug cartel in his spare time."

Jess considered another angle. "Larson's wife said he's been stressed lately."

"Drug cartel problems are not typical white-collar stress. Drug businesses present a whole different level of issues."

"Maybe Larson was working with a dealer. Given the size of the money transfers, the dealer would be a kingpin, don't you think?" Jess said.

"Charles Finnegan was shot at the warehouse. He's widely believed to have been the biggest dealer in Denver. Word on the street is that someone wanted his job," Henry said. "We've had a few names pop up from our network of informants. We're running them down. Nothing confirmed yet."

"If we've eliminated the system the new boss was using to funnel money to a Colombian cartel, he's likely to be enraged and unpredictable."

"And dangerous. Which means you're still at risk." Henry patted his own chest to emphasize the need for her bulletproof vest.

"Right." Jess nodded, putting the pieces together. "Rooney could have been the brains behind the scheme. Once Rooney was killed, Larson probably figured he couldn't keep the fraud going. Maybe he wanted to take the money and disappear."

"Without his wife and kids?" Henry asked.

"He mortgaged jointly owned homes in Denver and Florida without telling his wife. He needs money for something," Jess said. "If we're right about Rooney's activities, it makes no sense that Larson couldn't get money the same way, though."

Henry cocked his head. "Either there's a missing piece we haven't uncovered, or Larson's situation is not related to Rooney's money-making schemes."

"Could be just the usual tawdry stuff that clogs divorce courts around the country," Jess said. "Larson's broker is a woman he had an affair with years ago. His wife said Larson moved across the country to avoid her. But they're still in contact."

"Seems like there are many things Mrs. Larson doesn't know about her husband." Henry shook his head. "We're tracing Larson's credit cards and his name on airline lists. He's not that smart. We'll find him."

"Which leaves Lucy Cranfield," Jess said. "If they took her as a replacement for Rooney, she's in more danger now than before. She can't access Rooney's password system. When they figure that out, they'll kill her."

CHAPTER 55

HENRY LEFT FOR HIS office. Jess remained in the conference room for a few more minutes before deciding she should do the same. As she walked to her Jeep, Mandy called.

"Let me guess," Jess deadpanned. "Carter wants to know how the article is coming along?"

Mandy laughed and lowered her voice. "We are on deadline, you know. He's asked me every thirty minutes. It's beginning to get to me."

It was Jess's turn to laugh. "Beginning to?"

Mandy raised her voice to normal volume. "I have news about that Honda. There is no Colorado plate ending in 5273. But there is an EQS 273. Silver. Eight years old. Registered to Albert Hall living in Denver."

"Tell me you have the address."

"Coming your way, right now."

Jess thanked her and hung up. The address was twenty minutes away, maybe more with morning traffic. She texted the news to Henry and Norton.

Norton called immediately. "We'll send a car. Don't go walking in there alone."

"I could ride along. There's no risk to a passenger in an unmarked drive-by, right?"

He took a deep breath, blowing it out loudly. "All right. A ride-along. If the officers decide to approach, you stay in the car. Agreed?"

"Agreed."

"Stay safe, you hear me? If you get killed on my case, I'll be the one who pays for it," Norton warned. He ignored her snort of laughter and said, "I'll text you a rendezvous point."

The address came in and she put the location into the Jeep's GPS.

When she arrived, the officers were already waiting in a black Dodge Charger with steel wheels. The doorposts still had the marks where the spotlights had been removed. Only a complete idiot would fail to notice.

Jess introduced herself to the two officers, Stephens and Tomás.

"Won't notice from a distance," Tomás said when she pointed out the problems with the car.

"If these people are our suspects, they'll know you're cops from a single glance," Jess said.

Stephens shrugged. "Have to work with what we've got."

"We could take my Jeep," Jess offered.

"No way." Tomás shook his head. "We're unmarked but fully equipped. We have radio, guns, and video."

"Rules first," Stephens said. "We drive by. You stay back from the windows. No staring. No shouting. No fast reactions."

"Okay," Jess agreed. "Where are the video cameras?"

"Front and rear. Two on either side. We can replay after we pass. Ready?"

Jess nodded and they settled into the car.

"House'll be on the right," Tomás said.

She sat behind the driver. She'd be farther from the passenger window and therefore harder to see from outside. But she'd still have a clear view.

"How good are the cameras?"

"They're cheap. Like the rest of this car. But moving slowly we should be able to capture a license plate," Stephens said.

Tomás took the passenger seat and Stephens drove. He waited for a van to pass and then pulled out. The van turned right, and Stephens followed. They crossed two junctions and slowed to turn right again.

Small houses lined the street, brick with a small front porch and plain windows. Probably built in the 1940s. Maybe during the boom as soldiers returned from World War II. Most of the properties were well cared for and in good shape.

"Sixty-six fifty-four," she said, reciting the house number.

"Uh-huh," Tomás said. "Don't stare."

She kept her gaze on the passing homes, paying attention to the house numbers.

Sixty-six fifty-four was painted white over the brick. Decorative awnings covered the windows. The yard was bleak but tidy, as if the owner waited for spring for new flowers.

No garage. A driveway made from two rows of paving slabs with gravel between ran along the property from the street to the rear alley.

The silver Honda was parked alongside the house. It was reversed in the driveway. The front of the vehicle had no license plate, which was a violation of Colorado law. Although this seemed like the kind of neighborhood where residents were law-abiding.

Just as fast as the house had come into view, they passed, and it disappeared. She wanted to twist around and get more details, but she didn't. The viewing angle was wrong, and the Honda was out of sight behind the house, anyway.

Stephens cruised a few blocks before pulling into the parking lot of a local hardware store. Tomás took a tablet computer from the glove box and reviewed the video footage captured by the car's exterior cameras.

"Quiet," he said. "Drapes are open and lights are on. I see one person inside. Small. Probably female. No plates on the car."

"The yard looked well kept," Jess said.

Stephens turned and frowned.

"Hardened drug dealers aren't the gardening type," Jess said.

"Really. Who knew?" he said.

Jess gave him a cheeky grin. "The ones at the last drug dealer's house I visited weren't."

Stephens grunted.

Jess held out her hand. "May I?"

Tomás handed over the tablet. She ran the video several times and switched between the various cameras.

Finally sure, she handed the tablet back to Tomás and said, "No dent in the roof. The Honda we're looking for has a dent in the roof on the passenger side."

"Who said that?"

"I did. To Detective Norton. After I found someone at the site of the shooting who identified a suspicious person driving off."

Stephens offered a dissatisfied grunt.

Jess continued. "Point is, the plate may be a partial match, but it's not the same car."

"You're sure about the dent?" Tomás asked. "I mean, that there isn't one on this car."

"See for yourself." Jess gestured.

Tomás studied the picture for a few moments. "Nope. Car looks good. Not a scratch on it."

"We should knock," said Jess.

Stephens shook his head. "We talk to Norton first."

He stepped out of the car and paced back and forth as he made a call on his cell. A few moments later, he opened Jess's door and handed her the phone. "For you."

"You certain about the dent?" Norton asked.

"Sure as I can be. This car has no dent. The witnesses told me the Honda had a dent."

"Reliable witnesses?" Norton asked.

"Seemed reliable to me. And they'd seen the car before. Near their apartment," Jess said. "The dent makes the car stand out. Which is probably why they noticed and remembered it. There's a lot of Hondas on the road."

"Right," Norton said. "Let me talk to Stephens again."

She handed the phone back. Stephens closed her door and resumed his pacing. A minute later he returned to the driver's seat.

"Squad car is coming, and we'll approach the house." He looked at Jess. "You stay in the car until I'm satisfied it's safe for you to go in."

"Fine with me." Jess leaned back to wait.

The squad car arrived. Stephens and Tomás talked to the officers while Jess waited. After a few minutes, they returned.

"We're all set," Tomás said. "Remember, you stay in the car until we clear the house."

"Got it," Jess said.

They drove back to 6644 in silence. Stephens parked two houses before. The squad car parked two houses beyond.

Stephens and Tomás walked up to the front door. Neither looked relaxed. They rang the bell and waited, scanning the windows and sides of the house.

The front door cracked open a fraction. After a brief conversation, the door swung farther open.

A little old lady peered up to see the two men. An old man arrived and stood behind the woman.

The conversation continued. The man shook his head frequently. Finally they finished and the man closed his front door. Stephens and Tomás walked to the Honda, looked the car over and snapped a few photos with their cell phones, and then returned to the front seat of the Charger.

"Well?" Jess asked.

Stephens picked up the radio handset and released the officers in the squad car. The vehicle U-turned and left, going in the opposite direction.

"Who gave you this tip?" Stephens asked.

"Two people at the site of the second warehouse shooting."

"The car's owned by the elderly couple who live here. They say they haven't driven out of Denver this year," Stephens said. "Any chance those witnesses were just messing with you? Were they part of the gang, trying to throw you off?"

Jess shook her head. "What did the couple say about the car?"

"It's old, it's cheap to insure, and it hasn't moved in the past week," Tomás said flatly.

Jess looked along the street. She couldn't see the car directly. "What about the roof?"

"No dent in the roof," Stephens said.

"The witnesses who told me about this car didn't want to talk about it. Why would they lie?" Jess cocked her head and wondered aloud.

Stephens pointed to the house. "That old couple aren't doing drug deals. They're lucky they can still drive."

"Anyone else in the house?"

"We didn't see anything obvious to suggest another resident from our view at the front door. We'd need a warrant to search the house, and we can't get one without more evidence to support it," Tomás said.

Jess breathed out, letting the air hiss between her teeth. "I don't get it. There's got to be something we're missing here."

Stephens started the car.

"Wait." Jess opened her door.

"Wait for what?" said Tomás.

Jess stepped out of the car. "I'm going to talk to them."

Tomás opened his door. "I'll come with you."

Jess walked quickly and Tomás kept up.

She went straight to the Honda. The roof was pristine, the surface smooth to the touch and the paint unblemished. The interior was clean and uncluttered. The seats looked practically new.

A transparent sticker in the corner of the windshield showed an oil change was not due for three months. The back of the car had a few splashes of road grime around the wheel arches and rear bumper. The license plate ended with S273.

"Can I help you?" a man's voice asked from the side door.

"Mr. Hall, sir," Tomás said, friendly. "Last check. We'll be out of your hair in a few minutes."

Jess ran a finger across the license plate. No road grime. "It must be a challenge to keep your car so clean, Mr. Hall. Especially during our winter weather."

The old man came closer and stopped about six feet away. "People always want you to buy new ones, but if you look after 'em they can last a long time."

Jess sensed a tinge of regret. "You like cars?"

"Oh yeah." The man shrugged. "Had some good ones. In my youth. Seemed like money was no object back then."

"Vehicles eat you out of house and home these days," Tomás said.

Hall nodded. "That's why we bought this one. It was affordable for us. Probably be the last car we'll ever own."

The license plate holder was stamped PARKER MOTORS. Jess pointed to it. "Never heard of them. Is that a Honda dealer around here?"

"Fort Collins," Hall said. "Have a friend who works up there. Gave us a good deal."

"That's a long way to go for service," Tomás said.

"Yeah." Hall nodded. "Used to drive up there. See my buddy. Don't do that anymore. Not since the warranty ran out. I use a local place now. It's cheaper, too."

Jess moved to the front of the car. In the top right-hand corner of the windshield the transparent sticker with the oil change date had a telephone number underneath and the words "call for service."

"Where do you go for service?" she said, pointing at the sticker.

The man moved slowly around the far side of the car to stand beside her and peer at the number. "Oh. Easy Tire. Five miles away. Near where we do our grocery shopping."

Jess stepped around him and ran her hand over the front bumper. There were two small holes about six inches apart in the plastic. They were almost invisible against the car's paint.

"You had a license plate on here?"

"Yes, I had one," the old man said. "Must have come off somewhere."

CHAPTER 56

JESS RETURNED TO THE unmarked Charger and dialed Henry's number.

"They took the license plates," she said when he answered. "S273. The silver Honda."

She heard a loud click and Henry's voice boomed like he was in a conference room. "Norton's here. He needs to hear whatever you've got to say."

She pressed the speaker button on her phone. "I'm with Tomás and Stephens." After a brief round of hellos, she continued. "S273. The plate on a silver Honda owned by Albert Hall. Old guy. Had it for years. It's missing the front plate. The screw holes are perfectly smooth, so it was removed. And get this. The Honda is serviced at Easy Tire and Oil."

"Same place Rooney used," Norton said.

"Precisely."

"No one looks at their front plate. Some states don't even require them anymore," Henry said. "Put the front plate on another silver Honda and it's not likely to be noticed."

"Right. But if you're running a big-time drug operation, you don't want it brought down by a routine traffic stop," Jess said.

"So maybe they have fake IDs in Hall's name. And if they do have a problem, they just move on to another stolen plate."

"Easy Tire and Oil," Tomás said, looking at a map on his phone. "Less than five miles away."

Jess leaned over the front seats to look at the map Tomás found online. "That's the place Brantley visited when I followed him."

"I can park a car on that street right now to keep an eye on things," Norton said.

"Hold off on that for a few," Henry replied. "Let's get a plan together. Too many strangers showing up and we risk losing the dealer as well as his crew and his inventory."

"Okay," Norton agreed. "Planning it is. But let's get it done before we lose our advantage."

"Any news on Lucy Cranfield?" Jess asked.

"Nothing," Henry said, shaking his head.

"She's been missing more than twenty-four hours," Jess said, worried. "With the bank closed down, she'll be unable to tap into Rooney's system. These guys won't hesitate to eliminate her if she's not useful."

"You think they might be holding her at this Easy Tire place?" Norton asked.

"Possibly," Henry said. "But either way, Lucy is running out of time. Let's get to work."

Stephens drove Jess back to her Jeep in silence. Tomás spent the time on his phone. When they arrived at the Jeep, he held up his hand to indicate she shouldn't get out.

When he finished the call and hung up, Tomás said, "Found an apartment block down the street from Easy Tire. Four stories. And an empty apartment on the top floor. We can put a team up there to watch whatever is going on."

"Sounds good. Tell Norton." She opened the door and put one foot out. "Maybe we'll catch up later."

CHAPTER 57

JESS SAT IN A family restaurant. The sign on the door proclaimed they served the best burgers in Denver. She wondered how they'd prove such a claim, but if votes were required, she'd be happy to add hers. The burger and fries were excellent.

Customers came and went. The waiter topped off her coffee twice. She checked out the pictures of Colorado hanging on the walls. They showed either blue skies and mountain peaks covered in snow or towns and villages, lights glowing gold in nighttime scenes. She recognized all the locations.

She'd had very little time to travel for pleasure over the years, but she had toured Colorado. She enjoyed vigorously attacking the ski slopes even if she wasn't a powder hound.

The waiter had left the bill and passed by three times asking if she was ready to pay. Customers were waiting in line, and she was hogging the table.

Henry and Norton had surely made plans by now. She'd helped advance the investigation and she hoped they would keep her in the loop. Especially if she asked. Repeatedly.

Jess placed her company credit card down on the restaurant bill. The waiter swept the card and bill from the table and processed it at a register in the corner of the room.

Her phone buzzed. A text from Henry. He'd sent an address followed by "Park three blocks away. Use the back entrance. DL essential."

Jess smiled, realizing how little time she'd had to spend with Henry lately. His favorite phrase when secrecy was essential was "keep it on the down-low." They were developing their communication style and learning each other's habits.

What next?

No time to think about the future at the moment. She needed to stay focused on matters at hand.

She brought up the address on her phone. It was the apartment building Tomás had found earlier. Either Denver PD or the FBI had convinced the property owner to hand over the keys.

Norton would have camera and video surveillance in place. Perhaps long-distance audio. A good-size team. Probably packed into a two-room apartment.

They'd plan for an extended operation. Overlapping shifts, pacing arrivals and departures to minimize the risks.

The waiter returned with her card. She handed it back with an order for a dozen burgers and fries to go. After a brief discussion, he agreed to deliver them to her table in twenty minutes.

Twenty minutes turned into thirty, but everything was packed neatly into two large brown paper bags along with plenty of ketchup. Jess collected the bags and got on the road.

She located a street three blocks away, but all the street parking was full. She lapped one block farther away and squeezed in between two white panel vans.

Approaching the apartment, she struck up a conversation with a dog walker while the dog took an interest in the brown paper bags.

"Delivery," Jess said.

"Someone's lucky, eh, Sampson?" the walker replied, leading the disappointed dog in the opposite direction.

Jess entered the apartment building through a wrought-iron gate into a courtyard. She took the elevator to the top floor, found the apartment number from Henry's message, and knocked. After a moment, Norton opened the door, and she stepped inside.

The apartment was a tight squeeze. It had only two rooms, an open-plan kitchen and living space, and a separate bedroom.

She recognized Officers Stephens and Tomás. The others were strangers to her.

Some wore jeans and T-shirts, and some wore suits. All were placed well away from open-weave curtains covering the windows but providing little privacy.

In the living area, two cameras with long lenses had been placed on either side of a smaller video camera. The feed from the video appeared on a flat-screen television. The arrangement provided a good view of the garage's parking lot and entrance, but the angle obscured the side of the building.

An eager voice said, "Food?"

Jess hefted the bags onto the kitchen counter. "Burgers."

They lined up, collecting a burger.

Norton stood to one side. "We're collecting as much intel as possible. We don't want to go steaming in there only to bust a few hired hands."

"Makes sense." Jess nodded, scanning the open room. "Where's Henry?"

"He's out. Getting his oil changed."

Jess pointed toward Easy Tire. "Down there?"

"He's wearing a camera and a wire." Norton nodded. "He refused to let anyone else do it. He said he needed an oil change anyway."

She laughed. "Henry's always practical."

"Seems like he's not the only one." Norton pointed to the burgers. "Thanks."

"You almost had to share them with a dog."

Norton grinned. "Susie and Sampson."

"They're with you?"

"Susie's been with the department for years. Always works surveillance. Sampson's her dog. Good cover."

"You'll have to put him on the payroll."

"He does pretty well," Norton said. "He'll get a steak dinner on us when this is over."

"Morris's leaving now," Tomás said from his surveillance point across the room.

The television showed Henry's Subaru pulling out of the Easy Tire parking lot. He turned away from the apartment and into the blind spot, disappearing from the camera's view. He arrived at the apartment a few minutes later.

Norton cued up the video from Henry's body camera.

Henry picked up a burger and came over to join Jess.

"No great revelations down there," he said between bites. "Typical for the business. Tires, oil changes, wipers. That sort of thing. Didn't get to see upstairs."

"Expensive cars?" Norton asked.

Henry, mouth full, shook his head.

The video reflecting Henry's recon effort sprang to life on the television. The audio wasn't quite synced, but it was good enough.

The rectangular Easy Tire building was mostly garage space with a reception desk at one end. There were lines of roll-up doors, four on the front of the building and four on the rear, for drive-through service.

Henry's video circled the reception area. At the back of the room, a set of stairs led upward. A bored receptionist sat behind the counter. She offered Henry a small bottle of water when he checked his car in.

Half a dozen customers occupied plastic garden chairs arrayed around a coffee table with a pile of motoring publications. He sat a few moments sorting through magazines before holding up a six-month-old copy of *Taboo*.

"Who'd have thought I'd find this here," he said on the recording.

Jess grinned.

"Now you can tell everyone you got there before us," Norton teased without taking his eyes off the video.

"Morris," the receptionist called out.

Henry stood. She waved toward his car. "Bay four."

"Thanks." Henry left reception and walked the length of the parking lot. The video bounced with every step. He located his Subaru and approached bay four.

He drove into the last bay in the row. Each of the others was also occupied by a vehicle atop a hydraulic lift.

Neat stacks of tires, ten feet high and columns four deep, covered the width of one wall. A door marked OFFICE was at the opposite end of the garage. On the same wall, double doors with a large padlock hanging by its hasp led to what could have been a stock room.

An employee approached Henry and informed him he had to leave for insurance reasons.

"The receptionist asked me to drive in."

The guy shrugged. "We're the only ones allowed to drive the vehicles out when they're done."

"Okay. No problem."

Henry left through the door at the rear into a second, small parking area. Various older cars were squeezed into the lot, all parked around a high wire fence that enclosed the space.

He circled back through the garage and returned to reception. The girl behind the counter still looked bored. A couple of customers had departed.

A man walked down the stairs and left. Henry stood, stretched, and walked toward the stairs.

"No customers upstairs," the girl said without glancing up from her cell phone.

Henry pointed upward and put a foot on the first step. "Restrooms?"

The girl rolled off her chair. "No restrooms and no customers allowed upstairs."

"No problem," the on-screen Henry replied and returned to his seat.

Norton ran the video all the way to the end. A high-speed image showed Henry paying his bill, backing his car out of the garage, and racing off down the street away from the apartment building.

Norton stopped the video and the television switched back to the rear view captured by the video camera placed in the apartment window.

"I'll run facial recognition on the employees and customers," Tomás said as he set to work on his laptop.

Over the next few hours, the room settled into a working rhythm. They rotated the camera duty and Jess took a turn.

She learned that only two of the people in the room were FBI. Denver PD had supplied the majority of the manpower. Which meant this was Norton's operation.

Susie the undercover dog walker came by. She chatted with Jess and shared a burger with Sampson.

At Easy Tire, customers came and went. Tomás kept a running list of license plates on a sheet of paper on the wall, and his laptop displayed a rotating series of pictures when he fed the plate numbers into the software. He located criminal histories for both customers and staff, but none seemed especially relevant to the drug operation.

Jess studied the staff faces on Tomás's laptop. "I don't recognize any of these people."

"Why would you expect to?" Henry asked.

"From what I believe was the dealer's house."

Henry nodded. "Given the rap sheets Tomás has found over at Easy Tire so far, these guys are low on the pecking order."

"You thinking they just took the plate off the Honda and handed it on? No further involvement?"

He shrugged. "Could be."

Tomás whistled to capture attention in the busy apartment.

"I recognize this guy," he said, pointing to the video.

Tomás wound the video back thirty seconds. A man wearing a black parka got out of an old Volvo SUV, straightened his coat, and walked inside.

The video had only captured a few partial glimpses of his face, but Tomás said with confidence, "Louis Kemp. Bouncer. Beat a guy viciously a couple of years ago and we arrested him. The guy refused to testify, and we were forced to drop the charges."

"Could Kemp be involved in all this?" Norton said.

"At the time, we believed he bounced guys bringing drugs into the establishment where he worked on the door. We figured he kept the drugs and sold them," Tomás replied. "But Narcotics didn't come up with anything they could use against Kemp and dropped it after a while."

One of the staff backed Kemp's Volvo into the garage. Henry leaned forward, staring hard at the video. "They told me I had to drive straight in. Said insurance required it because the lifts were set up to have the front of the vehicle facing forward."

No one said anything for a moment. Then Norton picked up a handheld radio. "Susie. Do a walk-by. Soon as you can, please."

Jess watched the TV until Susie passed in front of the garage. Sampson, obligingly, stopped to relieve himself on a lamppost and they continued along the sidewalk out of the camera's view.

Susie called back on the radio. "They're loading something into the Volvo. I couldn't tell what it was from a distance."

"Can you be more specific?" Norton asked.

"Packages. About a foot square. Cardboard. Shiny. Maybe sealed in some kind of plastic wrap."

"We need to get someone in there," Henry said.

"Susie can't go again so soon. They could notice her," Norton replied.

"I'll go," Jess said without hesitation.

"No way," Norton replied, shaking his head.

She glanced around the room. "Which one of you doesn't look like police? And as you said, a woman is less suspicious to guys like this."

"Jess, these people are killers," Norton said. "We'll call in another undercover."

"I'll be fine." Jess patted her vest. "I'll get an oil change and come back. How difficult can that be?"

Norton pursed his lips. "It's obvious you're wearing that vest."

"I can take it off. I'll only be getting an oil change. I've done that hundreds of times before," Jess replied. "Simple stuff."

Norton sighed and gave up, probably realizing the only way to stop her was physical restraint. Which he wasn't willing to do. "Observation only. No prying, no pictures. You're just an ordinary person getting an oil change. Got it?"

Jess shrugged off her bulletproof vest and carried it as she hurried back to her Jeep four blocks away. She dialed Henry on the speakerphone as she drove, giving him the blow-by-blow.

"The Volvo is still inside the garage," she said when she pulled into the parking lot. "Bay one. Right next to the room you thought was the stockroom. A space in front of the bay is open."

Jess positioned her Jeep facing the Volvo and put the transmission in park.

"They are definitely loading boxes from the stockroom into the Volvo," she said quietly. "Several are stacked high in the back of the Volvo. They must be heavy. The Volvo's suspension is sitting lower than normal."

She waited a few more moments. Two men carried a large metal object out of the stockroom and struggled with the weight as they lifted it into the rear of the Volvo.

"They just loaded something metal. Took two of them to carry it, so it's heavy," she said.

The men closed up the Volvo. As Kemp walked toward the reception, Jess reversed the Jeep away from bay one.

When he came toward bay one, Kemp waved to the men, climbed into the Volvo, and drove away.

Jess watched as he passed. "Follow him?"

"Negative. He'll recognize your vehicle now. We have Stephens rolling in a car," Henry said.

Jess's phone buzzed with a message from Mandy. Her skin tingled as she read.

"Oh no," she mumbled.

"What's wrong?" Henry said.

"Got a text from my office. Turns out, there are two Easy Tire locations," Jess replied. "This could be the wrong one."

CHAPTER 58

JESS BROUGHT UP A map on her phone. She told Henry the second Easy Tire location was fifteen miles away.

Henry said, "Norton's trying to pull in more surveillance."

"I don't think we've been spotted by anyone here. It seems like business as usual. He should have enough time to get a second team briefed." Jess looked up at the garage.

The bay directly in front of her, bay one, was empty. "Think I should do the oil change thing?"

"Forget it," Henry said.

"Okay. Be back in a few," Jess replied and hung up.

The parking lot was a single line of spaces facing the four garage bays. There was only one driveway to the street, which served for entry and exit.

She reversed from her parking space and turned ninety degrees to drive out of the lot.

A large SUV with blacked-out windows backed out of a bay in front of her. It blocked the exit as the rear of the vehicle rolled toward her Jeep.

The SUV came uncomfortably close to the Jeep's bumper before Jess honked the horn. The SUV jerked to a stop only a few inches away.

The Jeep was blocked in. Jess couldn't move.

She swiveled her head left and right looking for a way to escape.

A big, older Cadillac sedan sped into the parking lot from the street. The SUV had to roll backward to clear a path for the speeding vehicle. Jess couldn't drive away, so she backed deeper into the rear of the lot.

The Cadillac braked hard, inches from the SUV, then reversed into the first servicing bay.

The driver of the SUV jumped out, waving a fist and shouting in full view of Tomás and his surveillance equipment.

Jess looked left and right for a way out. The Jeep was pinned in.

She punched the speed dial for Henry. The phone rang. Once. Twice. Three times.

A young man got out of the Cadillac and casually walked out of the bay toward the front door into reception. The SUV driver kept shouting as he dogged the man.

Henry's phone continued to ring.

The young man ignored the SUV driver and reception, crossed a grass divide into the next parking lot, and entered a coffee shop.

Tomás answered Henry's phone. "Henry's rounding up a new team for the second Easy Tire location and Norton's rotating cars to keep on Kemp's tail. What's up?"

"Did you see the Cadillac?"

"Yeah. You okay?" Tomás asked.

"So far." Jess checked behind her and made sure her doors were locked. "Weird behavior like that rings my alarm bell."

"Sit tight. Keep calm" was Tomás's advice. But he wasn't sitting here trapped between the SUV and the fence.

The SUV driver finally gave up shouting at the Cadillac and turned back toward his vehicle.

"Looks like the SUV guy is about to move," Tomás said.

Jess checked around her again. The workers in the garage seemed occupied with various vehicles. No one was even looking in her direction, let alone approaching her.

The Cadillac waited in the bay. Wisps of smoke wafted over the trunk because the driver had left the engine running.

The rear of the car looked wonky. Sloped up somehow. Damaged, perhaps? She leaned forward and realized that the trunk lid was ajar.

The SUV driver climbed into his vehicle.

"Cadillac guy just left the back of the coffee bar," Tomás said. He shouted for another car to follow the young driver.

Before she could ask anything else, Jess heard the unmistakable sound of loud gunfire. Sharp cracks somewhat muted by the Jeep's bodywork.

Jess released her seat belt and threw herself down behind the engine block. Instinctive. Automatic.

People ran from reception, spilling into the parking lot and running across the grass in the direction of the coffee bar, away from the garage.

More gunfire sounded. Single shot and automatic. Mechanics in the garage yelled and dived for cover. Some workers ran out of the building's rear exits.

A tall, muscular man raced from the stock room to the Cadillac, carrying two bags that flapped as he ran.

Jess caught a fast glimpse. A fraction of a second, maybe. No more. A quick snapshot of his face as he piled into the driver's seat of the Cadillac.

"Kahler," she said, instinctively, into the phone.

"Theo Kahler?" Tomás repeated.

Jess replied, "Definitely. Driving the Cadillac."

Tomás shouted something to the others in the apartment.

The Cadillac sped from the bay, turned away from the big SUV, and raced onto the street, burning rubber the whole way.

The SUV didn't move. The driver was still out of sight, probably crouched in the footwell.

Jess hammered on the Jeep's horn. The noise was loud enough to hear inside the SUV, but the vehicle didn't move.

"Kahler's speeding north!" she shouted into the phone.

"I don't have a vehicle," Tomás said. "I've called it in, but I'm the only one left here."

"I'll keep an eye on him until you can get a car free," Jess said as she twisted the steering wheel, drove over the grass, and dropped down the curb onto the street.

The Cadillac had already disappeared in the traffic.

She pushed the accelerator all the way to the floor.

CHAPTER 59

JESS PASSED A PICKUP truck and squeezed in behind a blue sedan. The pickup driver was enraged. He closed the gap between them and trailed inches from her rear bumper, honking his horn.

"Jess? You okay?" Tomás asked. "We've got a couple of squad cars coming. They're a mile behind you. Heading your way now."

Traffic lights ahead turned red. Jess braked hard, laying rubber on the road. The pickup behind her did the same and managed to stop before it slammed her into oncoming traffic in the intersection.

The pickup driver laid on his horn. She flipped her mirror up. She didn't need to see his angry face and shaking fist right now.

A block ahead she glimpsed a black Cadillac turning left. Was Kahler driving?

She waited for the light to change, still in the middle lane. The next light was green now and would be red by the time she got there. The Cadillac was already out of sight. She couldn't lose him now.

She checked both ways, put on her indicator, and turned across the left lane during a break in traffic, into a street on her left. The pickup truck driver behind her continued to honk the horn even as she put more distance between them.

The cross street was wide open. She raced to the next block and took a right and a left with no problems.

The Cadillac was only two blocks ahead.

She sped as fast as she dared until a car pulled out in front of her. She veered out but couldn't get around him because of oncoming traffic.

Up ahead, the Cadillac took a hard, fast right turn. The car's rear tires slid across the slick road. The Cadillac righted itself, and kept going.

Not an ordinary move by an ordinary driver. Nor one who was concerned about pedestrians, property damage, insurance claims, or jail time.

"I have Kahler in sight," Jess said to Tomás on the still-open phone line, adding the cross-street name.

"Keep back, Jess. Just watch from a safe distance. Our guys will be there in a couple of minutes," Tomás said.

Jess braked hard and followed Kahler's turn with an unintentional but similarly flamboyant slide.

"If they're behind me, they'll never catch up," Jess said.

"We'll have help up ahead of him, too. Just watch and stay back," Tomás said. "Or better yet, quit now while you still can. Morris will have my head if anything happens to you."

Kahler turned right. Jess slowed. Maybe Tomás was right. Henry would be worried and annoyed. She'd removed the bulletproof vest and she was chasing a known sniper. Which sounded a little insane, even to her own ears.

She turned right, following Kahler at a more reasonable speed. His Cadillac was four sedans ahead.

She could see over the roofs.

Which meant he could see her.

If he looked.

Which he surely had.

Jess had nowhere to go. No way to evade the Cadillac. Oncoming traffic and a vehicle close behind her. She couldn't pass or slow.

Again, she was trapped.

The road curved around and narrowed on a stretch where opposite lanes were blocked off for construction in both directions. Traffic slowed.

A truck turned off and a gap opened between Kahler and the vehicle in front of him. Brake lights flashed and then glowed steadily. The Cadillac, the first car following, then the next, all the way to Jess's Jeep.

"He's going to do something," Jess said. "He's stuck and he doesn't like it."

"Just stay in your Jeep. We're almost there," Tomás replied.

Before Jess had a chance to say anything, the Cadillac roared around a ninety-degree turn. Smoke poured from its rear wheels. The stench of burning rubber came into the Jeep through the ventilation system.

The cars between Jess and Kahler braked hard with squeals aplenty.

One veered into the orange cones that marked the roadwork, came to a stop when it left the pavement, and landed in road gravel.

Two of the other cars couldn't stop. They collided with a deafening crash.

Jess stood with both feet and all her weight on the brake pedal. It pulsed under her feet for an eternity until the ABS brought the Jeep to a halt.

Kahler leapt from the Cadillac, holding a gun with a giant magazine protruding from the middle. He fired four shots directly into the car behind him. The windshield shattered.

Jess couldn't see inside the sedan, but no one could have avoided those bullets.

"Kahler fired into a sedan. Probable multiple injuries," Jess said as she grabbed her gun case from the glove compartment. She dialed in the combination and pulled her weapon.

"Get out of there, Jess," Tomás ordered. "Four squads will be there within a minute. Keep back. Let us do our jobs."

She was all set to agree. Then Kahler ran.

Grabbing her phone, she jumped out of the Jeep and ran after him.

"He's on foot," she yelled to Tomás, still on the line. She could hear sirens on the way.

Kahler turned left into an alley.

She slowed and crossed the street at an angle, and she peered around the corner. He wasn't there. The alley was empty.

There were several doorways opening into the alley. The doors were set back to offer a foot or two of shelter from the elements. They also offered enough space to hide a killer.

While he was running from the car, Kahler had held the gun with his right hand. Jess reasoned that he'd shelter on the right side of the alley. Which would keep his shooting arm free and minimize his exposure.

She moved to the left side of the alley for a better view of the doorways. He had cover and protection and she was exposed.

Jess picked up a crumpled soda can and lobbed it down the alley. It rattled and clattered. Metal on stone. Loud in the confined space.

Nothing moved. No shadows shifted. No other sound followed the clattering can.

Her heart thumped hard. Where were Norton's backup teams?

Jess whispered her location to Tomás.

Out on the sidewalk, people were shouting and screaming. One man shouted about his lawyer, accusing everyone of causing the accident and demanding answers. A woman cried for help. No sirens were close. No engines roaring or slamming to a stop.

A stroller rolled into the far end of the alley. It bumped to a halt.

Kahler set off a round of gunfire. Jess counted five shots.

The stroller kicked backward, bucking and turning under repeated impact. A bundle wrapped in a blanket fell clear and rolled on the ground.

"He's shot a baby," she said into her phone. A sliver of doubt shivered her spine. Would Kahler have actually killed a baby?

Only one way to know for sure.

Her blood ran cold, but she could stand still no longer. That baby could still be alive. She had to act.

She raised her gun, unsteady but leveled, and ran toward the stroller.

The blanket flapped in the breeze, tattered and torn, separated from the baby bundle on the ground by six or seven feet.

She didn't have time to think. She hurtled past the gap between the buildings, turning sideways, both hands on her pistol.

She slowed her pace and steadied her aim. Gazed ahead, scanning as she moved. Watching. For Kahler. For movement. For innocents.

She kept moving toward the stroller. Until she spied him.

Kahler stood against the brick wall. Gun out. Arm locked in a steadying brace.

He fired.

She fired back.

His gun was on automatic. The shots kept coming. The air around her whipped into tiny deadly gusts, gone as fast as they arrived. Ricochet bullets slammed into walls and dumpsters and doorways.

Momentum carried Jess on. Past the gap in the buildings. Past the stroller. Past the edge of the next building.

She angled into a doorway, slamming against a wooden door. She aimed her weapon to cover the gap. She could fire the moment he moved. And she did.

He leapt forward, bringing his gun around toward her.

Before he had a chance to shoot, her bullet hit him in the biceps.

She saw the twitch of his clothing and the jerk of his arm.

She might have missed. Perhaps he was hit by a ricochet. She couldn't tell and didn't care. She fired again.

His finger stayed on the trigger and automatic fire sprayed the wall in front of him. Maybe shock and pain from her bullet caused his finger to freeze. Maybe she'd damaged something important. Maybe he'd lost motor control of his hand.

Shouts of "Stop! Police!" rang down the alley at the same time a helicopter thundered overhead. Kahler turned and ran, his boots stomping into the distance.

Jess had faith that Henry and the Denver PD could take over now.

"Jessica Kimball," she shouted. And in case they didn't recognize her name, she added, "*Taboo Magazine.*"

She placed her pistol on the ground and kicked it into the alley. "I'm unarmed. I'm coming out."

She took a deep breath and stepped out, hands up. Half a dozen officers approached.

The man on point checked around the gap between the buildings.

"Clear," he said, and ran after Kahler.

Detective Norton walked down the alley.

"Henry Morris has his hands full. You really know how to give a man sleepless nights." Norton picked up the rusty stroller. "A decoy."

Seeking certainty, she rushed to the bundle of blankets. They unspooled in her hands. Empty.

She threw the bundle against the wall, blood boiling. "He's one sick character."

Norton nodded. "Agreed."

She ground her teeth. Kahler had intended to trick her into risking her life. Even though she'd wanted to believe he wouldn't use a baby so callously, she had no reason to trust him.

She breathed loudly through her nose, knowing she would do the same thing again. She'd risk her life for the life of an innocent.

Because she knew. With plain and total certainty.

Kahler would have used a real mother and baby if he'd had to.

CHAPTER 60

WHEN HE HEARD THE sirens and the helicopter, Theo Kahler ran. He turned right at the end of the alley and darted across the two-lane road. He vaulted a four-foot-high divider in the median.

His arm hurt like hell. Kimball's shot was blind luck. That woman seemed to have nine lives.

Kahler kept running, glancing behind to confirm they hadn't spotted him. He entered a department store, took the stairs down a level, and exited into underground parking.

Earlier, he'd ditched the Volkswagen for a gold Camry. He'd left it on a corner, parked facing out, ready to leave Denver with a pile of cash.

The Camry started up. He put the car in gear and drove out. He'd seen no sign of police at the moment, but it was better to be moving in the open than cooped up in the concrete jungle.

Kahler had always hated cities. Abominable places to live. He couldn't breathe surrounded by all those people.

He hammered the Camry's dashboard with his fist. What the hell happened? He'd expected resistance at Easy Tire. Miller could have been there. He'd arrived with three loaded guns just in case.

But Miller wasn't there. Nor was the money. Or the drugs.

The place had been cleared out.

Had Miller screwed them over? Not likely. Some of the men were still there. Working on cars. Changing tires like good little saps. So where was Miller now?

And why was that damned reporter there? He'd noticed a Jeep in the parking lot but shrugged it off. There were thousands of Jeeps in Denver.

But that one really was hers. And she'd had the gall to chase him. Seriously? How did that make sense? What kind of reporter does crap like that? She had to know he'd kill her, given the chance.

Kahler gripped the steering wheel hard. He should have killed her long before now.

He rubbed his upper arm. His fingers came away bloody. He didn't look. The wound wasn't agonizing. He could still use the arm. He didn't care.

The army had taught him survival skills in the face of the enemy. Not to give up after a minor setback.

He punched the dash. He was sure as hell going to keep going. He had no choice. The cops had his picture and DNA, but with enough money he could disappear. Leave the country like he planned. A good beach and a good woman in South America and he'd be set.

But first he needed the money from Miller. The drugs, too. They could be sold. A different city. Farther south. To the right dealer, he'd get a few million. Enough to fuel his comfortable life.

He switched on the wipers as thin snow settled on the windshield, melting into icy slush, and zigzagged his way through the streets, away from the garage, watching everything, everywhere, all at once. Cars pushed past and slow cars dawdled. Nothing out of the ordinary.

He reached I-70 and took the entrance ramp onto the freeway.

Kahler needed to find Miller first. The obvious place to look was the other East Tire branch. But Miller would know what had happened by now.

Which meant his operational window of opportunity was slim. He pushed the Camry faster. The speedometer touched a hundred miles per hour as he weaved between vehicles.

He grinned. It'd be a bad day for some zealous rookie who decided to pull him over.

Kahler took the closest exit and slowed as he approached Easy Tire. Even before he pulled into the street, he saw the reflection of blue flashing lights from windows and wet rooftops.

A traffic stop gone wrong was too much to hope for.

The police were at Easy Tire. He swung a U-turn and worked his way over three blocks, working out a better approach as he drove.

The road from here to Easy Tire was long and straight. Cars filled parking lots and people milled around the sidewalks. Business signs dotted the street. Some flashed neon lights.

Easy Tire had a simple sign on a pole, illuminated now by the blue flashing lights from the mass of police cars surrounding the place. It looked like a cop convention with cruisers everywhere and officers posted to prevent gawkers from entering.

"Dammit!" How could the cops have organized so much manpower already?

Kahler turned onto another street and headed away from Easy Tire. He should never have trusted Miller. Guy couldn't organize a round of drinks in a brewery.

Kahler turned again, encircling Easy Tire, trying to plan a solid approach.

Ahead, a lone man wearing a hoodie walked with his head down. Kahler drove past him, only recognizing the guy in his rearview mirror.

He stopped and reversed the Camry. The man lifted his head and, seeing the car, turned to cross the street.

Kahler opened his side window. "Hassan. Stop. It's me."

Hassan stood in the middle of the road. He stared a moment, not approaching the Camry. "Need to get away from here, man."

"I know." Kahler motioned to the car. "Get in."

Hassan hesitated.

"Now," Kahler hissed.

Hassan shrugged and got into the passenger seat.

Kahler set off. A bell chimed relentlessly, getting on his last nerve.

"Put your belt on," he said.

Hassan secured his seat belt, silencing the chime. "Cops are all over Easy Tire."

"What did you see?"

"They swooped in on the place. Rounded everyone up."

"They get a tipoff?"

"How do I know, man?"

"Were they searching for drugs?"

"Don't know. I ducked out the back soon as I heard the noise."

"Where's Miller?"

Hassan shrugged.

"Was he there?"

Hassan shrugged again.

Kahler fisted his hand and punched Hassan in the biceps. "At the garage! Did the cops get him?"

"I don't know! I told you, I just got out fast."

"You got a gun? Knife? Anything we could use?"

"For what?"

"You want the cops to end up with all your money?"

"Man, you can't be—"

"Dammit. Do you have a gun or a knife? Yes or no?"

Hassan sighed and took out a small handgun. Great for concealed carry but not useful for offense.

Kahler gave a dismissive sigh. "Got a knife?"

Hassan pulled a Ka-Bar from an ankle holster.

Kahler swept his right fist around and connected with Hassan's nose. A hard blow this time. Bone and gristle crunched from the impact.

Hassan yelped as blood sprayed down his face.

Kahler ripped the gun from his hand, tossed it in the rear, and wrestled the Ka-Bar free.

Hassan wrapped his hands around his nose. "What the—"

Kahler flipped the knife around and drove it into Hassan's leg. Just an inch. Placed halfway between the knee and the hip. Far enough from vital arteries but plenty of flesh for pain.

Hassan screamed and howled. He clenched his fists.

Kahler twisted the knife a fraction.

Hassan cried out, "Stop!"

"Where's Miller?"

"I—"

Kahler leaned on the knife.

A guttural noise ripped from Hassan's throat. He tried to force back the pain and reach for Kahler's neck at the same time.

Kahler twisted the knife again. This time Hassan screamed, and he moved his hands toward the knife.

"Touch me and you'll die in that seat," Kahler said, turning the knife for emphasis.

Hassan's screams were deafening in the confines of the car.

"Last time. Where is Miller?"

"I...I..." Hassan choked his words out between grunts and snatched breaths. "I don't—"

"Tell me now and you can leave with one functioning leg."

"I...can't...I don't—"

"Or not."

"Ah, ah, ah. No, no, no." Hassan strained against the seat belt.

Blood bubbled from his nose. He had his hands close to the blade, but he didn't try to grab it. One wrong twitch and Kahler could backhand the knife into his stomach or any of his major organs.

He'd be dead before Kahler could stop the car and throw his body out.

Hassan took a deep breath. "P-please."

Kahler yanked the knife out.

Hassan screamed for several seconds before dissolving into a low grunt, his hands squeezing his leg hard in a desperate attempt to stem the pain and blood.

"Talk," said Kahler, holding the knife backhanded over the gear shift.

Hassan panted as he wiped blood from his face with his sleeve.

Kahler moved the knife. "We can do the leg thing again, if you like."

Hassan exhaled. "He...He left a couple of hours ago."

Kahler waited. "And?"

"Said we need to keep things moving." Hassan gulped air. "Took the drugs and money."

"And you let him?"

"He knows what he's doing."

"Yeah, yeah."

"I trust him."

"Where'd he take the stuff?"

Hassan kept quiet.

"Want to start the other leg?"

Hassan squeezed himself closer to the door. "I don't know where he went. Not for sure."

"Quickly."

"He ain't going to screw us over, man."

Kahler adjusted his grip on the knife. "I don't share your confidence."

Hassan took a deep breath. "Okay, okay. But you got to let me out. I ain't feeling so good."

"You don't say." Kahler sped up.

"Man…" whined Hassan.

"Talk."

Hassan breathed deeply. "The mountains. A hut…or cabin… or something. I heard him talking. Devon Peak. Road to the top."

"What's the road?"

"I don't know, man."

Kahler drew back the knife.

Hassan moved his hands to stop the attack. "No, no, no. I don't know. He didn't say. Nothing. I just overheard. It's a hike. That's what he said. West off the end of the road. That's what he said. That's what he said, man. Nothing else. I swear."

"Show me."

"What?"

"On a map, idiot."

Hassan fiddled with his phone a moment, then held it out, his hand shaking.

Kahler looked at the blood-smeared object. Devon Peak was in the center of the display. The satellite photograph had been taken in summer, when the ground and trees were green.

A narrow road wound up from the interstate to the top.

"Where is it? The hut?"

Hassan scrolled west and zoomed in on a tiny smudge. Even with the maximum zoom, it was hard to say for sure the smudge was a hut, but on balance, Kahler thought it could be.

"Good enough." He pulled over on the side of the road. "Get out."

Hassan opened his door. He pushed himself from his seat and stood on one foot, his injured leg off the ground.

"Wait," Kahler said. He reached into the backseat. "Your gun."

He threaded his finger through the trigger guard, aimed, and pulled. Four shots. Each one shoved Hassan backward.

The gun's punch was surprising. The noise inside the confines of the Camry wasn't quiet, either.

Hassan collapsed on the sidewalk.

Kahler threw the tiny gun into the backseat and stomped on the accelerator. Force closed the passenger door as he raced away.

CHAPTER 61

JESS STOOD BY HER Jeep, hands tucked in her jacket pockets. The weather report called for snow tomorrow.

Two people had been injured when Kahler shot into the car behind him. Paramedics had stemmed the blood flow and installed IVs in minutes.

"Fair" was their single-word assessment of the condition of the victims as they sped away to the hospital.

Norton took Jess's statement and released her from the scene at Kahler's Cadillac. He said she might prove useful at the second Easy Tire location, and she drove straight over.

Squad cars lined the street and officers bustled back and forth, radios crackling with updates. Jess didn't need the details to know there'd been no big drug bust here. The atmosphere didn't have a celebratory ring to it.

Grim faced, Henry left the garage and walked fast in her direction.

"Guess," he said when he arrived at her Jeep.

"Nothing here."

He nodded. "We sealed the area before we went in. No one—absolutely no one—got in or out. But…"

"Tunnels?"

"Nothing yet, but we're looking. We found a few guns and some drugs."

"Some?"

"Doesn't look like much, but the containment team is still assessing."

Jess knew one of the dangers in drug busts was exposure to the drugs. A combination of shoddy packaging and unpredictable potency meant even a small accidental exposure could be fatal for an unprotected member of the team.

"Any chance they were tipped off?" Jess asked.

"Not likely. Not enough time for that," Henry said.

"And if they knew, why is the gang still here?" Jess nodded. "So, no warning."

"But Denver PD raided both Easy Tire locations and found nothing." Henry pursed his lips and shook his head. "We're missing something."

"We connected Brantley to the theft of the K10. Kahler was the most likely shooter at Golden's warehouse. Killing Finny and his crew was definitely drug related," Jess said, going through the connections as if she were counting them on her fingers. "First Aurora Bank has been funneling money to Colombia. Rooney is dead and Lucy Cranfield is still missing. We have a license plate tied to Easy Tire, and both men ran when approached. Hell, Kahler tried to kill me. Twice."

Morris whistled. "Sounds more like a Hollywood script than a bunch of thugs fighting over drug territory."

"Kahler's an army-trained sniper gone rogue. Not your usual street thug." She glanced toward the garage. "There must be something here."

"We've still got a lot to go through." Henry checked his watch. "I gotta go. Probably going to be a late night."

She patted his arm. "Go. Don't worry about me."

Henry walked back to the garage and her phone rang. She recognized the number. "Armando?"

"Social media's buzzing. Lot of police activity. Might be connected with your warehouse thing."

"Not really a thing, but yes, it's connected."

"Thought it might be."

"I'm there now. Plenty going on, but you'll have to wait for an official statement."

"Might be connected with Lucy, right?" he asked hopefully.

"Believe me, this place is swarming with police and FBI. If there's anything to be found, they will find it."

"Have they looked into phone records?"

"I'm sure someone is." Jess frowned. "You got something you want to tell me?"

"No. Well…you're not police, right?"

Jess sighed. "Armando, if you're connected to these people or what's happened—"

"No. Nothing like that. It's just…I have a friend, works back-office stuff for one of the big wireless operators. And…"

"We don't have time to fool around, Armando. Say what you've got to say."

Armando breathed loudly into the phone for another couple of moments, still undecided.

Finally he said, "I looked up the address the police raided. Easy Tire? A bunch of burner phones have been used at that location."

"No surprise. Do you have numbers?"

"That would be illegal. But I have one. It's a mobile hot spot. Big one, like companies use. Been used at that location for a year. Occasional trips to other places. But last couple of days it's moved."

"Where is the mobile hot spot now?" Jess asked.

Armando replied, "I can send coordinates."

"An address would be better."

"There's no address. It's out in the mountains," Armando said. "I'm texting the coordinates now."

CHAPTER 62

JESS CONSIDERED ARMANDO'S TIP. Cell phones had the capacity to be a hot spot. But Armando meant something much more sophisticated.

But a big industrial-type hot spot at Easy Tire? Why would they need something like that?

Maybe it wasn't located at Easy Tire at all. Depended on how accurate the location services were, Jess supposed. Could the hot spot have been near enough to be mistaken for Easy Tire?

There were businesses all along that street. Some had living quarters above the business. Any one of them could have used a mobile internet connection.

As for moving this hot spot out to the mountains, that was not really remarkable. It was winter in Colorado and the ski season was well under way. Jess imagined there were lots of hot spots in cabins out there at the moment.

Still, it was worth checking out.

Armando's message arrived with latitude and longitude coordinates. Jess looked them up on a map.

Her phone listed the altitude as 11,300 feet on Devon Peak.

A satellite image taken during the summer showed a small group of trees surrounding a vague smudge that might have been a hut. A dark line meandered from a nearby roadway. Nothing but a narrow track in summer that was probably covered with snow now. Making it impossible to find.

Even if there was a link between the cabin and Easy Tire, would an internet hot spot actually work in such a remote location? She sent the question to Armando. He replied that the cabin was on the edge of service from Breckenridge.

Over at Easy Tire, officers were busy processing everything they'd found. They might not have the big fish they'd hoped for, but nothing was left to chance. Jess couldn't help at the moment.

She brushed a dusting of snow from her new parka. She had the right clothes and a Jeep with winter tires.

She could check out Armando's tip. Even from a distance she would be able to tell if the smudge on the photo was a cabin and whether it was occupied.

If the intel was confirmed, she'd call it in and let the professionals deal with whatever was going on there.

She put the coordinates into her Jeep's navigation system. It displayed a route via I-70 and a turn to the south. Bypassing Mount Evans and eventually winding up a mountain pass on the side of Devon Peak.

The last part of the route was highlighted in red and flashed a warning about unpaved roads.

"It's not like you're doing anything useful at the moment," she said aloud. She'd already decided to go. She punched the button to start the route guidance and headed out.

She stopped at a gas station on the outskirts of Denver, gathered a couple of fruit and nut bars and a black coffee and filled the Jeep's gas tank. The snow-laden mountains were not a place where she wanted to run out of gas.

Traffic on the highway kept up at a good pace, even as the road narrowed to two lanes. Icy patches began to form in the corners of the windshield. She kept the heater high and the wipers going, but the Jeep's heating system was struggling to keep up with the cold.

A column of vehicles took the exit for Mount Evans. Which lightened the traffic but did nothing to improve road conditions. Progress slowed.

A pickup truck with no weight in the bed careened sideways into a snowbank at a sharp turn, forcing traffic to a halt.

Another truck driver pulled up to help get the pickup out of the snowbank.

Waiting for the two trucks to clear, Jess sipped her coffee. Her phone had no cell signal here. She couldn't check messages.

She composed a short message to Henry, hoping it would go through when she drove into an available signal.

Once the pickup was back on the road, traffic moved forward but at a slower rate. Her navigation screen indicated she had passed eight thousand feet. Another six miles to reach the unpaved route leading to the coordinates Armando provided.

Vehicles in front of her peeled off to cabins and lodges dotted along the route. The altitude clicked up as she continued.

At ten thousand feet, the last SUV ahead of Jess turned into a narrow driveway. The SUV plowed ahead toward a majestic two-story log cabin with a view all the way down the mountain.

Now Jess was alone on the road.

Fine particles of dry snow danced and twisted across the snowy pavement. The Jeep slipped a few times when the four-wheel drive rebalanced, seeking to grip on the icy patches.

The trees thinned out as she drove, gradually changing from thick forest with a heavy canopy to small clusters.

She'd reached the timberline. The elevation where forests ended because conditions are too harsh for forests to thrive.

Another few hundred feet of altitude and the trees would disappear completely. She might see an occasional stunted trunk up there but nothing more. Low temperatures and high winds and other environmental factors made trees impossible once she passed the tree line.

Jess slowed as she approached a Camry parked awkwardly on the side of the road. The right rear fender stuck in the snowbank as if it had slipped backward on the icy road.

She drew up ten feet behind the sedan. Daylight had faded. She turned her headlights on full and peered into the vehicle.

Jess saw no one inside. Fine snow swirled around the car, but there was no buildup around the windows and doors. The sedan hadn't landed here long ago.

The driver and any passengers had left. With a quick scan outside the car, she spied a trampled patch of snow. She looked farther up the trail but saw no one.

"Hope you're trudging toward shelter of some sort," Jess said aloud, putting the Jeep in gear again and slowly moving forward. "You'll freeze to death out there tonight."

A half mile farther along and she reached what the map indicated was an unpaved road. She saw no sign of the snow-covered road.

Jess was between the timberline and the tree line now. Pines still dotted the landscape in small clusters along the edges of the road, giving her some indication of the invisible path.

She'd arrived at the mountain later than she'd planned. Which meant walking in the cold and growing darkness.

She was already wearing the body armor, which would give her more protection and warmth out there. So she left it on.

Wriggling into the rear of the Jeep, she swapped her jeans for ski pants, stashed fruit and nut bars, a handheld GPS, and the Glock in her parka, and finished her coffee.

She grabbed her metal flashlight dangling from a lanyard and slipped it into her pocket. Finally, she donned a fleece hat and pulled her hood over the top.

Stepping outside into the cold, gusty wind, Jess locked the Jeep, tucked the key fob into a zippered interior pocket, and pulled ski gloves onto her hands.

Her boots were waterproof, and she cinched her snow cuffs tight on her pants. The cold didn't worry her as much as getting wet. Water sucked away body heat without mercy.

Jess set off walking between the outcrops of trees. The top of the snow was soft, but about twelve inches down her boots met hardpack.

She made good forward progress using the fading light without her flashlight.

Her GPS indicated the hut was two miles away. She could cover that easily on the snow-covered pavement. But walking was harder work when she lost the trail farther along the mountain.

She was crossing an area where the ground undulated in big troughs and peaks. After ten minutes of exertion, she unzipped the top of her jacket, balancing body heat with the frigid air.

The few remaining trees still seemed to indicate a path that twisted and turned, but she was closing the distance to the cabin.

The last of her daylight faded fast. She switched to the flashlight and GPS. Every minute, she swung the light around the area to keep her bearings and plot her route.

Just over halfway, the dry fine snow turned heavy and wet. The gusty wind picked up speed. She regretted leaving her ski goggles behind. The cold air made her eyes water.

She felt her phone vibrating in her pocket. She pulled her hood down and turned her back to the wind when she stopped in a cluster of trees to read the messages.

Henry's text warned her to be careful and gave a quick summary of the situation at the garage, which hadn't changed much.

But the message from Armando sent a chill down her spine.

Confirmed bank systems accessed by hot spot used at garage and in mountains.

Jess forwarded the message to Norton and Henry and tucked the phone back into her jacket.

If the gang had used a hut in the mountains as their base of operations to purchase drugs through an underground network, would they have protective measures in place?

Cameras? Infrared heat sensors?

More importantly, if Lucy had been kidnapped to replace Rooney, was she being held up here?

Only one way to find out. Jess flipped her hood into place, turned to face the wind, and kept going.

CHAPTER 63

THE GPS SAID THE cabin was still a mile away. Jess turned off the flashlight to avoid being seen as she approached.

She exited the trees, holding her arms in front to avoid branches slapping her face. Visibility was poor. Wind blew the snow in sheets across her path. She could see only a dozen feet ahead.

Her greatest fear was stepping off an edge. In the ghostly white glow, everything blended together.

Even a short drop, ten feet or less, could break a bone if she landed the wrong way or hit solid rock. She placed her weight down slowly on her leading foot, reasoning that she could always roll backward if she sensed the ground ahead might fall away.

Progress was slow. Pacing her way around an outcrop of trees, she realized they descended to her right. She was on the brink of a steep slope, so she turned left.

Her phone buzzed. She reached into her pocket. A message from Henry. As she opened the text, her feet slipped.

Her knees hit the snow.

She slid between the trees, falling, grasping for branches. Rolling and sliding along the snow, she emerged from the trees.

Her boots hit something under the snow, spinning her around. Snow sprayed into the air and slapped her face.

She heard a muted cry ahead. She glimpsed a figure wearing white clothes tumble headfirst a few feet away. Icy lumps hammered into her back as she clawed at the snow to bring herself to a stop. Finally, she managed to roll onto one knee.

The white-clad figure came to a rest ten feet farther down the hill. It was a man wearing a ski mask.

He rolled upright holding a large rectangular box in his right hand. Had to be a rifle case.

He rushed toward Jess, hindered but not stopped by the snow and the slope.

She threw herself forward, shoulder down, closing the gap between them while she had the advantage of altitude and gravity.

She hit him in the stomach, folding him over.

They tumbled backward.

He swung a punch that hit her in the side. The hard bulletproof vest took the brunt of the force, but it still hurt like hell. She rolled away from him.

He leapt forward, swinging for her stomach. She turned quickly. His gloved hand glanced off her thick parka and vest, this time without pain.

The rifle case swung around toward Jess, carried by the momentum he'd put into his punch. She grabbed the end of the long case and twisted. The length of the case gave her enough leverage to wrest the handle from his grip.

She swung the case horizontally, hammering the far end into his face. He made an angry noise between a cry and a grunt.

He grabbed the case. She shoved forward, pushing it into his face again and levering him backward.

He fell, the case flying free and slipping down the slope at speed.

He followed, rolling uncontrollably on his back, grunting and growling.

Twenty feet away, he disappeared in the dark, buried in the snow. Seconds later she heard a sickening crunch and a furious cry.

Her heart was beating fast. She panted, straining to hear movement. The air froze the sweat on her brow. Her knees felt weak.

Was that Theo Kahler? He was still unaccounted for and who else would be out here tonight?

She breathed fast. Whoever he was, she'd been lucky. Damned lucky.

He'd obviously hit something down there. If he'd been injured, that might stop him. But maybe it would only slow him down.

Either way, he'd made it plain that he'd try to kill her if she engaged him again.

She kept going.

A minute later she risked glancing at her GPS, shielding the light from the display with her hand. Another half mile to the cabin.

With the possibility of Kahler coming up behind her, she was fully committed now. She composed a text message to Henry, but it waited in the outbox until the phone found a signal to send it.

She walked and counted to a hundred before stopping to listen and then walking again. Each time she paused she heard nothing.

Whatever had happened to Kahler might have taken him out of action.

He could stay where he was until she reported his position from the warmth and safety of her Jeep.

CHAPTER 64

THE SILENCE WAS ABSOLUTE now. Long gone were the sounds of the city. No car engine or freeway noise cut through the snowfall. Animals seemed to have abandoned any attempt to forage in these conditions.

Only Jess's footfalls on the thickening snow disturbed the peace.

The sun was far below the horizon and sunlight no longer touched any part of the sky. Jess's world glowed in the moonlight. Falling snow cut her visibility to ten or twenty feet, but within that range everything seemed unbearably bright.

She continued the rhythm of careful progress. Easing her weight onto her front foot, stopping every hundred paces to listen, and checking her GPS every five minutes.

The group of trees was exactly where the satellite picture showed. She walked around the edge, sensing the slope with her feet and working uphill seeking a higher vantage point.

She reached for her phone. Her pocket was empty.

She'd had it in her hand when the man attacked her. Where had she lost it? No way she could find it out there in the dark, even if she went back.

Jess hunched down and entered the trees, stepping slowly. Even so, she could hear the noise of her heavy tread.

"Nothing you can do about it," she murmured.

The trees were evenly spaced, branches heavy with snow. She moved from one to another, pausing behind each to check front and rear to confirm no one had crept up behind.

And then the trees stopped. She moved sideways twenty paces to confirm the area in front of her was showing as her destination and knelt behind a rock.

A deep rumble disturbed the silence. She turned her head, trying to pinpoint the source of that sound, but its low volume and frequency defeated her.

The snow's milky whiteness extended in all directions. The hut hadn't been clearly visible on the satellite picture, so it was likely close to one edge of the remaining trees.

The man must have been heading to the hut and might have recovered from whatever happened to him. She only had a few minutes to learn what she came to find out.

She pulled out her pistol. She didn't plan to break into the hut, gun blazing. But she would shoot if she had to.

Two options. Circle the trees or enter the clearing. Both approaches carried the risk of exposure. She opted to circle.

Halfway around, she saw a wooden structure in the gloom. She backed up until the outline was only just visible, realizing that even if she couldn't see them, they could certainly see her.

The building was a log cabin that looked built to last. From her vantage point, she couldn't judge the cabin's size. But the rumble she'd heard definitely came from the cabin.

She moved farther into the trees and skirted around the rear of the building. Steam rose from a small chimney. The cabin was occupied.

Steady light spilled out around what looked like thick paper stuck to double-glazed windows. The sort of energy-efficient windows used in modern homes. Incongruous for a rustic cabin like this one, but effective to keep the heat inside and the cold outside.

A tarp covered what she guessed was a snowmobile, probably with a large sled they could pull along behind it for supplies.

She found the source of the rumble. It came from a large box at the rear of the cabin. Probably a muffling enclosure for a large generator, which explained how they managed to run the steady light inside.

What else did they need electricity for?

Farther on she came to the cabin's entrance. A full-width porch ran across the front, thick with smooth snow.

The building seemed smaller up close. Likely a single room, twelve feet wide and twice as long.

She knelt by a small tree. The covered windows blocked her view of the interior. There were occupants inside. She saw silhouettes move past the windows from time to time.

It seemed unlikely vacationers would cover the windows with paper. But the cabin was occupied. Henry and Norton needed to know right away.

CHAPTER 65

LUCY CRANFIELD HAD BEEN tethered to the makeshift worktable a good long time. Her back ached and her wrists were throbbing. Eyestrain caused a massive headache. She was hungry, cold, tired. She desperately needed a break.

On top of all that, everything she'd tried to duplicate Rooney's passwords and get into the banking system to steal massive amounts of cash had failed. She was running out of options, which increased the tension and caused her to make mistakes, too.

But she couldn't stop. Miller, if that was his name, wouldn't allow it. He'd made that plain enough.

Not that he'd actually kill her. At least, not until she admitted she had no idea how to get a functioning password. Which she absolutely would not admit until he forced her hand.

His patience was already tested. It wouldn't last forever.

Besides, Miller had created this whole problem. He'd tried the one-time password Rooney gave him. When it failed, probably because of a glitch in Rooney's equipment, he'd rendered the password useless.

The system was set up to generate a new password when the existing one was accessed. Miller had failed to access the system using Rooney's password. There was no way to get into the system to generate a new one.

Lucy hadn't figured out all of Rooney's system. But she knew about cybersecurity.

To put it bluntly, Miller was screwed. There might be a super hacker out there who was as good as Rooney and could figure this out.

But Lucy was no hacker. And she had no desire to be.

She was buying time. But she needed an escape plan. Pronto.

While Kemp was gone to pick up supplies, Lucy had a chance. She couldn't fight them both. Together they were too much for her.

But Miller alone was not all that smart.

She made a plan, and she hoped it would work. The longer she waited, the more likely Kemp would return. It was frigid cold outside and dark as pitch. But waiting for morning light was just as risky. Maybe more if Kemp came back before dawn.

Now, she thought. *Go now.*

Lucy looked up from the laptop screen. "Sorry, but I need to pee."

Miller's face wrinkled in a fierce scowl. "You drink too much coffee."

"Hard to work if I'm falling asleep at the keyboard," Lucy shot back.

"How about I shoot you first?" Miller raised his pistol, pointing it at her foot. "Keep you from running. I've got no energy to chase you. And it's freezing cold out there."

For an extremely tense moment, Lucy worried that he'd actually shoot her. She stifled the nausea triggered by his threat and put a defiant look on her face.

"You shoot me and I'll be in too much pain to work at all," she replied.

"Yeah, well, I haven't shot you yet and you're not producing anything I can use, are you?" Miller snarled in return.

But he didn't pull the trigger.

Instead, he waved the pistol in her general direction as he approached to unlock her restraints.

CHAPTER 66

JESS BACKED AWAY WHEN the cabin's front door opened. Her heart skipped a beat. She held her breath and stopped moving.

Two figures stepped onto the porch, kicking through the fresh layer of snow.

Jess eased closer to the tree's shadow.

The first was a woman with long hair wearing a three-quarter-length coat designed more for style than protection. Lucy Cranfield. No question.

The other was a man wearing a knit cap and a parka. He pushed her off the porch with a gun in her back.

"I told you, I have to pee," Lucy said angrily.

He shoved her again. The gun looked big and fat. An automatic.

"Just get on with it. Frigging freezing out here," he growled, pushing the gun toward her for emphasis.

He looked around the clearing. His scan passed Jess without stopping. Had he seen her?

Lucy walked toward the woods, and he followed. Lucy stepped around a tree and squatted down.

Jess moved her gaze away and looked into the cabin. Light spilled out the open door. She saw a table and computer equipment with blinking LEDs.

Perhaps Lucy and the man were the only occupants.

He stomped back and forth, slapping his bare hands against his jacket. "Hurry up."

"I'm not doing this for fun," Lucy snapped back.

She turned her head and stared. A straight line. Through the gloom. Between the trees and across the clearing.

And then she saw Jess.

That almost electric connection when two people made eye contact.

Jess's heart leapt. She raised a finger across her lips.

Lucy stood with her mouth open.

The man with the gun said, "Are you damned well done?"

"I..." Lucy closed her mouth, zipped up her jeans, and rustled her coat. "Just finished."

She glanced back to Jess.

Jess kept her finger over her mouth and nodded.

"Kemp?" the man called out. He paced around and called again. There was no reply, just the deep thrum of the generator.

Lucy stepped around the tree and back into the clearing. "Looks like it's just you."

The man turned. "What'd you mean by that?"

"Kemp's late getting back. Maybe he's not coming."

"He'll be here."

"What then? When he arrives?" Lucy asked.

"Don't sweat it. Get the transfer done, then you're free."

Lucy took a deep breath. "You promised."

"I'm still wearing this itchy damned ski mask, aren't I?"

"True," she said, drawing the one syllable out for a while.

"Get back inside. Get our problem figured out. We'll all be happy, and you can go."

When she didn't dash into the cabin, he pushed Lucy toward the door and jammed the gun into her back.

Jess inched around the tree, keeping the pair in sight. The ski mask hid the man's face. He'd said they could let Lucy go because she hadn't seen their faces.

Which was a lie.

When Lucy outlived her usefulness, she'd be killed. Like all the others.

Lucy climbed the snowy steps to the porch. The man was one step behind.

Jess raised her pistol. He had his back to her. An easy target. One or two shots could incapacitate him until Henry and Norton arrived.

She licked her lips. The two were close. Thirty feet away.

Jess was a good shot. Accomplished even.

But could she shoot a man in the back? Cold-blooded?

Before she made the decision, he lost his footing on the steps and lurched forward, falling into Lucy.

She turned to fend him off, but he regained his balance and pushed her through the door, slamming it hard behind them.

The loud noise echoed all the way around the mountain.

Half a moment later, Jess heard a whooshing sound.

A wave of snow descended rapidly from up the slope.

The wave knocked her down, sliding her toward the cabin. She let out an involuntary cry and clamped her jaw shut.

The cabin door opened and slammed back against the wall. The same man stormed out, gun first.

The snow wave became a mini avalanche. It overwhelmed her body, turning her around to face the cabin.

He ran over before Jess stopped moving, holding his gun six inches from her face.

"Don't even think about it." He stamped his boot down on her wrist and kicked her pistol free.

"I'm lost. I'm lost," Jess said, raising her hands above her head.

"Bullshit." He wedged his gun under her chin. "Ain't nobody all the way out here for a stroll in the snow."

"Who is it?" Lucy called from the doorway.

"Get back inside," he yelled angrily.

"Look, I told you, I'm lost." Jess shuffled an inch farther from his gun and sat up in the snow. "I saw your lights. I was hoping you could shelter me until morning."

"Yeah, sure," the man growled. "We're running a friggin' Holiday Inn here."

He kicked snow over her pistol. He grabbed Jess's arm and pulled her upright.

"Move." He shoved her toward the door, nearly knocking her off her feet again.

CHAPTER 67

JESS TOOK THE STEPS up to the porch slowly, unzipping her jacket's side pockets as she walked. The man didn't push her again.

He'd likely fed Lucy a story about not wanting to hurt her in order to get her cooperation. Shooting Jess would blow the lid off his lies. He'd do it anyway. But not before he had to.

Lucy backed into the cabin to let them enter.

A dirt-covered floor crunched under Jess's boots. She scanned the cabin quickly.

Only one room. All the windows were covered in paper, not just the ones she'd seen from outside.

Bedclothes were heaped in the middle of a rusty metal bed in one corner of the room. A bright blue plastic tarp covered the large, rounded shape.

On the floor, a microwave and coffee maker were surrounded by food wrappers and drink cans.

In contrast to the bare-bones squalor of the rest of the place, the table was piled with wires and electrical equipment and occupied most of the room.

An RXP box rested on the top of a half-disassembled computer. Several chairs surrounded the table.

Jess frowned. "What are you doing?"

Lucy looked at the man.

He closed and locked the door and waved his gun at Lucy. "Get on with it."

She sat down. He handcuffed her right wrist and attached a cord intended to secure her to the table.

He pulled a chair away from the table and gestured for Jess to sit.

She didn't. Sitting would put her at a disadvantage. She needed room to maneuver.

He seemed conflicted. If he forced Jess to comply, he'd lose his advantage with Lucy.

Jess ignored him and stepped toward the bed.

"Sit," he said, hefting his gun in her direction. "I won't ask again."

"You're a long way from everywhere." She kicked the bed. A small cloud of dust bloomed. "But I understand the attraction of solitude."

He crossed the room to Jess in half a moment, leveling the gun toward her chest. He had his finger on the trigger.

"I said sit." He shoved her back onto the bed and leaned sideways to grab a length of cord.

Jess rolled from his line of fire and whipped the flashlight from her pocket, holding the lanyard and flinging the foot-long aluminum body as a cudgel.

The metal flashlight made hard contact. The two-pound mass, moving fast, slammed into his temple with a sickening crash.

His gun went off. The stray bullet shattered the window behind Jess.

He staggered toward the bed, head down, using one hand to stop himself from collapsing and maintaining his grip on the gun.

Jess whipped her arm around and swung the flashlight again. Horizontally.

This time she hit him on the other side of his head.

He stumbled, shaking his head while bringing his gun around toward Jess.

Lucy ripped the wires from a box on the table and hurled it.

A sharp corner of the box struck him in the back. High up, between the shoulder blades.

He cried out and fired reflexively.

The noise of both shots was deafening, but Jess barely noticed.

Until the second bullet hit the right side of her chest.

A glancing hit with a 9mm round.

The force and impact of the shot landed hard enough.

Pain bloomed out to consume her entire body.

Jess dropped the flashlight and stumbled back, clutching the wound.

Her legs weakened and she sank to one knee, struggling to breathe. Tears sprang to her eyes and overflowed, rolling down her cheeks. Her body's defensive mechanisms worked overtime to numb the shock and pain.

The man staggered forward, gun extended, his finger still through the guard and too close to the trigger.

Given the chance, he'd shoot her again. Lucy, too, now that she'd seen him for what he was.

Jess gritted her teeth and lunged for him.

Grabbed his arm. Forced the gun away.

She brought her knee up as hard as she could into his groin. Once. Twice. Three times.

He folded over, groaning and holding his crotch.

She shoved him forward with her boot on his back.

He collapsed, sinking to his knees, the gun still gripped against his chest.

His head smacked the blue tarp on the bed. His body followed.

Sliding downward, resting his weight against the tarp, he twitched, jerking to one side.

The gun went off again, jolting the tarp. The force of the bullet and expanding gasses tore the material, sending the blue tarp flapping, while a cloud of white dust rose into the air.

The man screamed.

Lucy grabbed Jess's arm and dragged her away. She was weak. Dizzy. The room was spinning.

"Get the gun," she mumbled.

"No," Lucy said. "No."

"Get the gun," Jess said, trying to shake Lucy off.

"No. We've got to go," Lucy said. "That white stuff is fentanyl. Very strong. Lots of it."

The man rolled over, sliding down the blue tarp, a growing bloodstain around his stomach. His face and chest were covered in white powder.

His mouth hung open. His eyes seemed paralyzed.

The gun thumped to the floor.

"Get the gun," Jess mumbled.

"Have you got Narcan?" Lucy said. "He won't survive without Narcan. The drugs are too powerful."

Jess shook her head, trying to make sense of the situation.

His head slumped forward, and his tongue protruded.

Lucy pulled Jess to the far side of the room. She unzipped Jess's jacket to check her gunshot wound.

"What the hell?" Lucy ran her hand over the frayed fibers around the bullet's impact point and tapped the hard shell of the ceramic plates.

"Bulletproof," Jess said. She slid her hand under the vest and massaged the pain in her ribs. "Thanks to some very helpful friends."

Lucy sank back on her haunches, panting. "I thought you were…"

"Not yet," Jess said. Her painful breathing was easing a bit. "I'll have a helluva bruise. Maybe a couple of cracked ribs. But still alive."

"You were at the Mellon Tree. For Justin Rooney."

"Yeah."

"I think…I think he's been involved with these people," Lucy said. "He was always looking for money to spend on those expensive cars. I guess he found it."

"How do you know that's fentanyl?" Jess said, pointing to the blue tarp.

"They moved it here a couple of hours ago. I heard them talking." Lucy pointed toward the man. "Name's Miller. The other one, Kemp, let it slip. Pissed Miller off. They didn't want me to know they planned to kill me. Like I was some moron who wouldn't figure that out."

"They killed Rooney. They weren't planning to let you go, Lucy," Jess said. "I came here alone. And I've lost my phone. We need to get help."

Lucy glanced at the pile of computer equipment on the table. "I can get a message out. But I don't know where we are."

Jess fumbled the GPS from her pocket and held it out, reciting Henry's phone number.

Lucy typed frantically for a moment and hit the send button. "Mr. Larson. They locked him up. A place called Toppers, they said. He might be dead by now."

"Tell Detective Norton." She recited Norton's number, which she'd memorized in case she needed it.

Lucy quickly sent the messages, then waved toward the blue tarp. "We need to get out of here. Away from that stuff. Even a small amount can kill."

"Yeah, and away from Kahler."

"Who?" Lucy frowned.

"A sniper. He's probably on his way here," said Jess, rolling onto her knees. "He's tried to kill me twice already."

Lucy's mouth hung open.

Jess used the wall to help her stand. She shook the tether that attached Lucy to the "We've got to get you free."

"Over there." Lucy pointed to the microwave. "An axe. They thought it was funny. Using an axe to open the meals."

Jess took a deep breath and held it while moving closer to the pile of drugs. She grabbed the axe and returned quickly.

Lucy stretched the cord on the ground and swung the axe to separate herself from the table. She found a hat and gloves and stared at the gun by Miller's body.

"Forget it," Jess said, looking at the white powder. "My pistol is outside in the snow. I can find it."

"He had a phone." Lucy worked her way around the edge of the hut to the opposite side of the bed, held her breath, foraged through the heap of bedclothes, and pulled out a burner phone. She pressed a few buttons.

"Doesn't work." She tossed it to Jess.

Jess tucked the phone into a pocket. "We'll take it anyway. And the snowmobile."

Lucy shook her head. "They screwed up. Kemp accidentally took the key when he left. Miller was really pissed. Said he'd kill Kemp when he got back."

"Then we'll walk back to my Jeep." Jess picked up a broom from beside the door and disconnected the brush, leaving a five-foot yellow pole. She opened the door. "Keep as quiet as possible. Kahler could be out there."

Lucy nodded and they stepped out into the increasingly cold night.

CHAPTER 68

THE SNOWFALL HADN'T SLOWED. The majestic pines surrounding the cabin were barely visible. Blanketed by the combination of faint moonlight and crystal whiteness, the nighttime scene looked otherworldly.

The snow blanketing the front of the cabin was deep and even. Jess and Lucy searched the ground, using the broom handle to stir the snow, until Jess uncovered her gun.

She cleaned snow from the mechanism, checked the magazine, and tucked the pistol inside her jacket.

Kahler might or might not be injured. He might have returned to his car, or he might be heading for the cabin. But he wouldn't hesitate to kill them, given the chance.

Jess pointed up the hill. "I have a Jeep. Two miles away. But Kahler's out there. We'll take the long route."

Lucy pulled her hat down over her ears.

Leaving the area closest to the cabin wasn't difficult. The trees provided handholds for stability and the ground was relatively flat. But as they left the woods, travel became much more difficult.

Ground and sky melded into one featureless white swirl, stealing Jess's vision and balance. Her boots sank six to twelve inches into the fresh snow with every step. The snow underneath the new powder collapsed as she moved her weight from one foot to another, rolling her to one side and challenging her ability to balance.

Lucy wasn't properly dressed. Her jeans were soaked with snow and rapidly became wet, further slowing progress.

After fifteen minutes, Jess paused to rest against a single pine. Lucy's face was flushed in a blotchy patchwork, and she wasn't breathing well. They were both covered with a layer of clinging snow.

"How much farther?" Lucy said, shivering.

"About two miles. We need to loop around to my Jeep. We don't want to be on the same path as Kahler."

Lucy nodded without complaint.

Jess brushed snow from the girl's coat and hat. "Let's keep moving."

Using the GPS, Jess located her Jeep and set off again. Lucy followed directly behind.

The broom handle worked well for detecting changes in the gradient and preventing them from falling into an unseen ravine. A couple of times, Jess veered downhill to stay on a level path, making the walk slightly easier.

Wind kept the snow angling down the hill, across their trail. Jess kept brushing the buildup from her hood to prevent it from melting and running inside her jacket.

Lucy grabbed Jess's arm.

"Stop, please," she gasped. She sank to her haunches, leaning forward, breathing hard and shivering uncontrollably.

A grating noise cut through the air. Jess turned back to look at the cabin. The grating noise became the thrum of a gas-powered engine. "Snowmobile."

Lucy closed her eyes. "Kahler."

"He'll never find us in this." Jess did her best to sound confident, offering the encouragement Lucy needed.

Jess didn't mention that Kahler had been an Army Ranger. By all accounts, he was a damned good one. He probably considered these conditions a mere challenge, not an insurmountable obstacle.

The GPS showed they still had to cover a mile and a half to reach the Jeep. Their footprints were disappearing with the fresh snow, but would the snowfall be quick enough to hide their trail from Kahler?

Lucy struggled to her feet. "We'd better keep moving."

Jess led off. Neither of them spoke.

The snowmobile engine revved and roared. The omnipresent sound filled the previously silent night.

Jess kept turning her head with the hope of tracking the vehicle, but the snow muted the frequencies that might have located him. Yet the noise was getting louder. Kahler was coming closer.

Lucy fell behind a few paces. Then a few more. Jess waited for her to catch up.

"Sorry," Lucy said, steam rising from her forehead in the damp night air. The girl's gloved hands shook. "I don't feel well."

"Did they feed you?"

Lucy shook her head. "Just a granola bar and coffee. Lots of coffee."

Jess took her hand, holding it gently with her fingertips. Lucy couldn't stop shaking. She wouldn't be able to continue much longer. Carrying her was impossible and exposure would reduce her body temperature to dangerous levels.

"We have to find shelter," Jess said.

"Maybe we should have waited in the hut."

Silently, Jess wondered if Lucy was right. Too late for that now.

She turned up the slope, convinced she saw a place that could provide shelter.

She held on to Lucy's hand as the girl trudged up the hill. They reached a cluster of trees stunted by the altitude's harsh conditions.

"Can we really hide here?" said Lucy.

"No. We're going higher."

"Higher?" Lucy's fear was clear in her voice.

Jess led them fifty feet farther up the hill to a rock overhang. The blowing snow had accumulated a massive drift. Jess steered Lucy around the side of the overhang to a single small pine.

"Stay here. No matter what happens."

Lucy slumped down. She didn't speak.

Jess turned back to the cluster of trees, carefully sweeping the ground behind her with the broom handle in an attempt to cover their tracks.

The trees were thin and a few feet apart here. She selected a four-foot-wide gap and lodged the broom handle at chest height between two trees.

She turned on the burner phone and tucked it into the crook of a branch behind the broom handle.

If Kahler hit the broom handle squarely while riding the snowmobile fast enough, she'd have the advantage. If he approached from a different direction, moving toward the phone's light, she would know exactly where he was when the light moved.

Twenty feet from the trees, she scooped out an indentation with her hands. Lying down, she dragged snow back over herself, starting at her feet and working up to her shoulders.

She tucked her arms to her chest and gripped her Glock with both hands.

Time crept agonizingly slowly. Her snow jacket kept her dry, but the cold invaded her bones. The snowmobile engine growled one minute and purred the next.

Kahler was working his way up and down the mountain. A steady search pattern. Disciplined.

As the snowmobile noises grew louder, she realized he was about a hundred feet lower down the mountain. He would pass by without seeing the phone's light.

But what then? He wouldn't simply give up. He'd recovered from their previous encounter and was still on the hunt.

With the snowmobile, he had a clear advantage. Even if he did miss them with this first pass, he would comb back over the mountain.

Or she would encounter him somewhere else when he was prepared and she was not.

Jess knew where he was. She'd take him on now while she had that small advantage.

She drew her arms out, pointed her pistol downhill, and fired a single shot.

The noise cracked through the cold night air. A single sharp retort, the echo dampened by falling snow, but still loud enough to be heard.

The snowmobile's engine quieted a beat while Kahler located the gunshot. A moment later, the motor roared.

Kahler was heading her way.

Moments later a single hazy light appeared some distance below her. As the snowmobile approached, Kahler cut the light.

He weaved the sled around the far side of the cluster of trees. His silhouette was barely visible.

Jess adjusted her grip on the gun.

The phone screen glowed like a blue beacon. Kahler saw it.

Light flashed from the snowmobile's direction as automatic gunfire rang out. The glow from the phone danced and rolled as the bullet hit the tree where Jess had placed it.

The snowmobile's engine roared, and the headlight burst back to life.

Kahler raced toward the light, running fast between the trees.

He hit the broom handle and fell backward.

The impact wrenched him from the snowmobile.

The sled veered left, hit a tree, and rolled on its side, engine still screaming.

Kahler howled. Not pain, but anger.

He staggered to his feet in the gleam of the snowmobile's headlight, grunting with the effort. The engine labored as the track continued grinding and crunching against the tree.

Jess waited for a clear line of fire. She kept her aim low and sent three fast shots at her target.

This time Kahler's scream was definitely pain.

She fired again.

His screams increased with intensity and anger.

He dove for cover behind a narrow tree and fired back. His bullets churned the snow on her right, but she was unharmed.

The labored throb of the snowmobile's engine reached a crescendo and abruptly stopped as the engine stalled.

Jess fired again in Kahler's direction.

He returned fire from another location. He'd circled left.

Jess ran for the trees, knelt and fired single shots, aiming low and counting each one. She saw him run across the slope in the moonlight.

She moved forward and retrieved the phone. The cracked screen glowed but didn't respond to her touch. She shoved it in a pocket.

Jess worked her way out of the trees, following dark patches in the snow. He was losing blood.

She found an automatic weapon half-covered with snow. Kahler's. How many other weapons did he have with him?

She felt the heat from the snowmobile's engine and knelt beside the machine. It looked intact. If she could start it, she might find Lucy and outrun Kahler since he was on foot. She'd need to move fast.

Using the handle grips, she rocked the vehicle back and forth on the slope, hoping to build enough momentum to right it. Metal and plastic creaked.

The falling snow would mute a lot of the noise, but she feared Kahler would hear if she took too long.

She grunted against the five-hundred-pound weight, swinging harder and harder until it finally lurched upright, almost pulling her over.

She wiped snow from the handlebar. The keys dangled from the ignition switch beside a cord pull.

Once she started the engine, there'd be no doubt about her location.

Kahler would close in fast.

She pointed the sled downhill through a gap in the trees. The slope would allow her to build up plenty of speed. She'd be able to leave Kahler behind and head uphill to find Lucy.

Jess stood beside the snowmobile, placed one knee on the seat, gripped the starting cord, took a deep breath, wincing at the pain in her chest, and pulled as hard as she could.

The engine turned over, coughing once.

It didn't start.

She let the cord retract and tried again.

This time the engine caught a moment and died.

The engine's noises eroded her advantage. Kahler would be on his way. No time to lose.

She cycled the cord in and pulled again with all her might. The snowmobile burst into life, roaring loudly before settling into a steady rhythm.

A massive pain shot through her back. Left side. Low down.

Her body was lifted and thrown over the seat. Her head landed beside the front skid. Her legs arced around and slapped down on the snow.

Her right hand still gripped the starting cord.

She gasped and groaned, the air and energy knocked out of her.

Kahler stood on the opposite side of the snowmobile, knife in his hand. The bulletproof vest had saved Jess again, and he seemed shocked the blade wasn't buried in her back.

He threw one leg over the machine, raising the knife, preparing to finish the job.

She reached for the throttle and squeezed.

The snowmobile jerked forward. The handlebar pulled from her grip.

Kahler lurched backward, pushed awkwardly on the seat, legs in the air.

The snowmobile slowed. She wrapped the starter cord around his leg as he slid off the opposite side of the seat, arms windmilling, grasping for any kind of hold.

Jess whipped off a glove and squeezed the throttle lever. The engine growled and the snowmobile bolted forward.

Kahler screamed, flailing his arms, attempting to grab the sled and lift himself up.

She scrambled onto the snowmobile, landing one knee on the seat and jamming a glove over the handlebar, pinning the throttle lever on full.

The engine screamed. The impulse threw Jess off the seat into the snow.

The snowmobile hurtled down the slope, dragging Kahler by the starter cord bound tight around his leg and smashing him against the trees.

She rolled across the snow to a stop, watching the snowmobile disappear down the mountain while his angry screams faded into the distance.

Jess didn't wait. She scrambled to her feet and turned uphill toward the overhang.

The falling snow grew heavier and the flakes thicker, wetter. Visibility dropped to a few feet and the only sound she heard was the wind driving snow across the mountain.

She weaved left and right until, eventually, she found the rock.

It took another few minutes to find Lucy, curled into a ball, shivering uncontrollably. "Did—did...did you get him?"

"Hit him, but he got away."

"May...maybe he won't come back."

Snow had drifted around Lucy's body. Jess cleared it away. The girl's face was almost white. She needed shelter and fast.

Jess worked her way around the rock to the snowdrift that filled the space beneath the overhang. Fifteen feet high and filled with snow, the space was far from ideal. But Lucy didn't have the strength to move to another location.

Kahler's gun had an open stock, the kind of skeleton frame that reduced weight. Jess rammed it into the snowdrift, twisting and turning to half drill, half dig a horizontal tunnel. The gun's frame chewed up the snow but proved useless to sweep it away. She had to stop regularly to drag the loose snow from the growing space with her one gloved hand.

The digging was slow. The trench needed to be wide and deep enough for two, and although the new snow was fresh and soft, farther down it was hardpack.

Lucy dragged herself up onto her knees to help spread the extracted snow and hide their tunnel. Jess was about to tell the girl to save her strength, when she realized the exercise might warm her up and keep her blood flowing.

Fifteen minutes later, the hole was deep enough. Jess helped Lucy into the space, then shuffled in beside her, piling up snow to hide most of the entrance.

"What if he finds us?" Lucy said.

Jess tapped her pistol. "I have two guns. Twenty-plus shots. I'll use them all."

"Okay."

Now that they were out of the wind, Jess almost felt warm. An illusion, she knew. Her body was still losing heat, simply not as fast.

Lucy's shivering slowed and her breathing reached a more normal level.

Jess wriggled a granola bar from her pocket. She had a second bar but decided to save it for later. They would stay hidden until daylight.

Lucy protested they should share.

Jess refused. "I had a huge meal before heading up the mountain. Enough calories to last me a week, at least."

Lucy seemed unconvinced but gave in.

"Thank you," she said as she gobbled the bar and licked the crumbs from the plastic wrapper.

Jess had nothing to say. She watched the swirling whiteness, a gun in each hand, waiting for daylight.

CHAPTER 69

LUCY SLEPT. JESS MIGHT have. It was hard to tell. The whiteout stole time and space alike. If they became sealed into the snow tunnel, they would asphyxiate. Jess reached out regularly to clear away the snow accumulation from the small open hole at the entrance.

The howling wind finally abated, and Jess sensed the snow's slight change in hue. Her watch showed five a.m.

"Getting light," she said as she shook Lucy awake. "We need to move while we still have some cover."

Lucy nodded. Ice had formed around her nose and eyelashes. She tried to wipe it away with the back of her glove. She groaned.

"I don't think I can move."

Jess handed over the second granola bar. "You'll feel better once we get going."

She scrabbled out of the snow hole, pushing aside the mound she'd used to hide the entrance. The wind had dropped to a whisper and fine snow drifted almost vertically.

Fifty feet away, the cluster of trees she'd used to trap Kahler was visible. Which meant she and Lucy would be visible, too.

Jess dragged Lucy from the hole. The girl groaned. Her face blanched. Her jeans were frozen so solid they cracked as Jess helped her stand.

Lucy shivered faintly and she had a vacant look in her eyes. She tried to wrap her arms around herself, but the effort seemed too much. Jess realized Lucy wouldn't last out here much longer.

"Come on. Let's get to my Jeep. I'll turn the heat on," Jess said as she threw Lucy's arm over her shoulder. She dragged Lucy along, forcing her feet to stumble forward.

The snow had settled, packing down to make the walking easier. Visibility improved to maybe fifty feet now. Jess kept checking. Left and right, back and forth.

Ten minutes later, a dark patch came into view ahead.

Jess stopped and eased Lucy down onto her knees.

The dark patch didn't move. It could have been Kahler. Or a tree. Jess was taking no chances. She rolled Lucy onto her back.

"Stay down. Lower is better." She handed Kahler's gun to Lucy and showed her how to fire it.

Jess headed uphill to arc around the dark patch. As she came closer, the dark shape became the outline of a hunched figure, large enough to be a man.

She squatted and waited.

He didn't move. When the snowfall relented, she saw a rock beside him. And the long barrel of a rifle.

Had to be Kahler. Only Kahler would be out on this mountain in these conditions.

He seemed to be watching, concentrating on movement downslope.

Jess could back away and collect Lucy. They could detour around him. The Jeep was still a mile away, but they might make it before he changed position.

A branch cracked, somewhere off to the right, beyond Kahler. Her heart rate spiked.

She swung her gun around, searching.

She heard an animal's tread moving away from Kahler. She took a deep breath to calm her nerves.

Kahler continued to look downhill. Had he known the noise was an animal? Perhaps seen it pass by a few minutes before? Seemed strange that he didn't check.

The snowfall thinned again. A moment's clarity of a few hundred feet.

Kahler was leaning against the rock, half-buried in snow. His head rested against the rifle, and the rifle angled upward. He was bareheaded and his hair was iced over.

He'd fallen asleep.

Jess stood. She was behind him. His large rifle would be difficult to maneuver. If he woke, she would be able to shoot long before he could.

She covered the hundred feet to his position, pistol ready.

Kahler didn't move.

Fifteen feet away, she shouted, "Drop the gun, Kahler!"

Still he didn't move. She stepped closer and shoved his shoulder. He rocked from side to side as one solid mass. Bloodstained ice had welded his clothes together.

She levered the gun from his fingers, found the safety switch, and tossed the weapon downhill.

He didn't seem to be breathing, but she found a weak pulse on his wrist. She went through his pockets and found his knife. She tossed it downhill, too.

Then she left him where he was and went to find Lucy.

The girl's skin had a definite bluish tint, and her body was shaking again.

"Come on, Lucy. Not much farther now." Jess lifted her out of the snow and helped her walk on.

Thirty minutes later, Jess heard the angry buzz of snowmobile engines. She led Lucy into a stand of trees and waited.

The first snowmobile approached. The rider's white cross on a red ski outfit marked him as local ski patrol.

Jess staggered out of the woods holding Lucy against her body. The rider looped around and stopped in front of them, already talking on the radio.

Seconds later they were surrounded by ski patrol and FBI agents.

They bundled Lucy into a sled pulled behind a snowmobile and left at high speed. Then they did the same to Jess.

She told the agents about Kahler before the ski patrol drove her away. She lay back, exhausted, confident the FBI would finish the job.

CHAPTER 70

SEVERAL WEEKS LATER, AFTER Kahler's expedited trial, Jess sat in the front row of the courtroom behind the prosecution team at the sentencing hearing. Her son, Peter, was beside her. Two rows behind them, Karl Oppenheimer sat upright, shoes gleaming, tie straight, and uniform freshly pressed.

All three had attended the entire trial. Turned out Theo Kahler had survived the night on the mountain in a catatonic state. His body temperature had hovered a fraction above the point of death. He'd been revived at the hospital and charged with multiple counts of murder, attempted murder, and assault.

Kahler sat silent and expressionless beside his court-appointed lawyer, even as Jess had testified against him. After four days of trial, the jury found Kahler guilty on all counts. The judge sentenced Kahler to life in prison because Colorado had abolished the death penalty.

After Kahler filed out under armed guard and the judge left the bench, Peter shoved his phone into his pocket. "Now we eat?"

"I have the feeling you're not cut out for the legal profession." Jess put her hand on his shoulder and smiled as they lined up with the crowd of spectators leaving the courtroom.

"No kidding. In the time it took him to wrap up, I coded a whole new obstacle avoidance package for my drone."

"On your phone?"

He frowned. "Sure."

Karl Oppenheimer remained in his seat.

"We're headed for lunch," Jess said when she reached his row. "Join us?"

"I'll stay here a while, thanks." Metal rattled as he patted his top pocket.

"Your brother's dog tags?" she asked.

He nodded.

Jess said, "They tried to connect Kahler to your brother's death. There wasn't enough evidence and Kahler didn't admit anything. But they won't give up."

"I know." Karl paused. "I don't feel good about it. I wanted him convicted for my brother's death. But locking him up for another reason is definitely better than not convicting him at all."

She gave him a sympathetic smile.

Kahler had murdered a lot of people, all of them criminals, except Herman Horatio Oppenheimer. Kahler had denied killing Karl's brother. Everyone knew he was lying, but the prosecutor said they needed solid evidence to convict him.

Karl stood and shook her hand. "Your boss sent me a check."

"Good," she said. "*Taboo* printed your story. Without you, Kahler might never have been convicted. The money is yours."

"It's a lot of money."

Jess smiled. "Carter has a lot of money. He likes to do good things with it."

"I'm not sure—"

"No strings attached, Karl. Cash the check. Do something nice for your family."

"Maybe I will," he said, and sat facing the bench. "Thank you."

Jess ushered Peter on, leaving Karl to his thoughts.

On the courthouse steps, lawyers offered competing statements about the outcome to TV interviewers.

Jess crossed the street and headed to an alley that led to a small diner. Peter checked a menu on the window and decided on his meal before they stepped inside.

Detective Norton was already seated in a booth, eating. He slid over to allow Peter and Jess to sit.

"You got here quickly," she said.

He grinned. "Left early to get a good seat."

"At least it's almost over," Peter said.

"Depends on what you mean by over," Norton said. "There's the rest of the Miller gang to deal with. The main supplier and a trucking company that was routinely moving the drugs across the border. And then the banking issues, which will be handled by the feds. We'll have court cases lined up for months."

"Don't forget Larson and his mistress," said Jess.

"When we found him locked up at Toppers, he was more than happy to tell us everything we needed to know. Which wasn't much," Norton said. "Turns out he wasn't part of the criminal enterprise and having an affair isn't a criminal offense. But the IRS is going to enjoy chasing them for tax evasion."

"Good news on that," Jess said. "His wife has filed for divorce, and Tsui has tracked down most of their legitimate assets. By the time the lawyers finish with Larson, he'll be lucky to escape with the clothes on his back."

"Love it when our plan comes together. Or"—Norton shrugged—"when we can make it look like we had a plan, anyway."

Henry arrived and sat beside Norton.

A waiter placed a carafe of coffee on the table, took orders, and left.

"What are you planning to do now that this case is over?" Norton asked.

"What makes you ask?" Jess replied.

"You know, you should think about joining Denver PD," Norton said. "You'd be good at the job."

"No, she shouldn't," Henry said.

Jess opened her mouth to argue, but Henry held up a hand.

"The Bureau should have the first chance to hire you. We don't have anti-nepotism rules anymore, you know," he said with a wink.

Norton gave Jess a look of mock indignation. "You can't possibly think of going to—"

"Guys, guys," Peter said with a cheeky grin. "If you seriously think you can tell my mom what to do, you really don't know her."

Jess laughed, wrapping her arm around his shoulder. She was always proud of him and never more so than at that moment.

She said, "Gentlemen. Listen to my son."

They all laughed.

"Besides," Peter said. "She's—"

"Whoa, whoa," Jess said, laying a hand on his arm. "Let's finish eating first."

She ignored the curious looks as the food arrived, and they ate enthusiastically. Peter kept grinning, and Jess had to keep elbowing him in the ribs to keep him quiet.

Henry made a show of finishing his meal and straightening his silverware on the empty plate. "So?"

"So, what?" she said.

"So are you going to tell us poor flatfoots your big secret?"

"Speak for yourself, Morris. My arches are just fine, thank you," Norton said.

Jess grabbed her bag and stood. "Follow me."

The group walked out of the diner, down the alley, and across the road to a gray four-story building that had once been a factory.

An investment company had bought the place and modernized it. The exterior doors and windows were framed in blue. The color went well with the occasional piece of industrial equipment dotted around the courtyard.

Jess waved a card in front of a reader and the front door popped open. She led them through a reception area. She climbed a metal staircase, original to the building, all the way to the fourth floor.

Henry and Norton looked in every direction as they ascended. Peter merely smiled. He'd been here before, helping his mom set up the place.

The fourth floor had one corridor that opened around each of the building's four sides. She stopped at a door flanked by waist-high frosted-glass windows.

The door was unlocked, and she stepped into a large oblong office. The industrial decor continued inside. Cables and pipes ran along the open ceiling. Small paned windows overlooked Colfax Avenue and the criminal courthouse.

Two desks faced each other, and another frosted-glass partition separated a small office from the rest of the space.

Behind one of the desks, Mandy Donovan and the audio engineer from *Taboo Magazine* were busy arranging computers and cables.

She straightened up. "Aha. You brought the whole gang."

"Time to make it official," Jess said.

"Wait." Mandy rummaged in a packing box and pulled out a rectangular shape covered in bubble wrap and held it out.

Jess peeled off the packaging and checked the lettering on a light wood sign. Everything looked correct.

"Do I have to guess?" said Henry.

"No," Jess said. "I've decided to stop simply reporting the injustices happening in the world and do something more."

She turned the sign over.

"Well, well," Norton said.

"No surprise," Henry said.

Jess had considered the idea for years and Henry knew it. But now seemed like the right time. She'd found Peter. She had Henry. Her personal life was in order.

She had business contacts in law enforcement and the legal system. She had a team in place. And more importantly, she still felt a burning desire to see justice done, even if the system couldn't always deliver.

Nothing could happen right away. She had licensure requirements to meet first. Carter, her good friend and longtime boss, had offered her the time and the money to complete her training and she'd already started her apprenticeship. He said *Taboo Magazine* would send cases her way, too.

She laid the sign on the desk.

Outlined in white, the simple, black lettering really stood out.

JESSICA KIMBALL
PRIVATE INVESTIGATOR

ABOUT THE AUTHORS

DIANE CAPRI

Diane Capri is an award-winning *New York Times*, *USA Today*, and worldwide bestselling author. She's a recovering lawyer and snowbird who divides her time between Florida and Michigan. An active member of Mystery Writers of America, Author's Guild, International Thriller Writers, Alliance of Independent Authors, and Sisters in Crime, she loves to hear from readers and is hard at work on her next novel.

Please connect with Diane online:
http://www.DianeCapri.com
Twitter: https://twitter.com/DianeCapri
Facebook: http://www.facebook.com/Diane.Capri1
http://www.facebook.com/DianeCapriBooks

NIGEL BLACKWELL

Nigel Blackwell was born in rural Oxfordshire in England. He has a love of books, a PhD in physical chemistry, and a black belt in pointing out the obvious. He has driven trains, crashed single-seat race cars, and traveled much of the world.

He now lives in Texas with his wife and daughter. Together they enjoy the sunshine and listening to the coyotes howl at night.

Please connect with Nigel online:
http://www.NigelBlackwell.com
Twitter: http://www.twitter.com/Nigel_Blackwell
Facebook: http://www.facebook.com/authorNigelBlackwell